I0763300

GARY AND BRENDA...

Sometimes!

By

Lyn Pike

MAPLE PUBLISHERS

GARY AND BRENDA ... Sometimes!

Author: Lyn Pike

First Published in 2025

ISBN 978-1-83538-498-5 (Paperback)
978-1-83538-567-8 (Hardback)
978-1-83538-499-2 (E-Book)
978-1-83538-694-1 (Audiobook)

For inquiries, or to contact the author directly, please email:
pikelyn485@gmail.com

Book Cover Design, and layout (in collaboration with the author) by:
White Magic Studios
www.whitemagicstudios.co.uk

Published by:
Maple Publishers
Fairbourne Drive, Atterbury,
Milton Keynes,
MK10 9RG, UK
www.maplepublishers.com

CONTENTS

Chapter 1 – January
First Class move, Gary! 1

Chapter 2 – February
Tooth be or not tooth be? 21

Chapter 3 – March
My scones are louder than yours! 43

Chapter 4 – April
Up North 67

Chapter 5 – May
A Handbag! 91

Chapter 6 – June
Oh Bronwyn, ti diawl bach! 113

Chapter 7 – July
Ah, her beautiful eyes and smile 133

Chapter 8 – August
Paul's a bicycle 153

Chapter 9 – September
Oh, bowls to prompting! 171

Chapter 10 – October
The newbies, the brazils and nearly a Dutch artist 195

Chapter 11 – November
The Battle of Archie, 2024 217

Chapter 12 – December
Waddle I do if I lose you? 243

Chapter One

January
First Class move, Gary!

A new year, a new beginning. It was a cold crisp January morning and the sun shone brightly. Gary and Brenda's belongings were either boxed up or wrapped in cloth for protection. The removal men had loaded everything onto the lorry. They were ready to drive the one and a half miles across town to Seymour Rise where their new home was located. Seymour Rise is a neat cul-de-sac in Wancott, a market town located about seven miles south west of Oxford.

It was a difficult time for the couple who were full of excitement and also fear of the unknown. They had lived in the home they were about to leave for thirty-five years and, on the whole, their memories were happy ones.

Gary placed two boxes in the back of his car. Their contents required special care so were given the luxury of travelling in style and not in the back of a lorry. One of the removal men waved at Gary to signal he and his mate were off and would see him at the new address. Gary nodded back.

Brenda was still in the house so Gary walked back inside and found her standing in the hall with her back to the front door. She was motionless as she stood staring longingly into the empty lounge. Her eyes were full of sadness, like those of a child being forced to give back a puppy they've been cuddling.

'Come on love, are you ready?' Gary asked but there was no reply. Her silence was deafening so he continued to talk to hide it. 'You know this move is for the best, don't you? This house is too big for us to manage now and we should be comfortable in our retirement.'

'I know,' Brenda said, at last submitting to the inevitable. 'But it's so sad as we've spent almost all of our married life here. Oh Gary, where has that time gone?'

'It's remarkable, I know,' he replied, 'but we are about to embark on the next stage of our lives and we'll have many happy years in Seymour Rise, I'm sure.'

'It won't be another thirty-five years though, will it?' she sighed.

'What? Don't you fancy hanging on for a birthday card from the King then?' Gary smiled and took hold of Brenda's hand to lead her outside.

'Bye number 9,' she said, glancing back. 'Please be as kind to the next occupants as you have been to us.' They walked towards the car but before Gary could open the car door, Brenda gave him an awkward stare.

'What?' he enquired. 'What have I done wrong?'

'You haven't done anything wrong yet, but you may do if you get into that car!' she replied, with a smile.

'What?' Gary repeated.

'A kiss? You haven't given me a kiss.'

'But you're coming with me, aren't you?' he protested. 'What do you need a kiss for?' Brenda pulled him towards her and planted a kiss firmly on his lips.

'There, wasn't too hard, was it?' she insisted. 'It's a good luck kiss as it's the last kiss we'll have outside number 9.'

'You are silly,' replied a slightly embarrassed Gary. 'Right let's go then, Mrs Good Luck kiss!'

The car pulled out of the drive. Brenda couldn't bring herself to look back but even so she couldn't stop tears rolling down her cheeks.

The journey across town took less than five minutes. As they turned into Seymour Rise they drove past three contractors digging up the road. They were Frank, the 50-year old manager of the team, Doug (45) and Steve (33), known affectionately by the locals as The Three Roadeteers, often shortened to Roadeteers. Unlike the great works of The Three Musketeers, the Roadeteers could always be found at the heart of any traffic jam. They take charge of approximately ten square miles of road around Wancott. If any business needs a hole digging, then the Roadeteers would be contracted to carry out the work. They are on the Oxfordshire Highways Department's list of approved contractors and once the necessary legal approvals are obtained, they will carry out the required job. When the customer's work 'down that hole' has been completed, it is the job of the Roadeteers to fill it in and resurface the road. Today was just a normal chilly January morning for the Roadeteers.

'Here Frank,' said Doug as he excavated shovels of soil, 'who is this work for then?'

'Water Company,' replied Frank, 'we're locating the water pipe so they can put in another stopcock.'

'Right,' continued Doug, 'so when are we scheduled to fill it in again?'

'In seven days' time, or so the paperwork says.' Steve looked excited by this news.

'So, we'll need the best tarmac and roller to make it all smooth,' he said, grinning from ear to ear. 'I love rolling out the road and making it all smooth.' It didn't take a lot to make Steve happy.

'That's good,' said Frank, with a big smile on his face, 'because a month later we've got to dig it up again for the broadband company, so if the road's a bit bumpy from your first efforts, you'll get a second chance, lad.' Doug looked perplexed by it all.

'What? That's madness,' he said.

'No!' Frank replied. 'That's what the paperwork says!'

'Right you are!' Doug and Steve exclaimed in unison.

The removal lorry had parked outside 19 Seymour Rise and Gary and Brenda's car was parked behind it. Gary walked to the front door and opened it allowing the first piece of furniture to be carried in. Brenda followed them inside unaware of the interest their arrival had generated. Trudie Grimsdale in number 17, the semi-detached house attached to Gary and Brenda's, was secretly staring out of her window. She watched with great concentration as the furniture and boxes were carried in. Trudie's husband, David, was on his laptop completing some paperwork for his job. Both Trudie and David are in their forties and have been married for twenty years. They both have careers in the health care sector.

'How do you spell pneumonia?' David enquired, looking confused as he typed.

'What?' replied Trudie, without averting her stare from her neighbours. 'Oh, that's one of those hard ones, isn't it? N-U-M-O-N-I-A, perhaps?'

'No Trude!' he exclaimed. 'Your spelling is worse than mine and the spell checker isn't offering an alternative.' David looked up and saw Trudie still standing at the window trying hard to hide behind the curtain.

'Ah Trude, come away from the window,' he exclaimed, 'there's being inquisitive and there's being nosy.' Trudie tried to plead her case by saying,

'It's natural to be curious and show a friendly interest in . . . ' David interrupted her.

'An interest?' he said. 'At this rate they could be your specialist subject on Mastermind! Why don't you make a nice gesture and pop round to see if you can help them?' Trudie looked horrified at that suggestion and replied,

'What, and look like a nosy neighbour? I don't think so.' Before Trudie could say anymore she spotted her friend Sarah Richardson walking up to her door. Sarah and Trudie had been close friends since school. 'Oh Sarah's here,' she said and rushed to the front door and opened it two seconds after Sarah rang the doorbell.

'Wow, that was quick Trude, you must have been passing the door as I arrived,' said Sarah.

'I was at the window and saw you coming,' replied Trudie.

'I see, well I'm on my way to the gym, so thought I'd pop in to check that you're still alright to come out for the pub lunch tomorrow.' She started walking through to the lounge and spotted David, 'Hi Dave,' she continued.

'Hello Sarah,' David replied, 'she'll come out with you tomorrow if she can manage to pull herself away from the window for long enough. She's spying on the new neighbours.'

'Oh Sarah, don't listen to him!' Trudie said firmly, 'We've got neighbours moving in and I've had a little look out of the window every now and then, you know what it's like?'

'I saw the lorry outside,' said Sarah.

'Every now and then?' retorted David. 'It's been constant staring. I should think by now you could tell us what colour underwear they are wearing.'

'David please!' Trudie yelled. 'That's enough of that, thank you!' By now Sarah had moved over to the window and took a quick peek out. Brenda and Gary were helping with the boxes outside, so were in full view.

'Oh,' she said, a little surprised, 'that's Brenda and Gary! I should really go and say hello but I haven't got time. I can't miss my slot at the gym.' Trudie's nosy side was intrigued.

'You know them?' she asked.

'Not as well as you by now,' David said. Both women completely ignored him.

'Yes,' Sarah continued. 'I met Brenda through the Women's Institute, you know the WI as it's known. She's really nice. She mentioned that she was moving but I had no idea she was coming here. I know Gary too from work, but haven't seen him since he retired over ten years ago.'

'He worked at Brookes Uni, with you?' Trudie said, she was determined to get as much information as possible.

'Yes, he's a bit of a drip really, but okay. To tell you the truth I think he fancied me back then.'

'Oh, here we go,' said Trudie. 'Sarah, you think everybody fancies you! I may regret asking this but why did you think that?'

'Well, I took an office pen home by mistake and he didn't get angry.'

'Oh my God,' said David. 'You can borrow my pen if you like!' Trudie looked puzzled by this comment, it almost sounded like verbal adultery to her so she hit back by stating.

'Don't bother Sarah, believe me it has run out of ink!'

Inside number 19, Gary and Brenda were trying to unpack. It was rather cramped with boxes everywhere but at least the removal men had placed the furniture roughly where it should be.

'I know why they say moving is the most stressful thing you'll experience after bereavement and divorce,' said a stressed Brenda. 'I know it's early on but I'm already feeling homesick for number 9. I do hope we've done the right thing moving here.'

'Oh love, don't worry. Everything will be okay,' said a reassuring Gary. Brenda turned around suddenly to face him looking shocked, like she'd just remembered something important.

'Gary, you should have carried me over the threshold, like you did at the old house.'

'Why? Do you want to give me a hernia?' Gary replied, 'that's what newlyweds do, isn't it?'

'Why would newlyweds give each other hernias?' asked Brenda. 'Oh, I see what you mean,' she continued, 'but we weren't newlyweds at number 9! Please carry me over the threshold or the house won't feel right. I won't give you a hernia as I'm only half a stone heavier than when you carried me before.'

'Yes, but I'm thirty-five years older now,' protested Gary, but to no avail. Brenda grabbed his arm and pulled him outside and he started to lift her up. Out of the blue a woman approached them and the lift was aborted with Brenda landing on the ground and Gary on top of her. They both stood up trying to regain their composure and look respectable. The woman was Aggie Parker, a 68-year old retired school teacher.

'Welcome to Seymour Rise! I'm Aggie and I live opposite. I thought you might like these to brighten your new home.' She handed Brenda a bunch of carnations. Brenda was still shocked by her sudden presence but took the flowers offering a smile in return.

'That's really kind of you, thank you,' she said. 'I haven't a clue which box the vases are in though.' Aggie looked serious and then nodding at Gary she remarked,

'Well don't let him carry any boxes as the vases will soon be broken if he drops them as readily as he just dropped you.' Gary and Brenda looked embarrassed and there was a short awkward silence before Brenda spoke again,

'This is Gary and I'm Brenda. Thank you for the flowers. When we've unpacked and found the kettle, you must come round for a coffee.'

'That'll be nice. Well I won't take up any more of your time,' and with that Aggie marched back to her house as quickly as she'd arrived. Before Brenda had time to say anything, Gary scooped her up and carried her into their new home.

'Oh, I love you,' she whispered in his ear.

'You'd better!' he replied, struggling for breath.

Back inside they started unpacking the boxes. Brenda pulled out a photo of her parents and placed it inside the display cabinet; it was the first thing to get put in there.

'Do you think my mother would have approved of this house, Gary?'

'I'm sure she would have, although she wasn't always easy to please,' replied Gary. 'I was always looking for her approval! I'm certain she would have liked us moving to a place with a posh name like Seymour Rise.' Brenda looked at him, smiled and said cheerily,

'Yes, you are right.' Gary could see a sadness behind her smile.

'You still miss your Mum and Dad very much, don't you?' he said and pulled her close and whispered, 'Well I'm sure they are looking down on you now and . . .' He aborted the sentence realising what he'd said, 'oh no, what have I just said! What an awful thought!' Brenda laughed and hugged him for a couple of seconds.

'I could murder a cup of coffee,' she said, 'which box is the kettle in, do you remember?'

'I don't,' Gary replied. 'The post-it notes I used to label the boxes all fell off so the removal men just put them anywhere there was a space.' Brenda looked a little annoyed at hearing this.

'Why didn't you write on the boxes with black marker pen, like I said?'

'If I'd done that they couldn't be used again, could they?' he replied.

'But we won't need them again, will we? You are stupid Gary!' Gary remained quiet and opened another box. He dug deep and although there wasn't a kettle, he did find something.

'I've found the mugs!' he shouted, triumphantly.

'Mugs Gary! Not in front of mother's photo, find the posh cups!'

Before he could answer the doorbell rang. Its ringtone was a version of Meat Loaf's song Bat out of Hell.

'Is that the doorbell?' Gary asked. 'We'll have to get that changed as that will forever remind me of your batty mother! Perhaps it's her at the door and she's come to smash the mugs!'

'Poor Mum, leave her memory alone and go and answer the door, our new front door that is,' Brenda said, with a broad smile.

Gary opened the door leaving Brenda sorting through the boxes. Standing outside were a man and a woman, Kai Peterson (29) and his partner Izzy Farmer (30). At first Gary thought what are the chances of having a visit from Jehovah's Witnesses on the first day in your new home? Surely not. They looked very serious and before Gary could speak, Kai started to blurt out words almost in desperation,

'Hi, I'm sorry to bother you with you moving in and everything but we live in the house that backs on to yours in Turnpike Road.' He'd not finished when Izzy started her plea,

'We've lost our cat. We haven't seen him since yesterday evening. I was hoping he'd be home when we got back from work but he isn't. He hasn't got shut in here has he, you know with the door being open as you moved everything in? Or perhaps he's in the shed?' She then ended her 'speech' by calling out, 'First Class, here First Class, where are you boy?' Gary was a little confused but was trying hard to take it all in.

'Sorry,' he said, 'but we haven't seen any cats. What are you calling him?' The pairs' desperate faces dropped still further in disappointment at hearing Gary's words. Kai responded,

'First Class, he's called First Class. His actual name is First Class Male but we shortened it to First Class after he had his balls cut off, I'm a postman you see.' Gary couldn't resist a little joke and said,

'Do all postmen have their balls cut off?' Sadly there was no reaction at all to his jokey question and he began to feel bad for joking at what was a sensitive time for this young couple. 'Okay, I see, I'm sorry. I'll keep my eyes open for him and if I find him I will *Return To Sender*.' Again, there was a stoney silence until Izzy, still very straight-faced said,

'Thank you, but we didn't send him to you. Thank you anyway, sorry to have troubled you. I'm Izzy by the way and this is Kai.' Gary now felt very guilty for making jokes at their expense.

'Nice to meet you. I'm Gary. I hope you find First Class soon.' He shut the door and went back into the lounge.

'I haven't found the kettle yet. Who was that?' Brenda asked.

'Well,' he replied, 'we've been here a short time and I've already met three of our neighbours.'

'More neighbours? I've already got flowers in the sink,' she said.

'That was the couple whose home backs on to us, from Turnpike Road. They've lost their cat and wondered if he'd made it in here while the door was open.'

'Oh, that's a worry for them, it puts finding the kettle into perspective, doesn't it? I'd love a hot drink though. It isn't that warm in here, is it? The radiators are warm though so the heating must be working.'

The room was a little chilly, but that was to be expected as the front door had been open for quite some time when everything was moved in. Their belongings were gradually being unpacked and placed where they would make memories in future. There were still at least eight boxes to unpack downstairs and a few upstairs. Brenda stopped and plonked herself down on the sofa.

'Oh Gary,' she said wearily, 'I hope I can get used to being here. I loved number 9!'

'I know, so did I but we'll be fine here too, I promise,' Gary said, as reassuringly as he could. 'Let's take a break and walk into town to get a hot drink and something to eat.' Brenda looked pleased by that suggestion and agreed, after all she found things always looked better after a break.

In Wancott town centre there is a café called Dolly's Delights, known locally as DDs. It is run by Dolly Pickford, a woman aged 55. Dolly and her husband Ian (58) moved to the town from Huddersfield ten years ago and live above the café. It was lunchtime and Sarah walked into DDs after coming straight from her session at the gym.

'Hello Sarah, how are you doing? You look hot, have you been jogging?'

'No Dolly, I've come from the gym,' Sarah replied, 'I've had a cold shower too but I'm still hot!' There was a very short pause before she changed the subject. 'I called in on Trudie on the way to the gym and you'll never guess who's moved in next door to her.' Dolly thought for a moment and said,

'George Clooney? No? Richard Branson? Well how should I know? Who is it?' Sarah didn't look amused at Dolly's reluctance to play her guessing game realistically.

'No Dolly, it's Brenda and Gary.' Dolly laughed.

'Almost George and Amal then,' she said. She thought for a little while and added, 'So that's where they've gone, they're not far away then. It's a bit of a come down from where they were before, mind. Brenda did say the old house was a bit too big for them now, well I think it has four or five bedrooms, and they are the other side of 70 now, you know?' Sarah listened intently before deciding to excitedly impart some more news to Dolly.

'You know that Gary fancied me when we worked together?' she said and got an immediate response from Dolly.

'Sarah, you think everyone fancies you!' she insisted. 'How have you managed to stay single, hey?' Sarah was not amused. 'That's not funny,' she protested, 'can I grab a coffee to go please?' Dolly poured a coffee, took the payment and handed the cup to Sarah. The cup slipped a little as Sarah took it and a small amount of coffee spilled down her jacket. Luckily as it was a takeout cup the design stopped it from spilling a larger amount. Dolly should have been sympathetic but instead started to giggle and said,

'Oh no look! Even the coffee needs to be close to you.'

'Ha, ha, very funny,' replied an annoyed Sarah, 'I'm off.' She headed for the door and upon reaching it she turned round and said, 'Oh George and Amal are here,' as Gary and Brenda entered.

'Hi Sarah,' said Brenda, 'how are you?'

'I'm great thanks! I hope you settle into your new home quickly.'

'Thank you, that's kind,' Brenda replied.

'Will you be at the next WI meeting?' Sarah asked.

'I'm not sure as I've lots to do in the house,' Brenda replied, as Sarah left and the door closed behind her. Gary and Brenda continued towards the counter.

'Hello you two,' said a welcoming Dolly, 'I hear you are moving today.'

'That's right. We are having a break from it though. Can we have two coffees please? We haven't located our kettle yet,' said Brenda, almost begging for her hot drink.

'Then we'll have a look at your menu, please,' added Gary, 'I'm starving!'

'Of course,' said Dolly passing over a couple of menus, 'and I'll bring your drinks over. Go and sit at a table and take the weight off your feet.' They did just that and started to look at the menu.

'I think I'll have the all day breakfast,' said Gary, 'what about you, love?'

'I think I'll have a bacon sandwich with a portion of chips,' Brenda replied.

The coffees were delivered and the order for food was taken.

'Oh, that's nice,' remarked Brenda, as she took her first sip. 'You know we will have to put a decorating schedule together? A plan for each room.' Gary pulled a face.

'Do you think they all need decorating?' he pleaded. 'Couldn't we redecorate slowly?'

'Depends on how slowly,' Brenda responded. Gary smiled before announcing,

'A room a year maybe?' Brenda didn't find that suggestion as amusing as Gary.

'No! You'll need to work faster than that! I was thinking a room a month!' The smile left Gary's face.

'Oh, I've had an idea, I'll decorate a room a month,' he said, sarcastically. 'When am I going to have time for playing bowls?' Brenda didn't offer an answer but she smiled. They sat in silence as they continued to drink their coffee. There was only one other couple in DDs. They were two tables away and holding hands under the table. Brenda smiled remembering what it was like to be young. She quietly placed her left hand under the table and touched Gary's leg. It brought an instant reaction from Gary, but not the one she had hoped for.

'Are your hands still cold, love? Well my trousers won't warm them up, best wrap them round your cup.' And they say romance is dead, she thought to herself. At this point Dolly walked over with their food and placed it on the table.

'Thanks, you are an angel, Dolly!' said Brenda. Dolly laughed.

'I don't think I've ever been called that before,' she said. 'Enjoy your food.' She walked away. Brenda stared at her sandwich for a while. Gary started to eat straight away.

'What's up?' he said, 'Is there something wrong with your food?'

'No, I'm sure it's lovely,' she said, tears were welling up in her eyes, 'but I just suddenly felt sick at the thought of not going back to number 9.'

'Oh love, don't worry,' said a concerned Gary, 'we'll soon make this our special home.' Brenda tried to smile as he continued, 'I'll decorate a room a week if it makes you happy.' He then placed his hand on her knee under the table. She giggled while the young couple looked on and pulled a face in disgust. What were they thinking of, daring to do something romantic when they are 'old' people?

Gary demolished his all day breakfast easily whilst Brenda ate her chips. She carefully wrapped her sandwich in her napkin to take it home, wherever home was now. They thanked Dolly, paid, left and started the ten minute walk back to Seymour Rise. As they neared their road they approached the roadwork sign which was a warning to traffic of the grand work carried out by the Roadeteers. In the distance they could see a fountain of water coming from the hole in the road which rose up about five feet.

'Oh dear!' said Gary, 'I think they dug too deep! That's the Roadeteers for you!' They both smiled and walked on.

As they reached their house the time was approaching 3:30 and it would be dark very soon. Gary was about to put the key in the lock of the front door when Brenda had a sudden thought.

'Hadn't we better check the shed? Just in case our neighbour's cat is in there?' she said.

'That's a good idea, love,' Gary agreed. They walked around the side of the house and through the gate leading into their back garden.

'I remember the garden as bigger than this when we viewed this house,' Brenda said.

'Ah well that's the power of the Estate Agent. They can talk you into seeing everything bigger,' observed Gary. 'Perhaps we could get one to look at our bank balance.'

Brenda immediately felt that all too familiar sick feeling that comes with her severe doubts about this house.

'We had a lovely garden at number 9,' she whimpered like a lost dog. Gary thought on his feet and tried to distract her thoughts. He peered inside the shed through the open door and said,

'Oh it's quite big inside! And the removal chaps have put our garden things in here! I wonder where the key is? I don't think it's wise to have it unlocked with our lawn mower and tools in it.' It worked! Brenda's thoughts turned from number 9 to the shed.

'Well, there's no cat in there, is there?' she said. 'Why did you bring so much rubbish, Gary? You'll need to sort that out.' Gary smiled inside though showing no expression on his face. He loved an excuse to sit on a chair in his shed daydreaming, or as he called it, solving the world's problems in his mind. He'd just been authorised to sit in there while he sorted it out, wink, wink! Gary's vision of shed paradise was suddenly disturbed by Brenda's voice.

'Right, let's go inside. It's starting to get quite dark,' she said. Gary closed the shed door and they walked towards the house, but before they got there Trudie, from next door, looked over the fence and said cheerily,

'Hello, you're Gary and Brenda, I believe!'

'Wow, are we famous?' chirped Gary. Trudie smiled back and continued,

'Apparently so! But don't worry I'm not after an autograph or selfie. It just so happened an old friend of mine was visiting this afternoon and they recognised you.' Brenda was intrigued to find out who this was.

'Oh no, I don't think much of this witness protection scheme. So who is the friend that knows us?' she joked. Gary thought he'd join in the fun and added,

'It wasn't killer Ken was it, looking to silence us from giving evidence against him?' Trudie laughed and immediately felt as if she'd known these new neighbours for years.

'No, it was Sarah Richardson. She knows you both.'

'Oh Sarah, yes! I know her from the WI,' Brenda responded. 'She's a lovely young lady. Of course Gary knows her from work, well, you know before he retired.' Gary looked less enthusiastic.

'Yes, I know her and I think I prefer killer Ken!'

'Gary!' exclaimed Brenda. 'He's only joking. He's just seen the shed and the excitement of a 'man shed' has gone to his head. So what's your name?'

'Oh yes, sorry . . .' Trudie started, but before she could continue Gary said,

'Funny name!' Brenda wasn't amused and let him know.

'Gary, let her speak or you can spend the evening in that shed!'

'Charming,' he replied.

'I'm Trudie and my other half, who is inside, is David.'

'I'm sorry,' said Brenda, sympathetically, 'how long is he in prison for?'

'He's indoors!' laughed Trudie. 'That's so funny.'

'I'm so sorry!' said an embarrassed Brenda.

'And she doesn't even like sheds!' Gary piped up. Brenda sensed it was time to go inside so decided to round off the conversation.

'Well, it's lovely to meet you. Once we've located the kettle you must come round for coffee,' she said. 'It'll be nice to get to know you.' Trudie looked pleased.

'Thank you, that would be nice. In the meantime would you like to borrow our kettle?' she offered.

'No don't worry, but thank you. Ours should turn up soon,' Brenda replied. All parties smiled and walked in the cold towards their homes.

As the evening began to draw in Gary and Brenda could be seen in their lounge. There were no curtains hanging and the light bulbs illuminated their space showing two people walking backwards and forwards between boxes and furniture. Izzy was a spectator of the couple as they sorted through their belongings. As her back garden backed onto Gary and Brenda's garden she had an excellent view from her lounge window. Izzy wasn't a naturally nosy person and was only drawn to observe her neighbours out of anxiety for her missing cat. Kai was sitting on their sofa. He looked up to see Izzy staring out of the window into the darkness.

'Try not to worry Izz, I'm sure he'll turn up soon. He's probably having a great time out there, cats do this all the time,' he said, trying to offer reassurance. Without even looking around she replied,

'I hope you're right.'

'I'll keep an eye out for him tomorrow when I'm delivering mail and ask around, someone may have seen him,' he said. Izzy moved towards the sofa and spoke wearily,

'I'll give him First Class! He's a first class worry!' Trying to lighten her mood Kai joked,

'He's like First Class letters, should be here today but may take three or four days to arrive.' Izzy, doesn't 'do' jokes. She found it hard to tell when someone was joking and Kai knew this but hoped he was cheering her up. Sadly, she didn't appreciate his efforts.

'Well,' she started to say, looking very serious, 'I hope our First Class is back before three days!'

'Fingers-crossed he'll be home tomorrow looking hungry,' Kai replied.

'If he isn't I'll print off some posters to display around telling everyone he's lost,' Izzy said. Kai looked puzzled by this, after all First Class had only been missing a day. So he joked again saying,

'I always think they look like, wanted posters. Have you seen this cat? He's wanted for crimes against mice and birds.' Again his efforts went straight over Izzy's head and she was puzzled.

'Well cats catch mice and birds, it's their nature so why would they be wanted for that?' she asked. Kai smiled and replied,

'You are a funny one. It's a joke that's all.'

'No,' she insisted, 'you are the strange one. How can you joke at a time like this?' Kai felt suitably told off and remained quiet.

It was now 9 o'clock and Gary was checking another box for the kettle. The couple were feeling pretty tired as it had been a long day. Brenda looked at the clock they had lodged in the display cabinet; they'd find a better place for it later.

'It's been a long day and it's only 9 o'clock,' she said.

'It certainly has, love,' Gary agreed.

'Thank goodness I managed to find all the bedding. Our bed is made and I think I'm ready for it. Oh Gary, this is our first night in 19 Seymour Rise, how romantic!' Gary was pleased by Brenda's positive attitude and wanted to encourage it so he said,

'Yes, the first of many happy years here love, I'll make you the happiest woman tonight.' That sounded very promising to Brenda and she smiled seductively as she asked,

'And how are you going to do that?'

'I'll find the kettle!' That wasn't exactly what she was expecting and a frown appeared to have taken refuge on her face. She got up and walked upstairs to get ready for bed and Gary followed her.

By 9:30 Brenda was in bed while Gary was still messing around somewhere.

'Gary, what are you doing? Come to bed,' she shouted. Gary shouted back from the bathroom,

'I've just finished brushing my teeth. I'm coming. I'm surprised you don't want to film me brushing my teeth.' Brenda was confused.

'What?' she asked. 'Why would I want to do that?'

'Because,' he said, 'it's the first time I've brushed my teeth in this house. Oh come to think of it you missed my first pee this afternoon!'

'Oh, shut up and come to bed, you fool,' she replied, too tired to argue or laugh. Gary entered the bedroom and stood in the doorway posing. He looked straight across the room into Brenda's eyes deciding it would be romantic to put on a French accent.

'I see a beautiful lady is living in this maison now. Would madam like some lovin'?' He winked at Brenda who couldn't take it seriously and laughed as she replied,

'Mais oui monsieur!' Gary moved towards her, still posing and performing a little dance. When he reached her he flicked off his slippers, kicking them under the bed. This resulted in the painful screams of a cat ringing out and First Class ran from under the bed, rudely tripping Gary as he performed his dance. Gary fell against the wardrobe shaking it. The box on the top was knocked over and a kettle fell out, hitting Gary on the head on its way down to the floor. He sat there moaning in pain with a shallow cut on his forehead. Brenda crawled across the bed to see him on the floor.

'Oh dear, never mind, it's just a little cut,' she said, trying to comfort Gary with her words. 'Wait there and I'll get something to clean it up for you.' She got out of bed and walked into the bathroom and after a few seconds she returned with some toilet paper and a bottle of Dettol. 'I can't find a clean cloth or sponge,' she said, 'but I'll use some loo paper.' She poured a little of the antiseptic onto the toilet paper she'd already wetted in the sink and started to wipe the cut on Gary's face. It stung and Gary jolted his head backwards instinctively.

'We'd better get it cleaned up properly,' she said, 'we don't want you getting kettleitis, do we?' Gary stopped groaning for a moment. 'Kettleitis?' he said, 'what's that?'

'Oh it's serious,' responded Brenda, 'it's where you start whistling when you get hot.' She burst out laughing.

'It's not funny! I could have been knocked out,' Gary protested.

'Never mind Gary, you've done a great job killing two birds with one stone,' Brenda said. 'You've found both the kettle and our neighbours' cat. Purrrrfect!'

Brenda finished washing Gary's cut and climbed back into bed ready to settle down for the night. Gary walked downstairs carefully carrying the kettle which he put on the kitchen table. First Class was waiting by the front door to be let out so Gary opened the door and watched as the cat walked up the road.

'Stupid cat!' he said out loud. He then made his way back upstairs and crawled into bed.

Two minutes later, while they were lying in the darkness,

'Brenda?' he said quietly.

'Yes,' she replied.

'Do you think we should have stayed in our old house? Perhaps you were right.'

Brenda turned over to face him and in a deeper voice, imitating his, she said,

'Don't worry love, everything will be okay!' They both laughed.

What a first night!

Chapter Two

February
Tooth be or not tooth be?

It was 13th February and a whole month since Gary and Brenda moved into their new home. The couple were eating breakfast with Brenda chasing some last cornflakes with her spoon around a pool of milk inside her bowl. She managed to manoeuvre some onto the spoon but, before she placed them in her mouth she glanced at Gary eating his toast.

'What was wrong with you last night?' she enquired. Gary stopped chewing and looked a little hurt.

'I do my best. You've never complained before. Well, not often anyway,' he replied.

'I was brought up to be thankful for what I've got however small and short lived, but I wasn't talking about that!' she said harshly. 'I mean what was wrong in the night? You were tossing and turning and muttering under your breath. What were you dreaming about?'

'I can't remember, it probably had something to do with cats and kettles! My head still hurts when I hold it in certain positions,' Gary replied.

'You were muttering something like, *I don't want to, I can't do it, I'm shy*. Who was bothering you and what couldn't you do?' Gary's facial expression suddenly changed.

'Oh yes,' he said, 'it's coming back to me now. I was being chased by this zombie. I fell over and when I looked back it was Aggie.' Brenda, having finished her cornflakes, pushed her bowl away abruptly reflecting her mood and sudden insecurity.

'Aggie? What, Aggie from across the road? Why did you dream that she was chasing you? Is this one of your fantasies? Do you fancy Aggie?' Gary looked stunned by this sudden eruption of questions.

'Me? I don't fancy Aggie,' he said, 'she frightens me! In fact she reminds me of your mother and I promise you I never fancied her! I was running away from her! Fancy her, what next?' Brenda thought about it for a couple of seconds and realised that what he just said made sense.

'I suppose not. Well, why was she chasing you?'

'I don't know,' insisted Gary. 'It was just a silly dream which I'd forgotten about until you reminded me. Perhaps she is still angry with me for dropping you outside the front door on the day we arrived here.' Brenda sensed that Gary was getting a bit annoyed so decided to remain quiet, but Gary had already decided to change the subject.

'I thought I might get some bowling practice in today,' he started. 'We've got a big league match coming up soon against South Marston and need all the training we can get.' Sadly for Gary, Brenda had other plans.

'You haven't got time for that today. We need to go to the supermarket this morning and this afternoon you can continue decorating the bedroom. It needs to be finished and you said you'd paint it. Oh, sometimes Gary you forget what you've promised,' she complained. It was only 8:40 in the morning but Gary was already feeling weary.

'Okay,' he said submissively, 'I've just had a great idea. I'll finish the bedroom.' Gary left the kitchen and Brenda started to wash up the breakfast things.

Across the road Aggie, the subject of Gary's dream, was talking on her phone while looking out of her window.

'Oh no! I'm sorry to hear that Michelle,' she was saying. 'Obviously I'm upset that you are pulling out a day before we are due to perform but I know it can't be helped. Please look after yourself and hopefully, with rest, your voice will return soon as strong as ever . . . What? . . . He says what? . . . . Well it doesn't matter what he says about enjoying the reduced volume; you've got a cheeky husband! You get well soon. I'm hoping Craig will be okay as he has got dental problems at the moment. He's going to a dentist this afternoon. Fingers-crossed they can sort him out. . . No, it's not toothache, apparently he's lost his front teeth . . . don't laugh, poor man. Yes, he has bridge work in the front of his mouth and the bridge collapsed yesterday evening, so to speak . . . No, he wasn't in a fight! He was eating dinner. I told him the vegetables should be cooked for longer next time,' Aggie laughed before continuing, 'hopefully he'll be available to perform tomorrow once the dentist has fixed his problem.' At this point Aggie spotted Gary and Brenda leaving their house and heading for their car. 'Oh Michelle I will have to go. I've just spotted a couple of reserves for tomorrow. I'll just need to persuade them that they'd like to take part, bye.' She ended the call abruptly and headed for her front door. Meanwhile Gary and Brenda were half way down the path. Gary was looking apprehensive.

'I can't get used to not having a garage. I don't like leaving the car in the road, it's vulnerable. You wouldn't leave a two-year-old child at the edge of the road, would you? Well this car is only two years old.' Brenda smiled at him.

'It's a car Gary! It's fine there. It spent most of its time on the drive before anyway, as the garage was full of your junk. The amount of, just in case I need it later, junk we took to the dump before the move was unbelievable.' At this point they had reached the car but Aggie was walking across the road towards them. Gary lowered his voice and leaned towards Brenda.

'Oh no, it's the zombie from my dream,' he whispered.

'Shhh Gary, she'll hear you!' was the hurried reply, followed by a cheery, 'Good morning Aggie, how are you today?' Aggie marched up to them like a soldier on parade and, in her usual abrupt ex-school teacher manner, replied,

'Morning Brenda, Gary. I'm a little stressed actually.' Gary found that ironic considering all things and muttered under his breath,

'Not as stressed as I was last night.'

'Sorry Gary, didn't quite catch that!' Aggie boomed at a volume so loud the whole neighbourhood could hear. Gary thought on his feet and came up with a genius line,

'Oh, I said I'm sorry to hear that.'

'Thank you, Gary,' she responded. 'You see my AmDram Group needs new members.' Brenda looked puzzled but felt she ought to contribute to the conversation.

'Oh,' she said, 'I don't know that group. What do you sing?'

'Sing? AmDram is not a pop group, Brenda. It's an abbreviation for Amateur Dramatics. I run the group.'

'Why doesn't that surprise me?' muttered Gary.

'You need to speak more clearly Gary, I can't make out what you are saying if you don't speak up!' demanded Aggie. Brenda grinned.

'Sorry Aggie. I just said I'm sure you are good at AmDram.' Again, Gary was impressed with himself at his smart reply.

'Well,' continued Aggie, 'I'm stressed at the moment. The group is due to perform at the local care home tomorrow evening and two of our cast may not make it now. It's a play I wrote too, so its success is important to me.'

'Tomorrow? That's close. You've got a problem there then,' Gary said.

'Yes, but we are well rehearsed and pretty much there really. There is a larger role for a male and a smaller part for a female which I need to fill. Would you two help me out?' Gary and Brenda started to turn pale and panic. Gary let his panic be heard first.

'Oh no, I can't act,' he said. 'I'm basically too shy. I didn't like having to make presentations at board meetings when I worked at Brookes University.' Aggie looked intrigued.

'You were at Brookes, Gary? Were you a professor there?' Brenda started to laugh but stopped immediately seeing that Gary was not amused.

'No, I was in management,' Gary replied proudly, 'I was Head of the Accommodation and Student Welfare Department.'

'Oh I see,' she replied. 'That's an odd combination! There's really nothing to acting Gary, you can do it.' Those words sounded familiar to him and he started having flashbacks of his dream.

'But, I don't want to,' he insisted.

'Nonsense. I'll put you down as a maybe then. Brenda, you'll do it won't you? Yes, that's brilliant!' Brenda stood still with her mouth open in shock as Aggie headed back across the road. As she marched off her commanding voice called out,

'I'll call in this evening to go through things.' Gary and Brenda stared at each other, both looked like they had been slapped across the face. Gary spoke first,

'What just happened? I think my dream was a warning.'

'Dream? It's a nightmare! And I'd be pleased if you kept me out of your nightmares!' Brenda replied.

'I didn't write it you know,' insisted Gary, 'it's an Aggie special, just like her play!' They got into their car and started to drive to the supermarket.

'You didn't want a kiss today before you got in the car then?' Gary joked.

'A kiss? I needed mouth to mouth resuscitation,' pleaded Brenda. There was a further minute's silence which Gary broke with a desperate plea,

'How are we going to get out of this? I can't act! I'll just make a fool of myself.'

'So, what's new there then?' she quipped. 'Why can't you be assertive with Aggie? You went on enough courses at work on how to be assertive. Didn't any of it stick?' Gary thought for a second or two and replied,

'Well I'm decorating the bedroom this afternoon instead of playing bowls so I suppose that answers your question!' Brenda gave the side of his head a hateful hard stare. She decided, however, it would be counterproductive to hit him while he was driving.

'Gary,' she started, 'you don't need to be assertive in the home, just outside it!' Before anything further could be said they approached roadworks. It was the Roadeteers who were digging up the road to enable the gas company to carry out work on the pipe below. Steve was on traffic control duties as the road was down to a single lane. Gary stopped the car as Steve was holding up the 'stop' sign. There wasn't any other traffic around but Steve continued to hold the 'stop' sign. Gary lowered the car window.

'Excuse me,' he said, very politely to Steve. 'Can I drive through?'

'Sorry Sir, it's not your turn,' Steve replied. Gary looked puzzled.

'But there's nothing coming the other way,' he pointed out but Steve wouldn't be persuaded to switch his 'stop' for 'go'.

'That doesn't matter, Sir. I've been on the traffic control course and I'm following them procedures I was shown.' Intrigued by this Gary needed to know more.

'What is them, err those procedures?' he enquired.

'In order to maintain a steady flow of traffic, I must allow at least a full two minutes to each lane of traffic. At the moment it's not your two minutes,' came the reply from the genius road traffic controller.

'But there isn't anyone coming from the other direction,' Gary insisted.

'Yes Sir, so that proves it's working as there's no build-up of traffic, so please be patient, thank you.' Doug and Frank had stopped digging and were laughing in the background. Gary looked annoyed but gave in. After a short while the board was turned around to 'go' and Gary drove off.

'THANK YOU!' he shouted.

'Oh Gary, that told him!' said a sarcastic Brenda.

'Well, I can't argue with them rules, can I?' replied Gary sharply. Meanwhile back at the roadside Steve turned to Doug and Frank.

'Well that bloke was an impatient one,' he complained.

'If there's nothing coming the other way Steve, you can let them through you know?' responded an amused Frank. He received an immediate rebuke from Steve who replied,

'And waste the public money spent on my course? I don't think so.' Doug and Frank smiled to each other as they said in unison, 'Right you are!'

It was 10 o'clock and Dolly had finished serving the early breakfasts in DDs and was enjoying the mid-morning lull in custom. Sarah was standing at the counter and they were enjoying a conversation when a woman burst through the door and looked around the café. Dolly and Sarah exchanged glances, they were puzzled by her behaviour.

'Are you okay, lass? You look lost,' Dolly asked the woman.

'I'm fine, thanks,' was the reply. 'It's my husband that isn't. I've lost him temporarily. We talked about coming for a walk round town so I wondered if he'd wandered in here. At least I think he's lost. We got up together, talked about what we were going to do but after breakfast I went upstairs to make the bed and when I came down he was nowhere to be seen. He'd put all the dirty breakfast things in the sink and disappeared.'

'Description?' asked Dolly.

'Just little white bowls and plates except for the ones you can't use in the microwave with little yellow flowers on,' she replied and Dolly looked amused.

'I meant what does your husband look like?' she said.

'Oh, a five-foot nine-inch pain in the arse,' came the reply, which Dolly hadn't been expecting. The woman continued, 'His memory isn't that good now and sometimes I wonder why I bother. Yesterday I made a list of pros and cons of being married to him. I had one pro and sixteen cons.' Sarah was intrigued by this.

'What was the pro?' she asked.

'He's tall enough to reach the top shelf of the kitchen cupboard, it saves me getting a chair to stand on! That's very handy!' she replied. It was at this point that the women noticed something out of the window.

'Oh there he is, he's outside,' she exclaimed with a sense of relief and she exited DDs as quickly as she'd entered. Sarah rolled her eyes in disbelief.

'That was odd,' she said.

'Yes, she needs to get greater control of her husband,' Dolly remarked, with a smile.

'No, I meant why did he put the breakfast things in the sink and not wash them up?'

'He's a bloke, Sarah,' replied Dolly, 'so it's a miracle he even moved them to the sink. It's easy to see you've never been married.'

'But Dolly, surely not all blokes are like that? Some must wash up, cook and clean?' Dolly smiled. She liked Sarah but was amazed at how naive she was for a 42-year old.

'Those that do live on Mars, not round here in beautiful Oxfordshire,' Dolly said.

'Well perhaps that's something we could bring up at the next WI meeting. Set a challenge for husbands to see whose husbands aren't completely useless,' Sarah said.

'Go ahead lass, bring it up at the next meeting,' Dolly commented.

'Surely we can train men better!' said Sarah. Dolly smiled again and said,

'Good luck with that. You don't know as much about men as you think you do.'

Gary and Brenda returned from their shopping trip. Thankfully Steve had his board set on 'go' as they approached so the return journey was easier. Brenda had unpacked the shopping and put it away. She made coffee and handed a mug of it to Gary.

'Thanks love. I'll drink it upstairs,' he said. He was holding a can of paint which he put on the worktop and carefully removed the lid. 'I'll carry on with the bedroom now. Are you sure about this colour as green isn't your normal choice?' Brenda looked irritated.

'It's not green, it's called luscious lime, Gary. It's soothing and will help us sleep.'

'Right, that's good,' he said, but after giving it a little thought he looked confused. 'Hang on, how can it do that? When we turn the light off we won't see the colour.'

'Maybe not,' Brenda replied, 'but believe me, if I'm happy then it will help you to sleep too.' Gary retreated to the bedroom with paint and brush in one hand and a mug of coffee in the other hand.

In Turnpike Road, Izzy was busy sweeping her garden path. First Class, her beloved cat, sat on the doorstep watching the movement of the broom with great interest. He was getting ready to pounce on it at any time. Mark, the local window cleaner, was cleaning the windows. Izzy stopped sweeping as Mark started to talk.

'How are things with you? How's work, are you getting jobs?' he asked.

'Yes, all is okay, thanks Mark,' Izzy replied, 'I clean for a lot of families now. Most are in the new houses in Tidy Corner Crescent and Manor Street. I've started an ironing and washing service too. A lot of people want their ironing done.'

'That's good,' he replied.

'What about you?' Izzy enquired.

'No thanks. I can manage my own ironing,' he replied. Izzy looked confused and then realised his misunderstanding.

'I meant how's business for you?' she continued.

'Oh yes, it's good although I have some free slots now,' he replied. 'Your neighbours at the back there in Seymour Rise,' he pointed to Gary and Brenda's back garden, 'left a slot when they moved.' Izzy looked thoughtful before offering some advice.

'Why don't you ask the new people, Gary and Glenda, if they want a window cleaner? They found First Class, our cat, in their house. They seem nice although he's a bit odd. He said - return to sender - when he talked about First Class.' Mark smiled at this.

'That's witty,' he said, 'considering your other half is a postman.' Izzy looked blank and continued,

'Well I didn't understand it.' Mark decided he ought to try to explain.

'It's a song,' he said. 'I suppose you are too young and don't remember Elvis. There's a young couple in Parker Road who thought Laurel and Hardy were the new solicitors in town when I was talking about them. It's all before your time.' Izzy still looked puzzled.

'No, the solicitors are Lauren and Parker. Who are Laurel and Hardy?' she asked.

'Yeah, never mind,' Mark replied, he had already given up on explaining things. 'Thanks for the tip about the new people, I'll have a word. They are Gary and Glenda you say?' With that Izzy continued her sweeping and First Class continued to supervise every movement of that broom.

It was 6 o'clock when Gary and Brenda sat down to eat their dinner. Gary looked pleased with himself as he proudly made an announcement.

'I've almost finished the bedroom,' he said. 'There are just little odd bits to finish off in the morning.'

'That's good. I'll sleep well surrounded by luscious lime!' said a smiling Brenda. Before she could say anymore the Bat out of hell doorbell rang. Gary walked to the door and opened it. It was Aggie. He tried to speak but, before he could, she pushed through.

'Good news Gary!' she announced in her forthright manner and continued walking on through the house.

'Come in why don't you!' he said sarcastically after the event.

'You are mumbling again, Gary!' Aggie shouted over her shoulder. She continued through and found Brenda eating her dinner. Brenda stopped eating and stood up.

'Sorry Brenda, I can see you are eating but this won't take long. I bring good news.' Aggie paused for just two seconds allowing Gary to interrupt with,

'The care home you are performing at has been closed down with immediate effect?' He was so hoping this was Aggie's good news.

'Definitely not,' Aggie continued, 'but Craig the leading man is okay to perform tomorrow. He's been to the dentist who's repaired his bridge so his front teeth are now fine. So we won't require you tomorrow, Gary.' Gary felt like a huge weight had been lifted off his shoulders and the relief was so great he couldn't help but smile. In fact he was beaming.

'That's great news. Not that I wouldn't have helped out in an emergency of course.' Brenda stared sternly at him.

'Sorry to stare Gary,' she started, 'but I'm just checking your nose isn't growing longer by the second.' Gary smiled back but he looked guilty. Aggie just ignored it all.

'Sadly, Michelle won't be able to make it as she has lost her voice, so I do need you Brenda,' Aggie insisted.

'Well my voice isn't very strong,' Brenda pleaded, 'quite weak in fact so you might like to find someone else.' Aggie's school mistress gaze turned on Brenda and she said,

'Now don't be silly, Brenda. I can teach you techniques on how to throw your voice.'

'She managed to throw her voice perfectly when telling me I wasn't playing bowls today,' Gary said. Brenda stared at him again with a stare that told him he was in trouble.

'You aren't helping, Gary!' she said, throwing her voice perfectly in his direction. Aggie was undeterred and carried on.

'Brenda, you will play the part of Ophelia.'

'Is it Hamlet?' asked a surprised Brenda.

'No,' replied Aggie, 'I told you it's a play I've written. Ophelia is a woman in her fifties.'

'Fifties?' Gary said. He laughed and realised immediately that he shouldn't have done that out loud as before long Brenda would be throwing more than just her voice his way.

'Ophelia only has a few lines. Then Peter, (played by Craig), kisses her and that's it really.' No matter how many other words Aggie managed to include in that sentence, the word *kisses* was the only one that firmly stuck in both Gary and Brenda's minds.

'Kisses?' they said, in perfect harmony. Gary continued 'I don't like the sound of that!'

'It's acting Gary, it's no threat to your relationship,' Aggie insisted.

'Is Craig, er Peter good looking?' Brenda asked.

'It's acting Brenda. It won't matter if he looks like the back end of a bus,' Aggie responded, getting a little agitated.

'Yes maybe,' Brenda exclaimed, 'but it would help if he looked like …' Before she could finish Gary interrupted,

'Me! Like me!'

'Yep, that's what I was going to say,' Brenda insisted although it was a little white lie, but Aggie couldn't have cared less and just carried on booming out her instructions.

'Right, well we are holding a final rehearsal at my house tonight at 8 o'clock. So pop over then and you can meet the others and we'll go over everything. See you then!' With that Aggie turned around and marched to the front door. Brenda looked at Gary.

'Well it looks like your nightmare has turned into mine - what fun! I've gone right off my cold dinner.' Gary was looking thoughtful.

'I hope he isn't good looking!' he said. Brenda didn't have any time for his self-pity.

'Shut up Gary and eat your cold dinner!'

'Yes love,' he replied.

As much as Brenda didn't want them to, the hands on the clock kept moving. Before she knew it, she was standing outside Aggie's front door ringing the doorbell ready for the rehearsal. Aggie opened the door and in her domineering style she said,

'Hello Brenda. What, no Gary? I thought he might have come along to support you.'

'And I thought,' Brenda replied, 'he might have come to get a look at this man who's going to be kissing me, but no, it seems he's got more interesting things to do like watching paint dry on our bedroom wall.'

'Oh well, go through,' Aggie continued. Brenda was taken into the lounge where the members of the cast were assembled. Aggie looked at the group and spoke to introduce Brenda,

'This is Brenda everybody, she is covering for Michelle. Brenda this is Neil, Freddy, Daniel, Connie, Susie and Craig.' They all nodded but didn't have time to say anything before Aggie's phone rang. She glanced at the screen.

'Sorry, I've got to take this, won't be a minute,' she said and left the room. Brenda felt self-conscious as she didn't know anyone there and they were obviously a close knit group. Luckily Connie broke the ice,

'Hi Brenda. Welcome aboard Aggie's wonderful stage!'

'Thank you,' she replied. Connie smiled and continued,

'I wonder why Aggie gave one of her characters the name Ophelia?'

'It probably makes her feel like Shakespeare,' said Daniel which made Connie smile.

'Yes, but Craig's no Hamlet, is he?' she said. Craig looked irritated by this.

'So it's a good job I'm playing Peter then, isn't it?' he responded.

'Okay Craig, keep your hair on, or should I say keep your teeth in?' taunted Freddy. While the others laughed Brenda wondered just how she'd got involved with such a bickering group. She also imagined what it would be like to be kissed by Craig. The sooner it was all over the better. Her thoughts were interrupted by Connie who had more to offer.

'I wouldn't want to be one of Shakespeare's women,' she said, 'it most often ended badly. If they were on a dating app then they could have avoided the bother by swiping left. Ophelia and Desdemona could have avoided early deaths.'

'What are you talking about, you dozy twit?' Susie said. 'Apps in the 1500s? And Desdemona isn't in Hamlet, is she?' Brenda looked bored and was pleased when Aggie walked back into the room. The rehearsal started and Aggie had been telling the truth in that Brenda's part was very small. They had been rehearsing for over an hour and a half and they were now reaching the end of the play. Aggie had written a shorter play with care homes in mind as her main audience.

'So here we have the final scene,' she explained. 'Peter is annoyed with Jean and wants to make her jealous. He's known Ophelia, as a friend, for about two years. Knowing Jean is watching he pulls Ophelia close and kisses her. Jean is jealous and realises she's been silly and grabs Peter's arm and pulls him away. They embrace and leave. Happy ever after!'

'Really?' questioned Brenda. 'It's not happy times for Ophelia.' Aggie felt agitated at being challenged. It wasn't something she was used to as her pupils at school never had the power to challenge her.

'Yes Brenda, that's life. Ophelia hasn't been developed as a personality in the play so the audience will have more sympathy for Jean than Ophelia.' Brenda was in a bad mood by now. In for a penny, in for a pound she thought and continued to fight her character's corner.

'So she's just been used! You should have called her Tartitius, not Ophelia. Her name could be lovingly shortened, by her friends, to Tart.'

'I like you already, Brenda!' laughed Connie.

'Please don't be silly Brenda,' demanded Aggie, in her best director's voice. She turned to address the others. 'I think we are as good as we are going to be now. Remember it's 7 o'clock at Later Years Care Home, see you there tomorrow and I'll bring your costumes.' There were nods all round as they got up and left. Brenda walked across the road and entered her home. Once inside she placed her back against the door and put her head in her hands and let out a scream. Gary shouted from the lounge,

'Is that you love or has that cat got back in here?' Brenda suddenly felt very alone.

The following morning Brenda decided to go for a walk. She hadn't slept well for worrying about her new acting role and thought some fresh air was what she needed. It seemed that luscious lime wasn't as soothing as she'd hoped. Her walk took her past DDs so she popped in for a chat with her good friend Dolly.

'Oh Dolly, how did I get dragged into this?' she asked. 'I hate this type of thing, I'd rather be in the background than in the spotlight. I wouldn't mind but the audience is in a care home and so probably won't know what's going on.' Dolly looked on sympathetically.

'I feel for you Brenda. I know Aggie can be very bossy, but you should have told her you wouldn't do it,' said Dolly. 'Why didn't you pretend Aggie was Gary? It would have been easy to be forceful then.'

'Why didn't I think of that?' Brenda smiled.

'Don't worry, this time tomorrow it'll all be over. I wonder why they chose Valentine's Day to do it?' she pondered. 'Still I suppose they won't know what day it is in the care home.' Brenda shook her head.

'Thanks for listening to me going on, Dolly. Let's hope you are right. I'd better get home and see how Gary's getting on with finishing the bedroom, oh yes and learn my four lines!'

'Good luck Brenda, stay positive!' Dolly said.

'We semi-pros don't need luck, we've got talent!' replied Brenda, smiling as she left.

'That's my girl!' said Dolly.

Brenda enjoyed the walk home. It was a mild day for the time of year and although cloudy it was quite pleasant. She walked down Seymour Rise and was two steps away from her front door when a postman walked up behind her. She turned around to find it wasn't Kai.

'Here you go!' he said, handing Brenda a letter.

'Thank you,' she said as she took it from him. 'Are you new?'

'No, I'm just covering this area today as Kai's on leave,' he replied and walked on.

The letter was in a yellow envelope addressed to 'Brenda Pilkington'. It felt like a card inside. She was intrigued and opened it before she reached the front door. Inside was a Valentine's card showing a pink pig asking Brenda to be his Valentine and press his 'oink'. She smiled. It wasn't signed so who could it be from? Gary had never sent her a Valentine's card. To be fair they weren't the thing back in the early 1980s and by the time they had become popular, Gary and Brenda were married and more for saving money than spending it on romantic gestures. Now she had a dilemma, should she thank Gary for the card and risk it not being from him, or should she ignore it and keep quiet so as not to make him jealous. He did have a slimy friend, Anthony, with whom he played bowls, who flirted with every woman he saw and she wouldn't have put it past him to have sent this to annoy Gary. With all these thoughts running through her head, she decided to ignore the card. Gary wouldn't have sent it so just ignore it for a peaceful life. She entered the front door with the card hidden away from Gary's line of vision. She hung her jacket up with the card zipped inside a pocket and then walked into the lounge where Gary was sitting.

'Hello love. Had a nice walk? The bedroom is completed and I'm pleased to say it looks good in green.'

'It's luscious lime!' Brenda insisted.

'Sorry, of course it is. Have you learnt your luscious lines for tonight? Did you see what I did there with luscious lines?'

'Oh yes, great.' Brenda said sarcastically. 'At least I don't have a lot of lines. I just hope I get them right.'

'What is Craig like?' Gary asked in a casual manner so as to appear only slightly interested.

'I'm surprised you didn't ask me that last night. I suppose you were playing it cool, trying to seem uninterested? Anyway what do you mean by, what's he like?'

'Well, I'm only showing an interest in the bloke who's going to be kissing my wife,' blurted out a green-eyed Gary. This reaction only strengthened Brenda's belief that she shouldn't let him know about the card.

'You're jealous!' she teased.

'I'm not jealous, just curious! Is he good at kissing?' he continued.

'Oh terrific! It's worth being in the play just for that kiss,' she lied.

'Oh really?' said a very disappointed Gary. Brenda couldn't go on with the façade any longer. Gary's sad eyes were displaying how hurt he had felt by that last comment and it was too much.

'Oh Gary, sometimes you are an idiot,' she started. 'Don't worry, no one could kiss me better than you.' A big smile lit up Gary's face. There's no fool like an old fool.

'Well,' he started, 'I know that but I still don't want any competition, do I?'

'You'll see him tonight,' Brenda continued. Gary looked perplexed by this.

'What? Do you want me there? I thought I'd stay here and watch Emmerdale.' Now it was Brenda's turn to look perplexed.

'You've never watched Emmerdale,' she said.

'I thought I'd start. It seems like a perfect time to start. Coronation Street is on tonight so I could start that too.' Well it was a nice try but Brenda wasn't going to let him off the hook.

'Oh no,' she insisted, 'you'll be there, Gary. After all this is your nightmare I'm acting out.' Gary smiled at her.

'I've had a great idea,' he said, 'I'll come along to watch the play tonight so I can keep an eye on Craig.'

'Gary!' she replied, but couldn't say anymore before the Bat out of Hell doorbell sounded. 'I'll get it,' she continued and walked to the door. On opening it she found Mark, the window cleaner, standing there.

'Hi, I'm Mark. I used to clean the windows for Nancy, the lady who lived here before you. I also clean for others in this road plus Izzy your neighbour in Turnpike Road. Are you Glenda, by any chance?'

'I'm Brenda, but a few people have called me Glenda recently. Is that coming from Izzy?' Brenda replied. 'She must think my name is Glenda for some reason.'

'Oh sorry. I was wondering, Brenda, if you would like me to clean your windows on a regular basis?' Mark asked.

'Thank you Mark,' Brenda said, 'but I haven't really given it much thought to be honest.' Undeterred the enthusiastic Mark handed Brenda a leaflet.

'No problem, you think about it,' he said, 'that's a leaflet with my contact details and prices.'

'Do you use a ladder?' asked Brenda. Mark smiled before replying,

'Yes. I'm tall but not tall enough to reach upstairs without one.' Brenda already liked him as he demonstrated he had a great sense of humour.

'I meant a ladder as opposed to a pole,' she explained.

'Oh yes, it's just me,' explained Mark, 'the Polish window cleaner went home a year ago.' Brenda wasn't sure about him anymore. Was he still joking or just a bit slow at understanding?

'I meant a long pole and a hose as opposed to cloth, bucket and water,' she explained. The penny had dropped and Mark realised what she meant.

'Oh yes, sorry. I don't use a pole and hose just a bucket with water, cloth and ladder.'

'Right, thank you,' Brenda continued, 'leave it with me and I'll be in touch if I need you.' With that they exchanged polite goodbyes and Brenda walked back into the lounge.

'Was that the post?' Gary enquired. Brenda immediately wondered why he was asking that as he wasn't expecting anything. Again, she wondered about the Valentine's card.

'No,' she started, 'it was a window cleaner offering his services. He left me his price list.'

'Oh,' said Gary, 'I wonder if he's a good kisser?' At this point Brenda picked up the nearest cushion and threw it at Gary. They both started to laugh.

The afternoon went by in a flash. In the evening Gary and Brenda arrived at Later Years Care Home and were met at the reception area by Trudie who was surprised to see them.

'Hi you two. I didn't know you were part of the dramatics group,' she said.

'We're not, Aggie just asked me to cover for someone at short notice and I'm not looking forward to it at all,' Brenda replied. 'I didn't know you worked here, Trudie.'

'I work for the Day and Night Agency and this home has booked me for a couple of nights this week, it's to cover for staff shortages,' Trudie explained. Brenda was interested in her neighbour's choice of career, anything that took her mind off the impending play was a bonus.

'Do you like your job?' she asked Trudie.

'Well, I've been doing it for over twenty years so I've got used to it really,' she replied, 'I fell into this career.'

'A bit like me and this play then!' Brenda said, with a smile.

'Seems like it,' agreed Trudie. 'Now let me take you through to your audience.'

'If you have to!' Brenda sighed. Gary had remained quiet throughout, just smiling at the appropriate times. He was similar to a dog out on its walk but standing patiently while his owner talks to a friend. Trudie led them into the lounge. Several residents were in there sitting on the comfy highbacked chairs. There was a television on in the corner in front of what was a make shift stage. At this point Aggie appeared and ushered Brenda into another room to get changed. Gary sat in a chair between two of the residents, Terry an 88-year old and Martha a 98-year old. Both turned their heads to stare at Gary who felt uncomfortable at receiving so much attention.

'Hello!' he said. Martha looked at Gary but addressed Terry,

'Is that the new chap in room 24?' she asked.

'I don't know,' Terry replied. He turned to Gary, 'Are you the new chap?'

'No, I'm here to watch the play,' replied Gary. 'My wife is in it.'

'What did he say?' asked a bemused Martha.

'He's here to see the play,' Terry replied. Martha rolled her eyes up towards the ceiling and said,

'That will be rubbish, they always are.' Gary smiled back uncomfortably. Another resident Winifred, a sprightly 86-year old, was sitting quietly at the front by the makeshift stage. Winifred turned around to glance back at Gary and asked,

'I'm ready for my tea now. Have you got it?' Terry came to Gary's aid straight away.

'No Winnie, you've had your tea. This man is here to watch the play.' He turned to Gary. 'Sorry about that, she gets a bit confused,' he explained. Gary nodded and smiled awkwardly. About a dozen more residents drifted into the lounge. Trudie then entered with the actors and Aggie followed them in. Trudie turned off the television and pushed it to the side.

'Good evening everyone!' Trudie said, with an enthusiasm Gary admired. A few residents responded with a grunt. 'We are lucky to have the Amateur Dramatics company here this evening,' Trudie continued. 'They are performing a new play called, *Evil thy name is Fennesy.*' Aggie responded immediately in her domineering voice.

'Jealousy!' she boomed! 'It's, *Evil thy name is Jealousy*!' Gary did well to stifle a laugh but couldn't hide his grin.

'Oh yes,' said Trudie. 'Sorry Aggie.' As she walked away she grinned back at Gary. A few residents clapped as the actors walked forward whereas Winifred turned again to Gary.

'Is it time for breakfast yet?' she asked.

The play started and everyone settled down. Gary watched intently working out in the first five minutes who Craig was. He didn't think he was anything special.

An hour and forty minutes had gone by, Terry and Martha had fallen asleep in their chairs and Gary was very bored. In the play Peter (Craig) is getting upset by his wife's lack of attention and to make her jealous he has approached Ophelia. He grabbed her arm and pulled her towards him.

'Oh Ophelia!' he said. He was about to kiss her when Winifred moved slowly but surely behind him. She must have been the only member of the audience who had been following the plot carefully.

'Let her go you dirty, cheating git!' she shouted and swung her cushion at Peter which hit him across the back of his head and neck. The force of Winifred's blow dislodged Craig's temporary bridgework and his teeth flew out onto Ophelia's (Brenda's) chest.

'Oh no!' Brenda screamed. The audience who were awake, laughed. The scream and laughter woke Martha from her sleep.

'I didn't know it was a comedy,' she said disappointedly, 'I love a good comedy! Right, if you've finished could you put the tele on so I can catch up with Corrie?'

Gary and Brenda drove home without a word being exchanged between them. He didn't know what to say to console his wife who was feeling humiliated. Once home she lay in a hot bath until it got too cold to bear anymore and then she went straight to bed. Gary crawled into bed with her just a little later. He still didn't know what to say and was hoping she had fallen to sleep but as they lay there in the darkness he heard Brenda utter an odd sentence, all things considered.

'I hate this colour Gary, we'll have to change it,' she said.

'What do you mean, love?' a confused Gary replied.

'The paint on the walls!' she explained. 'I'll choose another colour and you can paint them again. Luscious lime reminds me of the colour of the carpet in that home!'

'Got it!' replied Gary. Then there was a slight pause before he spoke again.

'I'm pleased he wasn't good looking. What a luscious slimeball! He doesn't look so good without his teeth, does he?' Brenda felt the pain of Gary's words hitting that raw nerve.

'Enough Gary! I can't bear it,' she pleaded but Gary just couldn't help himself.

'At least he didn't kiss you,' he continued, 'but he bit your breasts remotely, the bastard! Hey, perhaps this is the long lost book by Agatha Christie called The *Mouth* Trap!' Brenda sat up swiftly and shouted,

'That's not funny, really not funny!' In the darkness you could just make out Brenda's silhouette hitting Gary with her pillow.

Chapter Three
March
My scones are louder than yours!

After the unfortunate event at the care home, the rest of February passed by relatively quickly without incident and suddenly March had arrived. It had taken a while for Brenda to choose a new colour for the bedroom walls but she had found one at last. Gary hadn't painted the walls yet, but he had managed to locate a can of the preferred colour.

'I like March,' Brenda informed Gary. 'The jolly month of crocuses in full bloom and the promise of daffodils very soon.' Gary looked at her and smiled.

'Well, that's not quite Wordsworth, but it does rhyme!' he said.

On the evening of 5th March, Brenda was attending a meeting of the WI. The attendees were in the Town Hall, sitting in chairs positioned in a semi-circle facing the chairperson, who happened to be Susan Perringer. Susan is a 62-year old local magistrate. Others present were Sarah, Dolly, Jane Smith (52), Mandy Buckly (42), Lucy Avery (35), Violet Turner (41) and Vera Pascoe (70).

'Good evening ladies,' Susan said. 'It's nice to see you all.' Sarah found this amusing.

'All?' she replied. 'You should get your eyes checked! We are down to a handful of us this evening.'

'Thank you, Sarah,' replied Susan. 'I know we aren't all here but . . .' Before she could finish Jane butted in.

'Some of us haven't been all here for years. I put it down to my age,' she said.

Susan began to feel that the women were a bit hyperactive this evening and ready to challenge everything she said in the interest of making a joke. The best way forward was to go straight to the guest speaker.

'Okay Jane, let's get on now,' she continued. 'We are fortunate to have a local business woman, Margaret Ashwood, with us this evening. Margaret will give a talk on what it's like to run a small business. In 1996, she set up Cowley Blinds and Shutters, a company that is still trading today. Thank you Margaret, over to you.'

Up stepped Margaret, a woman who oozed confidence. Brenda hadn't really wanted to come to this presentation but, as she hadn't managed to make the January or February meetings, she felt an obligation to attend this one.

'Thank you Susan,' Margaret started. 'Thanks for inviting me here to talk. Starting up a business is exciting and frightening at the same time. When I decided to go down this route I had no experience of the business world and, quite frankly, I was unprepared for all the things that could go wrong.' Her talk continued for about thirty minutes.

The ladies listened intently for the first ten minutes but many had lost interest after that. They were more interested in the product than the business model. Their eyes lit up when Margaret announced she had finished.

'And that's about it really,' she said. 'Thank you for listening. I'm happy to answer questions.' Mandy put her finger in the air to attract Margaret's attention.

'I'd like to ask about the physical side of the business,' Mandy started, 'how did you learn how to fit the blinds and shutters? Do you employ men to fit them?' Before Margaret could open her mouth to reply Lucy, a primary school teacher and one of the younger WI members at 35, jumped in to rebuke Mandy.

'That's a bit sexist, isn't it Mandy?' she started, 'You are assuming that men fit them when I'm sure women fit them too. Who fitted your new blinds, Violet?' Violet jumped at the mention of her name as she wasn't expecting to be dragged into the conversation quite so abruptly.

'My husband fitted them,' she replied, 'it took him all day and I'm sure a woman could have done a better job.'

'Why do you think that?' Lucy asked.

'Because five minutes after being fitted they came crashing down! They took out a vase too.' At this point Margaret intervened.

'Well we have a mixed team of fitters, male and female,' she said. 'Anyone with proper training can install the products be they blinds or shutters.' Sarah had been listening and saw this as her opportunity to raise another topic.

'The trouble is,' she started, 'there always seems to be an expectation that men do certain jobs and women do other jobs. The truth is women can often do men's jobs but men can't do some basic things that women do. It's startling really.' Dolly laughed and looking at the others said,

'Sarah love, you are the only one who finds this startling, I'm sure. I think most married women aren't surprised at all. Men are good at barbecues and putting wheely bins out and that's about all!' Lucy was getting a little agitated at this point.

'That's not true of them all,' she protested.

'Well Luce, . . .' Sarah began but was stopped in her tracks very abruptly by Lucy.

'My name is Lucy!' she bellowed in a manner that would have made Aggie proud.

'Sorry! Well, Lucy,' Sarah continued, 'a woman in DDs the other week said her husband doesn't even wash up. He dumps the dirty things in the sink.'

'That's right,' started Dolly, who felt she should back up her friend, 'but I think that's probably them being lazy rather than lacking the skills to do the washing up.' Lucy was undeterred and responded with,

'Perhaps that woman's husband was waiting for a full load for the dish washer. My husband carries out all the normal chores. He's a great cook too.' The other ladies raised their eyebrows; it wasn't the first time they'd heard all about perfect Jake, Lucy's husband.

'Yes well, Lucy,' replied Dolly, 'that's probably a generation thing. You are from a younger generation and times are changing.' At this point Vera felt obliged to add her opinion. Vera, like Brenda, is one of the older members and the WI's resident comedienne.

'Yes,' she said, 'I've got a generational problem in my family. The male short-comings keep passing down the generations!' The others laughed. 'And Lucy,' she continued, 'we don't all have a dish washer you know! In my house the dish washer is called Vera.' There were some mumblings amongst the women and most were agreeing with Vera. Dolly thought it was an ideal time to bring up the subject of a challenge.

'What about everyone else here?' she began. 'Can your partners manage the house work? What about cooking? Are they up for a cooking challenge? We could ask them to bake any cake they like one evening in the cafe and we'll judge their efforts. Oh, I suppose we'd need an independent judge though.' Susan was listening carefully and looked across at Margaret who'd been totally ignored for the past five minutes or so.

'I'm so sorry Margaret,' she said, 'we seem to have veered off the subject of your marvellous talk. You are neutral though, as far as the WI is concerned, so would you please consider acting as judge at the cooking competition?' Margaret, still oozing confidence, looked interested in what was going on.

'I'd love to,' she replied, 'but I'm fairly busy right now.' She pulled up her diary on her phone. 'I could do Friday evening this week if that's any good? Otherwise I'm not free for a few weeks.'

'That would do nicely,' Dolly said. 'By heck, my husband's in for a shock.'

'I look forward to that,' said Margaret, smiling. 'Wancott's own bake off. I love cake.'

'She might not be so keen once she's tasted Gary's offerings,' Brenda muttered to Vera. Vera smiled back and they watched Margaret leave the hall.

'This will be great,' exclaimed an excited Lucy. 'My Jake is a great baker, he'll win this no problem! I can't wait to tell him.'

'You're confident Luce, er Lucy,' Sarah observed. Lucy ignored Sarah and addressed Dolly. 'I suppose your Ian is a good cook as he's living above DDs with you?' she commented.

'Not at all,' replied Dolly, 'he's never baked a cake in his life but he's eaten mine enough times. I think he'll struggle but that will make it more enjoyable for me to watch.'

'You're evil Dolly!' said Sarah, with a broad grin. The other women present who had partners were adamant that their partners would not take part with the exception of Brenda and Vera.

'I'll tell mine he is entering, he won't like it though,' Vera said.

'What kind of cake have they got to bake, Dolly?' asked Brenda.

'Any type,' she replied. 'So 7 o'clock on Friday at my café then. Let me know tomorrow who is definitely competing.'

Brenda's two-minute drive home was full of dread. How could she get Gary to make something edible on Friday? Was it even possible? At least the drive time was shorter than if she had been walking so there was less time to fill with worry. In the summer she would have walked home as it was barely a ten minute walk but in early March the evenings were still dark by 7 o'clock. She arrived in Seymour Rise and parked Gary's only true love, the car, on the road outside their house. Once inside she found Gary in the lounge looking at something on his laptop.

'Well how are you love, how was the presentation?' he asked. 'Did you learn much about running your own business and how to earn us loads of money?' Brenda frowned and replied,

'I don't know about running a business but I'd like to be running away!' Gary's interest was aroused by such a weird statement and he put the laptop down.

'Why? What's wrong?' he asked.

'I'll tell you what's wrong, I sat through thirty minutes of a boring talk on blinds and shutters.'

'Well they are trendy at the moment, aren't they?' Gary went on, 'all the houses around here seem to have them. What's wrong with good old-fashioned curtains?' Gary smiled with pride as he prepared to deliver his next sentence and said, 'Curtains are best, it's an open and *shutter* case, get it?'

'Very good, I'm glad someone's amused!' replied Brenda. She took a breath and continued, 'After the talk we had Lucy telling us how perfect her husband is at everything.' Gary took an extra interest in that statement but his face dropped a little with anxiety.

'Everything, really?' he said, 'I do my best you know? I'm getting older and realise I'm not always as capable as I used to be. Anyway, you're not always up for it!'

'What are you on about now?' said Brenda. 'I'm not talking about in the bedroom!' Gary's face lit up on hearing this.

'Ah - ha! So he's no good in the bedroom then! I suspected as much,' said a delighted Gary.

'I'm sure super Jake is good at that too, but we weren't discussing that. What's the matter with you?' Brenda enquired. She wasn't expecting a reply but got one anyway.

'I guess I'm just getting *blinded* by your information,' Gary said proudly. Brenda was already tired of Gary's jokes so thought she'd play him at his own game.

'Okay,' she started, 'but you can *shutter* up now. Have you ever considered applying for a job as a joke writer for Christmas crackers? Your jokes are bad enough.' Gary considered himself to be the king of dad jokes so took that as a huge compliment.

'Why, thank you madam,' he exclaimed with a smile.

'Anyway, there is a WI competition on Friday evening and you have been entered!' Brenda announced firmly. Gary was quiet for a second or two as his brain worked overtime to think what sort of competition this could be. A smile appeared on his face and he asked,

'What, me with all those women?'

'For goodness sake, Gary,' said an impatient Brenda, 'it's nothing to do with the bedroom or sex!' Gary jumped up from the sofa almost dropping his laptop.

'Brenda!' he shouted. 'Don't mention the s – e – x word in front of your mother's photo, the glass may smash!' Brenda couldn't help but smile in response to that remark.

'Oh yes,' she said, 'sorry mum.'

'So what is the competition?' Gary asked.

'It's a baking competition,' Brenda replied, 'you will be competing with some of the other WI husbands.' Gary looked troubled.

'No,' he shrilled, 'but I can't make anything. Why didn't you make an excuse for me?'

'What! And let Lucy boast for evermore about her perfect husband?' she replied, 'No way! You will beat him or at least equal his skills.'

'Why baking? I have other skills,' he protested.

'Oh yes?' Brenda said, trying to work out what they might be. 'Like what?'

'I'm good at jokes as you've just heard! I could do a five minute standup routine!' he pleaded.

'That would take guts Gary and your jokes are awful!' said Brenda who wasn't giving Gary an inch. He couldn't manoeuvre out of this challenge!

'I heard a good one at the bowling club last week,' he continued determined to make his case. 'A bloke comes in looking down and . . .' He was interrupted immediately by Brenda.

'Looking down where?' she asked.

'No, not looking down anywhere but down, depressed,' he responded, 'now stop interrupting as you are spoiling my delivery.'

'What are you delivering?' she asked, with a smile.

'I'm delivering or trying to deliver my joke. Now stop it!' he demanded. 'So this bloke walks in looking miserable. *What's up?* said his mate. He says, *oh I got mugged by six dwarfs last night, not happy.*' Gary looked at Brenda who wasn't smiling as she'd already decided to pull his leg.

'Right,' she said, 'he wouldn't be happy, would he? He's been mugged!'

'No love!' said Gary. 'Not happy as in six dwarfs, not all seven, so excluding Happy. Oh never mind you've spoilt it now.'

'Sorry Gary,' she said laughing, 'but those women would give you a harder time than that if you were delivering a five minute standup routine! So you will be baking!'

'Okay love, I've had an idea. I'll bake something,' he said. Brenda had got a submission!

'Good idea Gary!' she said, 'I'll help you as I can't have you showing me up.'

'Up where?' asked Gary, deciding this was an opportunity to get his own back.

'Shut up, Gary!' was the answer.

'See, you can't take your own medicine, can you?' he chirped.

'I'll give you 'not Happy' in a minute,' came the immediate response to that!

The next morning Gary and Brenda were in the kitchen putting away breakfast dishes.

'I thought I'd have a go at sorting out the garden,' said Brenda. 'There are so many weeds coming through and I need to make room for bedding plants to go in next month. Are you going to help me?' Gary looked confused by the question; he didn't *do* gardening and Brenda knew that!

'Very funny,' he replied, 'you know I'm terrible with plants. I can't tell a weed from a flower. I'm useless in the garden.'

'No different from anywhere else then!' said Brenda, with a smile.

'Watch it, you!' warned Gary, 'I'm good at decorating! The bedroom will be finished this week now we have the paint.'

'So what are you doing if you aren't going into battle against weeds with me?' asked Brenda. 'Are you going to decorate then?'

'I will decorate later, I promise, but I thought I'd go to the great Wancott Bowling Club today,' he replied, 'a few of the team are going to be there and we do need to train ahead of the match with South Marston.' Brenda frowned followed immediately by a smile.

'It's amazing how training involves sitting around just talking at that club!' she remarked. Gary looked a little guilty as that was so close to the truth.

Brenda spent a little time tidying up and dusting around the house before changing into some older clothes, those no longer presentable for wearing in public places! She went outside and started to weed at the top of the garden. This was an area by the small fence which formed the border between her home in Seymour Rise, and Kai and Izzy's home in Turnpike Road. After ten minutes on her knees she decided to stand up for a little break as she was already getting stiff. At the age of almost 71, she found she needed more breaks now to avoid her knees seizing up. Once up she noticed Izzy hanging out washing. During the three months she'd lived in Seymour Rise, Brenda had grown fond of Izzy as she had got to know her through their little conversations. Izzy seemed a little different to others, slightly aloof in her own world but with a pure innocence you couldn't help but admire. She seemed vulnerable at times and naive for her 30 years of age.

'Hi Izzy. How's everything with you?' Brenda shouted, while stretching her legs.

'Hi Glenda,' Izzy shouted back.

'Izzy, my name is Brenda.'

'I know, that's what I said,' Izzy replied.

'No, you called me Glenda.'

'That's right,' Izzy insisted, 'I know your name, Glenda!'

Brenda looked totally confused. Perhaps she'd been wrong all these years and should check the name on her birth certificate once back inside her house. No, now she was being silly! Izzy walked over to the fence.

'Are you busy? What are you doing?' she enquired.

'I'm trying to tidy the garden,' Brenda explained. 'We've got more weeds here than anything else. I think the mild spell of weather has led them to believe it is spring. I need to sort this out.'

'Weeds are a pain, aren't they?' remarked Izzy. 'I hope First Class doesn't cause you any trouble. The problem with cats is they can disturb new plants when they dig to do their business.'

'Business? Is he an entrepreneur?' Brenda joked, but Izzy's world is black and white with nothing in between, so she looked at Brenda and with a very serious expression said,

'No, he's a cat, as you know. But he does poo a lot.' Brenda forgot her joke and continued, 'Oh, a First Class mess, you mean!'

'Certainly is, Glenda. Now I can't stand here talking, I must go. I'm working from home today so I'd better get on. I've got lots of ironing to do for my clients.'

'Working from home in the garden,' Brenda joked.

'No Glenda, the iron is in the house, silly. It's the thing that gets hot. Perhaps you're getting confused with the hose pipe.' Brenda turned away admitting defeat and continued weeding her garden.

Gary was by now driving to the Bowling Club. It is situated in the Wancott Memorial Park and only a five-minute drive away. En route the Roadeteers were resurfacing a patch of road. Doug was driving the roller which had disappointed Steve as rolling out new road was a favourite part of his job. As Gary approached, Steve raised his hand to signal that he should stop. The road was down to single file and a van was about to drive through from the other direction. Doug and Frank were now shouting at each other and the roller came to a stop.

'Doug, you are a f*****g idiot!' Frank shouted. The noise of the passing van made it hard to be sure of the exact adjective used. 'You've driven over my sandwiches!' On hearing that, Steve started jeering and laughing.

'What are you complaining about, Frank?' Steve asked. 'You've gone from a ham sandwich to a ham roll-er!' Doug and Steve were both highly amused by this mishap.

'You are both idiots!' exclaimed an annoyed Frank. 'Get on with it!' Doug and Steve answered in unison,

'Right you are!' The road was now clear and Gary drove off, he smiled as his went. Some entertainment on a winter's morning was always welcome.

It was only three minutes later when Gary pulled into the car park of the Bowling Club. He parked the car and walked inside where he found Cyril, the 81-year old club captain talking to Tim, Paddy and Anthony. They turned and nodded in Gary's direction as a 'hello' gesture. The one thing the Bowling Club had in common with the WI is that it had older members. Tim is 72, Paddy 65 and Anthony 66.

'Well then,' said Gary, 'do you think we are up to beating South Marston next month? It may be near impossible.' Cyril looked a bit disappointed by Gary's negative words.

'Yes, we can beat them,' he said, 'you need to be more positive about this, Gary.'

'I am positive,' Gary insisted, 'I'm positive we can't beat them. They are unbeatable and that's why they are top of the league.'

'I'm with Gary on that,' said Tim, 'there's fat chance of winning that one.'

Paddy's ear pricked up immediately although you'd only have noticed this if he were a dog with big ears to prick up!

'Now,' Paddy started, 'why do we say, fat chance?'

'Here we go, he's off already!' Cyril observed. Paddy went on to explain himself.

'If it's a fat chance,' he started, 'then that's surely a bigger chance than a slim chance. Nobody has said slim chance.'

'Good point, Paddy,' said Gary, 'so I'll make it easier for you. We have no chance.'

Paddy looked happier with that explanation. He hated sayings that didn't make sense to him.

'Okay, no chance it is then,' he responded.

It went silent for a few seconds until Gary thought he would unburden himself of his most recent worries.

'I've got a problem at home,' he announced.

'You could try marriage mediation,' advised Anthony. Gary looked puzzled.

'What for? It's not that sort of problem. It's that the WI has decided to hold a cake baking competition for men and I've been entered.' Now it was Paddy's turn to look confused.

'What?' he said, 'So the woman who bakes the winning cake wins a man, you?'

'No, no. I'm not a prize,' Gary replied. Anthony smiled and added quickly,

'If he was he'd be the booby prize!'

'Thanks for that,' Gary said pulling a face at Anthony. 'It's a competition where the men make the cakes.'

'And the winner wins a WI woman?' asked a still confused Paddy.

'What?' Gary replied, not quite believing what he'd heard. 'No, of course not!'

'Are there any nice WI women?' Paddy asked; his imagination running wild.

'Gary's Brenda is alright,' Anthony said, with the sole purpose of annoying Gary.

'She's more than alright and she's not a prize!' said a worked up Gary. 'You never stop do you, Anthony!' Tim thought he'd change the subject back to cakes to try and diffuse the situation.

'Are you good at making cakes then Gary?' he asked.

'His hands look soft enough for him to have a feminine cake baking side,' said wind-up merchant Anthony.

'Ha, bleeding ha!' said Gary. 'No I've never made a cake in my life. I'm useless at cooking. The first time I made toast I got it wrong.' Cyril looked amused.

'How can you get toast wrong?' he asked.

'Easy, I buttered the bread before I put it in the toaster. It made a runny mess.'

'You idiot!' said Cyril. 'So why are you doing it? Tell the wife you're not doing it.' Gary nodded his head in agreement with Cyril but admitted,

'I dare not Cyril. Brenda is relying on me to outdo another woman's husband. I don't want to upset her and, believe me, letting her down would upset her.' Cyril understood Gary's predicament.

'You are quite right there, Gary,' he said. 'A woman is like a heaped spoonful of coffee. You don't know how strong she is until she's in hot water.' The others all nodded except Paddy who had immediately tuned into another saying.

'Hot water, why do we say in hot water?' he asked. 'When we're in trouble what's it got to do with hot water?' The others looked bored with Paddy's 'wonderings' already and left it to Cyril to sort him out, after all Cyril is team captain!

'Oh Paddy, you're thinking too hard today. Try to relax a bit and shut up,' he said. 'Right, let's get out on the green and get training for this upcoming game. It will be hard to beat South Marston but we'll have a good go.'

'It'll be hard alright, like pushing water up hill,' Gary said, deliberately to irritate Paddy.

'Gary,' Tim moaned, 'watch what you are saying.' Tim knew what was coming next and, yes, sure enough Paddy had a question for them all.

'Pushing water uphill?' he queried.

'Shut up, there's a good chap!' was Cyril's response to that.

It was now 2 o'clock and Brenda was back indoors when the doorbell rang. She opened the door; it was Kai with her post.

'Hello,' she said, 'I was talking to Izzy just this morning in the garden.'

'Oh nice, yes she's ironing today,' he said with a smile. 'I've got a signed for parcel for Gary here, Glenda.' Brenda thought what is it with this family and my name?

'It's Brenda,' she said.

'No, it's definitely for Gary. Be careful it's quite heavy.' He handed over the parcel.

'Thanks,' she said, already giving up on her name and signing for the parcel.

'Could you take a parcel for your neighbour, please?' he continued. 'He isn't in so it'd be nice to leave it somewhere close.'

'Who David?' asked Brenda.

'No, the other side,' he replied, 'I can leave a card through his letterbox saying it is here and he'll collect it from you.' Brenda, looked slightly hesitant.

'That's fine but I don't really know them,' she started, 'we've never said more than hello, but I'll take it if you don't think they'll mind.'

'Mind? Of course they won't mind,' Kai insisted. 'You are saving them the bother of rescheduling the delivery or a trip to the sorting office. They'll bite your hand off.'

'I hope not,' she said anxiously, 'I'm fond of both hands.' She took that parcel too and went back inside.

The time was 2:10 and Sarah and Trudie were sitting at a table enjoying afternoon cake in DDs.

'You know that bloke that works on the market, the tall slim guy on the fruit and veg stall?' Sarah asked. Trudie thought for a couple of seconds and said,

'Not really, but what about him?' Sarah wouldn't accept that answer.

'You do know him!' she insisted. 'He sometimes dyes his hair blonde, really bleached white blonde and it all sticks out! The other bloke calls him 'toilet brush' because he said that's what he looks like! You know, Trude?'

'He drives a VW Golf, sporty version?' asked Trudie.

'I don't know but he might do.'

'He's on the stall Wednesday and Saturday?' was the next question from Trudie.

'Yes!' said Sarah.

'Serves the fruit and veg?' Trudie asked.

'Yes!' replied Sarah getting excited.

'No, don't know who that is,' Trudie said laughing, 'I rarely go to the Wancott market.' Sarah was not amused.

'Oh Trude, that's mean!'

'Sorry, but you asked for it,' said Trudie, 'what about him anyway?'

'I think he fancies me,' said a happy Sarah.

'Oh no! All that for you to tell me one of your fantasy stories!' moaned Trudie.

'No it's not, Trude!' Sarah insisted, 'I don't even like him. Who wants to go out with a toilet brush anyway?' Then she thought for a second, 'Mind you if he's got a new WV Golf, I might reconsider.' Trudie couldn't believe she was serious.

'I made that up. I don't know what he drives, I don't know who you are talking about!' Trudie explained. 'Anyway, I may regret asking this but why do you think he fancies you?'

'He gave me two free plums,' Sarah replied, proudly.

'What?' moaned Trudie. 'What a build up for that! That's five minutes of my life I won't get back.'

'So sorry,' Sarah said sarcastically. 'I've got other news though. You'll never guess what's happening in here on Friday evening.'

'Go on, surprise me,' said Trudie, 'as long as it doesn't involve plums.'

'No, well,' Sarah thought for a brief spell before continuing, 'not unless they are part of the ingredients. Anyway, there's going to be a cake baking competition with a difference.'

'Oh, wacky cakes?' Trudie teased.

'Nothing like that. The bakers are the male partners of WI members. Well not all of them though, I think there are four contestants.' Trudie looked genuinely surprised.

'Wow, that's brave,' she said. 'I wouldn't trust David to bake anything. I dread to think what would happen. I swear he thinks a fairy cake is found at the bottom of the garden.'

'Ah Trude,' said Sarah, 'you are mean to him. He knows they aren't just at the bottom of the garden, they are at the bottom of the garden under giant mushrooms.'

'Mushrooms?' questioned Trudie, 'We are back to wacky cakes!' Both women started to giggle. Sarah stopped as she saw Dolly come out of the kitchen.

'Hey Dolly,' she shouted to get her attention, 'is your Ian ready for Friday's challenge?' Dolly was shaking her head as she walked over to their table.

'Is he heck!' she said. 'He says he's got a prior engagement playing darts at the King's Arms. So we are down to three competitors now. They are Louise's Jake . . .'

'Oh Mr Perfect!' Sarah interrupted.

'That's him!' Dolly confirmed. 'And there's Vera's Syd and Brenda's Gary. Mind you I've only got two cookers here so three competitors is plenty as two of them will have to share one. One can use the main oven and one can use the top oven.' Dolly had clearly thought this through and had everything in hand.

'May the best man win then!' Trudie declared.

'Did I tell you that Gary fancied me back in the day?' Sarah said. Dolly and Trudie shouted in unison,

'Not again Sarah!'

'You two are mean to me,' Sarah complained. Then she completely changed the subject.

'Dolly, do you know the chap that works in the market they call Toilet Brush?'

'I think I know who you mean,' Dolly began, 'I go to the market to buy eggs now and then for the café, why?'

'Does he drive a WV Golf?' Sarah asked.

'Oh for flicking-fluck sake Sarah! I made it up!' said Trudie, in a raised voice.

The time was 3:15 when Gary returned home after his time playing bowls. He walked up to his front door and noticed Mark was cleaning the windows.

'Hello,' he said to Mark.

'Hi mate,' was Mark's reply. Gary stopped walking and asked,

'How long have you been cleaning the windows?'

'Oh about fifteen years now,' was Mark's reply.

'That long? I didn't know we had that many, they must be very dirty,' Gary said, with a mischievous smile. Mark smiled back.

'I've heard about your sense of humour from Izzy,' he started. 'Return to sender!' Gary carried on through the front door, he hadn't got a clue what Mark was referring to. His brain had worked hard to eradicate any memories of the awful times involving cats and kettles.

'Hello, all trained and ready?' Brenda said. Gary pulled a face at her which indicated not all was well.

'To tell you the truth, I don't think we are good enough,' he admitted.

'I'm sure you'll walk it or, should I say, bowl it!' Brenda replied.

'Thanks for the vote of confidence, love,' he sighed.

'A heavy parcel arrived for you, I signed for it,' Brenda said. 'It's on the table in the hall.' Gary looked excited, like he did as a child receiving his first bike at Christmas.

'Ah that's great, that'll be my new bowling ball. I'll add it to my set. The younger they are the better they move.'

'A lot like men then!' said Brenda. 'There's a parcel for one of the chaps next door too. Kai asked me to take it in for him as there wasn't anyone in.'

'Right. We've never really met them properly, have we?' said Gary. 'The little nods and hellos seem friendly enough though. It's father and son, isn't it?' Brenda looked confused.

'Really? I heard they're a married couple.'

'No it's two men love . . oh!' replied Gary, the penny had dropped!

'Oh what, Gary?' asked Brenda.

'I just realised,' Gary replied, 'I didn't know, well I'll go to the foot of our stairs!'

'What for? Gary sometimes!' said Brenda, 'it's not a shock now you know, it's normal!'

'I know and I didn't mean anything by it,' Gary continued, 'but in my Dad's day it was an awful thing.'

'Thank goodness times have changed,' Brenda said. 'Be careful what you say to them though. I know you won't mean anything nasty by it but you may innocently cause offence and I don't want you cancelled,' warned Brenda. 'Mind you . . on second thoughts,'

'Straight people have a sense of humour,' Gary butted in, 'so I'm sure gay people do too, but I'll be careful, as the bishop said to the actress.' Before Brenda could respond the doorbell rang. The Bat out of Hell tune had been replaced the week before by a normal chime.

'Someone's at the door,' said an informative Gary.

'Well spotted, Sherlock,' said Brenda, 'I'll answer it then. You know, I miss Bat out of Hell now it's not there!' She opened the front door and found her neighbour Kristian Penbroke (44) standing there.

'Hi, sorry to bother you but I think you've got a parcel for me?' he said.

'Yes, I have,' Brenda confirmed. 'Come in and I'll get it.' Kristian walked into the hall as Brenda retrieved the parcel.

'Here it is.' She passed it to him and continued, 'I'm sorry we haven't really introduced ourselves, have we? I'm Brenda.'

'Not Glenda? It says Glenda on the card,' Kristian said.

'No, it's definitely Brenda, since birth in fact, and this is Gary my husband.' Gary nodded in acknowledgement.

'Are you settling in well?' Kristian asked.

'Oh, yes thanks,' Gary replied. 'Still some decorating to do but we are getting there.'

'That's good,' continued Kristian, 'if ever you need anything you can always call next door. Josh and I will help if we can.'

'Thank you, that's nice of you,' said Gary.

'Yes, thank you,' said Brenda.

'I must go, thanks again,' continued Kristian. 'Don't worry I'll show myself out.' Kristian opened the front door and walked outside.

'Yes, just shut that door,' Gary called as he left. The door shut. Brenda was mortified at what Gary had said.

'Oh my God, Gary! You just couldn't help yourself, could you?' she said, 'I'm surprised you didn't go the whole way and say, what a gay day!' Gary looked annoyed at that missed opportunity.

'Why didn't I think of that? But I never go the whole way and use all of Larry's catchphrases on a first meeting,' he remarked, jokingly.

'Unbelievable!' said Brenda. 'It's not funny.'

'I simply said shut that door. He's younger and to him it'll just be an appropriate comment as he was going out of the door. I didn't mean anything. The only one offended is you!' Mark opened the door and looked through.

'I've finished the windows, Glenda,' he said. Brenda turned round and still feeling annoyed with Gary took her anger out on Mark.

'It's BRENDA!' she yelled. Mark looked shocked.

'Sorry Brenda,' he said, 'I'll be off then.' He left quickly.

'Now look what you made me do!' she screamed at Gary.

'What?' he asked.

'I've terrified the window cleaner. We'll have smeary windows from now on!'

The next day was Thursday and Gary had great plans to finally start painting the bedroom again. Luscious lime hadn't worked out well and Brenda had chosen a new colour. Gary cautiously opened the can of paint while Brenda looked on. He kept his fingers-crossed that she still liked the colour. Her moods and tastes were known to change frequently.

'That looks better, Gary,' she said, so Gary uncrossed his fingers.

'That shade will go better with our bedding too. A lovely pale pink! What's it called? Oh yes, Pink Passion. I'm much happier with this colour.'

'That's good,' replied a happy Gary, 'I'll get painting a little later and have it finished in no time. Will this be a soothing colour? Sounds a bit passionate to me.'

'Oh yes, which is good news for you,' she said, winking at Gary, 'passionate and soothing!'

'Yes, I know how soothed you are will determine how soothed I am,' Gary replied, 'and how passionate you feel will determine how much …' Gary was interrupted,

'You've got it!' she said, winking again.

Gary painted that bedroom in record time. Every bit was finished, first and second coats, by Friday lunchtime. That was a good job too as it was completed just a few hours before the baking competition.

'Right then Gary, let's make this scone mixture,' Brenda said, enthusiastically.

'I'll sit in the other room and read my book then,' Gary replied, less enthusiastically.

'No, you won't,' she insisted, 'I won't have you showing me up this evening. I'll prepare the mixture and you can watch me. That way you have sort of done it yourself.'

Brenda had a bowl in front of her. She had rubbed the ingredients into a bread crumb like mixture and added the egg and milk. Gary was watching although every now and then he was distracted by what was going on in the garden and looked out of the kitchen window.

'Are you paying attention?' she asked.

'Yes, my honey bee,' Gary replied, placing his hand on her shoulder while still looking outside.

'I'll give you honey bee, I can sting, buzz!' she said, smiling at Gary.

'Why will my scones taste better than anyone else's?' he enquired.

'Because I add a secret ingredient,' she continued, 'it's a tip passed down by my mother. It gives them a bit of a kick.'

'Is it gun powder? That's what I think your mother would have added. That would make them as explosive as her tongue.' Brenda was not happy with that comment.

'Gary, sometimes you are so rude!' she protested. 'My mother was a lovely woman. It's a couple of pinches of cinnamon, that's all! That will give them bite and zing.'

'Surely, they are hot cross scones then . . . again a good description of your mother,' he said, with a smile.

'There you go again being rude about my mother. Watch it!' She then turned her thought back to her mixture. 'So here we have the scone mixture.'

'Right, so what will I need to do tonight?' Gary asked. He already looked nervous.

'When you get there,' she started, 'you can roll out the mixture and use the cutter to cut out six evenly sized scones. Then place them on the baking tray.' She then produced a pastry brush from the drawer. 'Then,' she continued, 'take this brush and dip it in the milk and brush the milk across the top of each scone. You'll get a nice brown finish once they are cooked. They'll need around thirty minutes on gas mark 6.'

'Okay, I think. Will I have all this stuff with me?' he asked.

'Yes, I'll put it all ready to go including the milk in a little bottle,' Brenda replied, in a calm reassuring tone.

'Right, good,' he said, 'can I read my book now?' He picked up his book from the side and started walking to the lounge. The book was entitled, *The basics of survival in a woman's world.*

Gary spent the next couple of hours relaxing. He had spent yesterday and that morning painting and so was due some downtime before the cookery competition. He wasn't looking forward to it at all, but it was soon early evening and he was standing in the kitchen at DDs. Several of the WI members plus the other two competitors were present. Dolly started the welcoming speech,

'Welcome to our little cooking competition, it's Wancott's own Bake off! Thank you Margaret, for agreeing to carry out the tasting and choose the winner. We have three competitors, Jake, Syd and Gary. They've all prepared their cake mixtures prior to this evening. Now they will make final preparations and cook their offerings. I have been told that Jake is making Chelsea Buns, Syd is making Rock Cakes and Vera tells me they will probably live up to their name.' There was laughter amongst the audience. 'And Gary is making Hot Cross Scones. That's a new one on me.'

'No,' Brenda said, 'just scones with a little kick, Dolly. Gary gets carried away with his descriptions.'

'Right then, that's great. Are you ready gents?' Dolly asked. The men nodded their heads to indicate that they were. 'Well then, off you go. And good luck to you all.'

All three men got their cake mixtures out. The two café main ovens were already on and the top oven in one was also on. This was to ensure they would reach the right temperature in time for baking the offerings. Gary rolled out his mixture and cut it into evenly sized scones and placed them on the baking tray. He was feeling confident and pleased with himself but then he realised he had the milk but not the pastry brush. He was becoming stressed and started muttering to himself. By this time Jake and Syd had already placed their cakes in the oven leaving Gary the top oven.

'Oh no, where's the brush? What am I going to do? I need the brush to put the milk on the top of the scones. I know what to do, I'll use a spoon. I'll spoon it on gently.' He immediately felt more confident. Problem, think, solution, solved! He turned to Dolly and made a request,

'Dolly, can I borrow a teaspoon please?'

'Of course, Gary.' Dolly handed him the spoon. 'By the way,' she continued, 'the main ovens are both being used now so you'll need to use the small top oven.'

Gary was now the only one in the kitchen as everyone else had congregated in the café and they were sitting at the tables. Dolly had made them some hot drinks and went back into the café to join them. Gary finished spooning the milk onto his scones and put the spoon down on the baking tray. Again, he muttered to himself 'Now I need to place them in the oven for thirty minutes, where's my oven? Oh yes, Dolly said the one on the top, here we go.' He placed the baking tray in the microwave which was on the worktop next to the cookers. He set the timer for thirty minutes and pressed the start button. Feeling happy with his efforts, he walked into the main café to join the others who were drinking their coffees. Meanwhile, there was sparking inside the microwave caused by the metal tray and spoon. The microwave started to bang as sparks flew, then there was one very large bang. Everyone rushed into the kitchen to see what had happened. Dolly ran over and turned the microwave off at the switch. Gary looked surprised and turned to Brenda.

'Are you sure it is thirty minutes, Brenda?' he enquired.

'Oh, Gary what have you done?' Brenda asked.

'Are you sure it wasn't gun powder in the scones?' he said. Sarah had already got over the shock of the bang and was now laughing. She looked at Gary and said,

'Well they were obviously hot and cross after all. That was certainly a kick!' A few others had begun to laugh and then came the moment Brenda was dreading, the sarcastic remark from Lucy.

'You obviously don't make these that often Gary . . . in the microwave,' she said smugly. By this time Brenda couldn't take any more and had disappeared out of the door.

The rest of that evening was very quiet in the Gary and Brenda household. Brenda sat around sighing a lot, in deep thought, until she had a bath and went to bed.

As they lay in their bed in the darkness, Brenda broke the silence as she exclaimed,

'I hate this colour on the walls Gary, we'll have to change it. Passionate Pink my foot!'

'Don't worry love, I know just the colour,' Gary piped up, 'Gun Powder grey!'

Brenda screamed and all that could be seen was her silhouette picking up her pillow and bashing Gary with it.

Chapter Four

April
Up North

The beautiful month of April had arrived full of the promise of Spring and Easter bunnies. A few weeks had passed since the baking ordeal in DDs. Brenda had promised never to involve Gary in a WI competition again and Gary promised never to mention gun powder. It was the best way to help Brenda's mental health remain non-explosive and stable.

The big event of April, apart from Gary and Brenda's wedding anniversary, had to be the bowls match between Wancott and South Marston. It had finally arrived. South Marston were top of the local league whereas Wancott were tenth of fifteen so by far the underdogs. However, underdogs very often bite back and this match had been very close with everything depending on the very last bowl which was Gary's turn. It was crucial and he was very nervous but released his bowl. It was a very good shot in that it stopped closest to the jack, but sadly it took out two of his team's bowls making South Marston the winners.

'Well done, Gary,' said a sarcastic Phil, 'that couldn't have gone worse if you'd tried!'

'I'm sorry, my hand slipped so that I let go too early,' Gary insisted.

'You can say that again,' was Anthony's contribution.

'He just said it. Why does he need to say it again?' questioned Paddy who was listening, as always, for things that didn't make sense to him.

'It's just a saying Paddy, don't start,' said Anthony. 'Why do you take everything so literally?' Paddy shrugged his shoulders.

'Never mind,' Cyril piped up, 'it was just one of those things.' Anthony didn't want to let it drop though. He liked winding up Gary normally so why not make him feel bad now?

'One of those annoying things!' he said.

'It can happen to anyone. Don't worry Gary, we'll beat them next match,' Cyril said trying to offer comfort.

'How?' asked Phil. 'Will Gary be on holiday?' Anthony found that amusing and laughed. Gary sat quietly feeling like the footballer who missed in the penalty shootout.

'Who's up for a quick drink in the pub then?' Cyril asked. 'That'll make you feel better, Gary.' And so, the Wancott Lawn Bowling Club members, well five of them at least, went to the Merry Oak, just a two-minute walk along the road. Gary bought them all a drink by way of an apology.

'Don't take it to heart, everyone makes mistakes,' Cyril said again.

'Thanks, Cyril,' Gary replied. Phil thought that Gary had suffered enough now and began to feel sorry for him. He decided that changing the subject would be a good move.

'What are you up to for the rest of the day?' he asked Gary.

'It's easy for people to criticise,' said Cyril, 'they should be more understanding.' This was an incredible remark from someone who just couldn't let it go. Gary chose to ignore Cyril and answered Phil's question. He looked more excited as he explained,

'I've got to put a plan of action into action, if you know what I mean. I'm celebrating my wedding anniversary; forty years married on Saturday.'

'It cost us the match but anyone can misplace a shot.' Cyril was still rumbling on in the background like a dormant volcano about to spring back into life. Phil, like Gary, chose to ignore him.

'Forty years,' said Phil, 'that's quite an achievement, Gary.' Paddy looked impressed too and asked,

'What are you thinking of doing?' The volcano was still rumbling on and now said,

'We'll beat them next time.' That was enough for Phil who turned to face Cyril and said,

'For goodness sake Cyril, shut up about it now. It's forgotten.' He looked at Gary and continued, 'I'm sorry I went on earlier Gary, after all it's only a sodding game, isn't it?' Gary smiled; he appreciated the support. Paddy looked up from his pint.

'Are you having a party?' he asked.

'Why would we? We lost,' Cyril said, he just couldn't stop thinking of that match.

'For his wedding anniversary,' Paddy told Cyril.

'No, not a party. I'm going away,' Gary replied.

'On your own?' asked Paddy.

'No, of course not. I'll take Brenda. I'm not going to celebrate on my own, am I?'

'Sometimes it is more enjoyable if you're on your own,' Phil said. Cyril and Paddy nodded in agreement.

'No, I won't be on my own,' Gary confirmed. 'My problem is choosing the right place to go, not who to go with. If I get it wrong I could find myself between the devil and the deep blue sea. I've got to get it right.' Paddy looked concerned but before he could speak Gary assured him he didn't need to worry about the devil or the sea, it was just a saying like the others and it had no valuable relevance.

'Whatever I choose,' he continued, 'I want it to be a surprise. Brenda likes a surprise.' Paddy looked thoughtful.

'Women are strange things,' he said, 'I've never understood them. When I was at work, a few years back now, I went out with a lovely lady. It lasted about two months, Patsy she was called.'

'What happened?' Gary asked.

'It all went wrong but I don't know why really. I took her away to a four-star hotel and everything,' Paddy replied; he looked sad just remembering it.

'Perhaps you said something wrong,' Gary said, looking puzzled. 'I hope you didn't challenge everything she said like you do with us.'

'No, not at all although she did say some funny things like, *on the other hand.* I couldn't see what her hands had to do with anything,' Paddy said.

'You must have some idea why she dumped you,' Phil said. 'Were you mean to her?' Paddy looked a little hurt at that suggestion.

'No, I was always kind,' he insisted. 'It was a smashing hotel and we had a romantic meal in the restaurant with candles and everything. I even ordered flowers to be delivered to the table. Anyway, it got to about 9:30 and I said how about an early night?'

'Oh yes,' Phil said, winking at Paddy.

'And she said, yes, she was keen for an early night too. So we had an early night but in the morning she'd gone, just left. No note, no message, nothing.'

'Oh well,' said Cyril, 'perhaps she thought that was as good as it gets so left at the height of passion.' Paddy looked thoroughly confused by that and thought Cyril made more sense when he was consumed by the match loss.

'That's terrible Paddy,' Gary sympathised, 'you must have done something to upset her.' Paddy thought for a second or two and then added,

'I did ask her friend what I'd done wrong and she said that Patsy might have been expecting to have the early night with me. She couldn't have liked her own room that's all I can think. It cost a lot too.' There was silence as all the men looked stunned. Cyril then asked,

'What happened just then? Has the trauma of losing the match interfered with my ears?'

'Paddy, didn't you want to be with her?' Gary asked.

'When I go away it is to relax and have a rest,' Paddy started, 'I was getting all the other at home.'

'I suppose you didn't fancy the away match then?' said Phil.

'Well, I want Brenda with me, in the same room, in the same bed and . . .'

'Too much information,' Cyril said, interrupting Gary.

'I don't know, I like to hear the details,' Anthony said, with a smile.

'I'm thinking of taking her up north to stay over and experience the aurora borealis,' Gary continued.

'You devil, Gary!' said Anthony. 'What position is that? I admire your stamina, mate.' Gary grinned as his macho side took that as a compliment, but reality soon took over and Anthony was corrected.

'It's the Northern Lights!' Gary explained. 'The great spectacle of wonderful colours in the night sky. It will be both beautiful and romantic. I hope the weather doesn't muck it up though. I'll book it all tonight. I'm going to tell her we are off to see my sister Mary, in Huddersfield. Instead of coming straight back we can travel on to somewhere where we can witness the Northern Lights.'

'I'm sure she'll love it,' said Cyril, 'if not you can always take Paddy, separate rooms and all that.' The men all laughed, except Paddy for some reason.

Meanwhile in Seymour Rise, Trudie was walking to her car. Kai was delivering the post and started to walk passed Aggie's house. Aggie opened her door and rushed to catch up with him. Trudie ducked down behind the side of her car. She didn't want Aggie to see her as the last time they had spoken Aggie was trying to get Trudie to commit to playing a role in her next stage production.

'I say Kai,' Aggie bellowed, 'are you sure you don't have anything for me? Perhaps it's out of order in your bag?'

'Sorry, I don't have anything. What are you expecting, a parcel, a letter?' he asked.

'It'll be a large letter containing a script for my next AmDram production,' she explained. 'I've had a few specially printed and I was expecting to have received them by now.'

'Oh right,' he said, 'I heard about your show at the old folks' place the other week. Trudie told me about it. She said it was an experience she'll never forget. It's not every day a resident attacks an actor and knocks his teeth out.' Trudie was cringing as she crouched beside her car. She would have appreciated it if Kai had kept her name out of the conversation. Aggie was not amused but was resigned to the fact that this would be a talking point for a while.

'Yes, well that was all very unfortunate. Most of the audience enjoyed the play though until that point.'

'Well it turned drama into comedy in one go,' Kai observed. 'The experience hasn't put you off drama then?'

'Oh no, definitely not,' Aggie insisted. 'This is my hobby and since retiring from the school it keeps me going.'

'Good for you. I'll see you later, bye for now.' Kai moved on with his bag full of letters still to be delivered and Aggie headed back inside. Trudie rose slowly and got into her car.

While Trudie had been playing hide-and-seek at the front of the house, Brenda was in her back garden inside the shed. She was trying to sort out the mess. Boxes were put there when they moved in and some other things were left by the previous homeowner. There was also a picnic chair which Gary sat on when daydreaming. Brenda came outside for some fresh air and spotted Izzy in her back garden. Izzy waved and both women walked to the fence.

'How are you, Glenda?' Izzy asked. Brenda didn't have the energy to attempt to correct her name so just accepted Glenda, after all she was beginning to feel like a Glenda.

'I'm fighting a losing battle in the shed,' Brenda said.

'Oh no, who's in there? Shouldn't you phone the police?' Izzy exclaimed in horror.

'There's no one in there. It's just a figure of speech. I'm trying to tidy it up a bit but as soon as I've made a space Gary will fill it with some other rubbish. Of course, he insists it isn't rubbish but, I tell you, it's man rubbish.'

'Why does he collect rubbish?' asked a puzzled Izzy.

'It isn't strictly rubbish but it is stuff I don't think we'll need again.'

'Oh,' said Izzy, still not understanding what was meant. Her thoughts moved on to something else and her face lit up with excitement as she announced,

'Glenda, I can't keep my secret anymore.'

'Don't tell me it's you that has been filling our shed with rubbish?' Brenda joked.

'Why would I do that?' asked a confused Izzy.

'Sorry Izzy, just joking.'

'Oh,' she said again, making this the second 'oh' in the last few seconds. Izzy's mind soon turned back to her news and she announced,

'You mustn't tell anyone this yet as we haven't told our parents, but I'm pregnant.'

'That's lovely, Izzy. Congratulations! It's so nice to hear good news!' Brenda replied. 'So are you hoping for a girl or a baby for life?' Izzy looked blank, yes it was another wasted joke.

'A baby, either a boy or a girl,' Izzy said, very seriously.

'Yes! Wonderful news!' Brenda said, quickly trying to gloss over her joke.

'Don't tell anyone else, will you? I'm so excited I had to tell someone. You can tell Gary though.' Brenda reassured her that her lips were sealed to everyone other than Gary.

'Do you have a due date?' she asked.

'It will be nine months from conception, Glenda,' came the precise reply.

'And when is that then, November time?' Brenda asked.

'No, it'll be early October as I'm twelve weeks now but I didn't want to say anything until I reached twelve weeks, just in case anything happened, you know?' Brenda knew exactly what she meant. She had had terrible heart-breaking experiences of miscarriages herself.

'Well, you'll have to start thinking of names next,' she said. Brenda was growing fonder of Izzy by the day. She no longer felt annoyed by her calling her by the wrong name, in fact she had started to actually enjoy it. Izzy had told her a lot about her childhood growing up in Wancott and the bullying she had encountered for being mixed race at a time when the town was predominantly a sea of white faces. Times had changed but twenty-five years ago things were different. Brenda wondered what life would be like for the baby. One thing was for certain, he or she would have a loving home which was the most important thing of all. That loving home would be missing jokes from Mum though.

Still on a high from Izzy's news, Brenda decided to go into town. She had to go to the jewellers and afterwards she could visit Dolly for a chat and a coffee. She wasn't expecting Gary home from his bowls match for a while because the after match drinks always lasted longer than the match itself. It was around 3:15 when she reached DDs. Dolly was behind the counter and a couple of people were sitting at a table eating cake.

'Hi Dolly,' Brenda said cheerily, 'it's only me today. There's no Gary so your microwave is safe. How's the new one?'

'It's great, thank you Brenda, love,' she replied. 'I'm not angry about that anymore. In fact I have a smile when I think of it now. Hot Cross Scones, indeed! Only a man could think you can cook scones in a microwave with a stainless steel spoon added for good measure. Where is he then? Probably too frightened to come in?'

'Bowls, Dolly,' was Brenda's response.

'Well there's no need for language like that!' Dolly joked. Brenda smiled and continued,

'He's got a match today. I expect they are in the pub by now though. I'm pleased he's got his bowls mates and leisure time. He gets a social life and I get four hours without him under my feet.'

'What would you like?' asked Dolly.

'To have him out from under my feet for four hours every day!' joked Brenda.

'No, I meant what would you like to drink?' Dolly smiled at Brenda.

'Yes, sorry. I'll have a black coffee and a chocolate brownie, please Dolly,' Brenda began. 'Can I pull a chair up to the counter so I can talk to you? I need to sit down after walking into town.'

'Of course, take the weight off your feet. Come and sit here.' Brenda pulled a chair from under one of the tables, positioned it at the counter and sat down.

'Ah, that's better,' she said, 'it's good to have a rest.' She paused for a second to sip her coffee and then continued, 'It's my wedding anniversary on Saturday. I've just picked up a little present for Gary from the jewellers. I don't know if Gary will remember though.' At this point, now 3:30, in walked the Roadeteers. They had finished work for the day and walked towards the counter acknowledging both women with an, 'Alright ladies?'

'Can I have three teas to go?' Frank requested.

'Of course you can,' Dolly replied whilst passing Brenda her chocolate brownie. 'Have you finished for the day then?'

'Yes, we've dug out a large hole for the telephone company to lay cable,' Frank replied. 'Not sure what they are doing but that's not our worry. They should start work tomorrow.' Frank looked at Steve and asked, 'Is all the equipment secure? I don't want anything nicked. Steve, did you put all the road signs and barriers out?'

'Yes, boss.' Dolly passed the takeout teas to Frank and took payment. He became distracted as something passed the window. It was a digger being driven down the road.

'What the fuck!' exclaimed Frank. Realising where he was, he immediately apologised to everyone else in DDs for his bad language and then continued, 'I thought it was all secure?' Doug couldn't help but smile, the scene reminded him of something out of a 1970s sitcom.

'I turned it off and covered it,' insisted Steve.

'Where are the keys then?' Frank asked.

'Ah yes, probably on the seat,' Steve replied.

'Get after it then! Oh give me strength!' Frank was not happy.

'Right you are!' Steve replied and left quickly. At least diggers can't move fast. The other two quickly followed Steve outside. Dolly and Brenda smiled at each other.

'No hope, is there?' Dolly giggled.

Brenda filled up the rest of her afternoon walking home and preparing dinner. When Gary arrived back she tried to console him but he continued to blame himself for the lost bowls match. The beer hadn't eased his guilt and he worried about having let everyone down. The pain appeared to wear off a little after he'd eaten his dinner and his mind focussed back on the surprise trip he was planning. He disappeared for a while from the lounge with his laptop and booked the hotels.

It was now 6 o'clock and he was sitting on the sofa. Brenda was next to him reading a book.

'Is it worth putting the news on or are we depressed enough already?' he asked.

'It'll be humans bombing other humans, people starving and when will the world end?' said a pessimistic Brenda.

'And that's just Swindon!' Gary joked. 'Let's leave the tele off. I wanted to ask how you feel about something anyway.' He paused for a second before saying, 'It's our anniversary on Saturday and . . .'

'You remembered!' Brenda interrupted.

'I've only ever forgotten it once and I dare never make that mistake again,' Gary said, protesting his innocence. 'How about we go out for a nice meal in Huddersfield?' Brenda found his suggestion amusing.

'What Huddersfield, Europe's capital of romance?' she said.

'We could visit Mary as we haven't seen her for a while and it will be easier on a Saturday for travelling,' Gary said, laying out his plans. 'We could have a nice romantic meal out in the evening and stay in a hotel for the night.'

'That all sounds lovely,' Brenda replied smiling. 'It'll be nice to get away from here for a day and the romantic evening will be lovely. It'll be great to see Mary, you know I get on well with my sister-in-law. I feel sad for her now, all on her own. We'd better warn her that we are coming so she's prepared.'

'Yes, she'll need to get some Rich Tea biscuits in,' Gary said. He grinned and continued, 'Leave the preparations to me, I'll see to it all.' In reality Gary had, of course, already booked it but he hadn't wanted to admit this just in case Brenda hadn't found the idea appealing.

'By the way, I tried to tidy your man cave this afternoon,' Brenda started, 'you know the one you call a shed and visit regularly to tidy but end up sitting in there looking into space?'

'I hope you haven't disturbed things too much. I know where all my precious junk is!' Gary said, with a worried look on his face.

'While I was out there I saw Izzy and I have news.'

'What's that then, Glenda?' Gary laughed.

'Very funny!' she replied and continued, 'Izzy is pregnant. It's a secret for now but she told me.'

'Oh no,' exclaimed Gary, 'can you imagine what they'll call that poor baby? A cat called First Class and a baby called Special Delivery?'

'No, don't!' Brenda laughed. The happy mood changed in a second when Gary asked,

'Do you ever wonder where our children would be now and what they'd be doing?' Tears immediately welled up in Brenda's eyes.

'Sometimes, but I try not to,' she started, trying hard to hold it together. 'I'm past crying over what might have been. It just didn't happen and they've never existed past fifteen weeks in my womb and that's that.'

'Yes, you are right,' Gary said, already regretting that he had asked such a stupid question. 'Sorry I mentioned it, I didn't mean to bring it all back. You would have been a great mum just like you're a great aunt to Mary's two girls.' He put his arms around her and she snuggled into his chest.

'By the way, stupid,' she said, with a weak smile, 'I am literally a great aunt to Verity and Tammy, aren't I?'

'Yes, but you are the best ever aunt and great aunt!'

'Ah, thank you,' Brenda continued, 'perhaps it's all for the best really, at least we haven't got children to force us into an old folks' home.'

'What? You don't fancy sitting in a comfy chair and watching one of Aggie's plays?' Gary laughed, 'OMG, shame on you!'

'What's with OMG? You've never said that before!' said a surprised Brenda.

'Oh yes, OMG is youngster speak, innit? I may not have kids but I can still be down with the kids.' They both started to laugh as Brenda attempted some of that herself.

'Wicked! Or is it sick?' she asked. Gary started to tickle her. 'No, stop it! Stop!' she begged. Brenda is very ticklish.

Saturday morning soon came around. Brenda had packed the suitcase ready for their trip and left it by the front door. She had planned to put it in the car the day before but Gary was worried it might encourage thieves to break in. He had always been a worrier!

'I'm really looking forward to this, thank you for being so thoughtful,' Brenda said. 'Happy Anniversary, Gary!'

'Me too love, and Happy Anniversary to you,' Gary replied. 'You deserve to be spoilt and a night away will be a lovely break. Let's go! It'll take nearly four hours to get there and Mary is expecting us early afternoon.' They walked outside with their suitcase and a bunch of flowers.

By 2:30 they had arrived at the flats where Mary lives. They were in a good mood as their journey had gone very smoothly. Brenda was quite excited at having arrived at the destination as she was looking forward to her break. They entered the lobby and headed towards the lift.

'Well we were lucky there, no hold ups at all. That's the type of journey I like,' Gary said, happily. 'Right, we want the 4th floor - number 406, oh no.' Gary's perky mood had been knocked for six by a sign on the lift doors that read - OUT OF ORDER.

Gary read it out loud, slowly and softly,

'Out . . of . . order.' This made Brenda laugh.

'Gary! Reading it slowly won't change it. So it's the stairs then!' she chirped merrily. She turned to the stairs on her right and walked towards them but Gary didn't move.

'What?' he moaned. 'Four flights of stairs will probably kill me.' Brenda giggled.

'I'll take that risk,' she shouted back from half way up the first flight of stairs.

'Charming!' Gary muttered. 'And Happy Anniversary to you too!' He hadn't moved from the lift and couldn't resist pressing the call lift button. He pressed it and the doors opened. With a smile of relief on his face, he entered the lift. He pressed the button for floor 4 and the doors closed. The lift then ascended about three feet and stopped. At this point he became anxious and started to shout,

'Brenda, I'm stuck! Brenda!' Brenda had come back down the stairs wondering where Gary had got to. Her giggles turned into full blown laughter as she asked,

'Oh Gary, why did you get in? It said it is out of order, oh no sorry it said,' (she was now impersonating Gary), 'out . . . of . . . order.'

'It's not funny. I can't get out and I'm feeling claustrophobic. Do something! Brenda? Are you there, Brenda!' came the plea from inside the lift.

'Claustrophobic? How come you can sit in a little shed for hours and not feel claustrophobic, it isn't much bigger?' she laughed. By this time Gary was getting very panicky.

'It's not the same,' he protested, 'I'm not trapped in the shed. Do something . . you won't be laughing if this lift plunges to the bottom and I die!'

'What? You are only a couple of feet from the bottom. Oh Gary, sometimes!' was Brenda's exhausted response. At this point Gary managed to prise open the doors about ten inches and Brenda could see him. Brenda's laughter now stopped.

'For goodness sake don't put your head through there!' she shouted. 'If it moves you'll be beheaded. I don't fancy watching that, or even worse, clearing it up.' She had a further thought and smiled again.

'Blast! I should have increased your life insurance,' she joked.

'It's not funny, will you please help me?' Gary pleaded.

'How?' asked Brenda. 'Have we got some lift door cutters in our luggage?' Whilst talking Brenda had walked over to a notice showing the emergency telephone numbers for the lift and pulled out her phone. She rang the number shown. Gary could no longer see her and started to panic.

'Brenda!' he shouted, 'where are you, love?' Brenda walked back to stand in front of the lift.

'Do you want the good news or the bad news?' she teased.

'Good news! I'll have the good news,' Gary replied.

'I've found the phone number for assistance,' Brenda said.

'Brilliant . . so what's the bad news?' he asked.

'It's unobtainable,' she giggled.

'No!' he gasped. Brenda climbed the stairs back to the first floor saying nothing as she went. Gary could no longer see her through the crack in the lift doors.

'Brenda, where are you? Brenda!' he asked with a note of panic in his voice.

Brenda walked across to the lift call button on the first floor and pressed it. The lift doors could be heard slamming shut on the floor below and the lift travelled up to the first floor. The doors opened and Brenda reached in and pulled Gary out abruptly greeting him with,

'You pillock! Don't do that again. Now we use the stairs and if they don't kill you, I just might!' Gary looked at her and smiled.

'I've had an idea love,' he started, 'let's use the stairs, at least it's one flight less now.'

Gary puffed a bit but he made it up the stairs and, after a few minutes, they were standing outside flat 06 on the fourth floor (known as 406). When the door opened Mary stood there with a welcoming smile; that beautiful smile could light up any room, or corridor for that matter.

'Hello you two. It's lovely to see you,' she said. They hugged each other before going into her flat.

'Shame about the lift, how long has it been out of order?' Gary asked.

'It's a pain. It happened a couple of days ago but should be fixed today, apparently,' she started. 'Trouble is idiots are ignoring the sign and trying it.' Brenda gave Gary a long stare and said,

'You don't say!'

'Yes, they really need to put tape across the front of the doors to stop that,' Mary continued. Brenda's smile then left her face as she realised she'd forgotten something.

'Oh Mary, we have some flowers for you. They are in the car. Gary can you pop down and get them?' she requested. Gary answered that request with a resounding 'No!' Mary smiled on hearing his commanding refusal.

'That was definite,' she observed.

'Sorry Mary I . . .' Gary started to explain but Mary interrupted him saying,

'No, don't be silly. Don't worry, I'll walk down with you when you leave and you can let me have them then. Thank you for thinking of me, you shouldn't have wasted your money on flowers for me!'

'He thinks he'll die if he has to go down more than one flight of stairs,' Brenda joked.

'It's not going down that'll do it, it's the coming back up,' Gary replied. 'Anyway, how are you, sis?'

'I'm well thanks. I keep fit by climbing stairs!' she said. 'Well, sit down you two. The kettle has boiled and I've opened the Rich Tea biscuits!' Mary headed to her kitchen and Gary and Brenda smiled at each other, oh Mary loved Rich Tea biscuits.

Back in Wancott, Kai was enjoying a rare Saturday off work. He and Izzy had visited both sets of parents to tell them their baby news. Izzy was excited as she had other plans for their afternoon. She wanted to discuss names for the baby.

'Now our parents know I'm pregnant, I feel better about having told Glenda,' Izzy announced.

'Glenda? Glenda who?' asked Kai.

'Glenda, from over the back fence. I saw her in the week when she was battling something in her shed. To be honest what she said didn't make much sense to me.'

'Right, you mean Brenda? I found out her name is, in fact, Brenda,' Kai said.

'No, Glenda,' said Izzy, 'lives with Gary! Anyway, Glenda said we'd be choosing names soon for the baby so I've been thinking.'

'Watch out world!' laughed Kai. Izzy looked over at Kai with a straight face.

'What? Why?' she said.

'Never mind,' he said giving up. 'I should know better by now.'

'I think Goofna is a good name for a boy,' Izzy declared. Kai looked stunned.

'Goofna?' he repeated, in disbelief.

'Yes,' confirmed Izzy, 'it comes from Africa and I think it's quite rare here.'

'I'm not surprised! Where did you hear of it?' enquired Kai.

'From one of my clients,' she replied, 'I was cleaning her house and she has a Saluki dog called Jasper. They said the Saluki breed originates from Africa and they nearly called him Goofna.' Kai looked even more confused.

'So the dog breed is African, but that doesn't mean the name Goofna is African. Goofna sounds like a good name for a dog though,' he responded.

'I like it and it will be rare,' she insisted. 'And if we have a girl, I thought Camille. What do you think?'

'Let's hope the baby's a girl, that's what I think!' Kai remarked. 'Goofna? Can you imagine what trouble a boy will have going through school with the name Goofna? It'd be shortened to Goofy for a start.'

'You don't like it then?' she said. 'How about Tittimus?' Kai knew his partner didn't see the world like others but this was a real puzzler for him.

'How about Daniel or Elliot, you know something normal?' Kai replied. 'No son of mine is going to have Tit as part of his first name, unless it's Titan.' It was now Izzy's turn to look confused.

'You are being awkward now,' she declared. 'What surname will the baby have?'

'Mine of course, unless there's something you aren't telling me,' Kai said.

'But we aren't married, so I think they should have my surname,' she insisted.

'But we're engaged, and anyway they take the father's surname,' Kai said, getting agitated.

'Well you think hard about the first name choices then and I'll think hard about the surname.' Izzy felt she now had bargaining power!

Gary and Brenda spent a lovely three hours with Mary. The flowers were safely passed on to her and the pair made their way to the hotel. They were directed to their room on the third floor and started to settle in.

'It was nice to see Mary looking well and happy,' said Gary. 'She's had a rough couple of years.'

'Yes, it's always nice to catch up in person,' remarked Brenda, 'she copes well on her own.' Brenda was looking around the room as she spoke. 'This is a lovely room, isn't it? It's a nice hotel. Good choice, love,' she said which resulted in Gary smiling proudly. A couple of minutes went by as they unpacked their little suitcase, then Brenda said,

'Would you mind if we didn't go out for our meal but ordered something from the Room Service Menu instead? We've had quite a tiring day, haven't we? With the travelling, seeing Mary and . . .'

'All those stairs!' Gary interrupted before continuing, 'This is a treat for you so you can choose to do what you want to. If you want to eat in the room that's fine with me.'

'Yes, then let's look at the menu and order to our room,' Brenda continued, 'we can have a happy anniversary in our room.'

'That sounds nice and cosy,' Gary agreed. 'I've got a surprise for tomorrow, we are going on to another hotel but only for one night.'

'What? Another night?' said a surprised Brenda.

'Yes, we are travelling across to a seaside town.' Brenda smiled but the smile suddenly left her face to be replaced by a worried look.

'Why didn't you tell me before we left home?' she asked. 'I only brought enough clean underwear for one night away.'

'It's only one extra night!' Gary replied. 'We'll be okay with what we've got. You know what we men say, don't you? If you throw your pants against the wall and they don't stick to it, then they are still okay to wear.' Brenda looked horrified.

'That is disgusting!' she said, in a raised voice. 'Only an unmarried man would say that. You're married to me and should know better! Has that filth come from your bowling mates?'

'It's just a joke love, just a joke. Now what do you want to order to eat?' Gary said, trying to change the subject.

'I'm feeling a bit sick now. I'll choose later,' she sighed.

'Sorry,' Gary said feeling just a little guilty for causing her nausea.

In Seymour Rise, Trudie had just received a text message from Brenda. When she left, Brenda had told Trudie that the house would be empty for one night. The text was explaining that it would now be two nights due to Gary's surprise. The message was a little muddled but Trudie understood its meaning. As Trudie read her message, David walked over to the side table in the lounge and picked up a large letter. It was addressed to Aggie.

'What's this doing here?' he asked.

'Oh that, it was squeezed through our letterbox but it's for Aggie. I think Kai was off today and the postman covering put it through the wrong letterbox. It's probably scripts as she was saying, a couple of days ago, that she was expecting some.'

'What's the play this time?' David enquired. 'Is it the great Agatha Christie's Death by flying teeth? Or perhaps it's, a dental bridge too far. You've got to hand it to her . . .' Trudie interrupted him,

'I'm not handing it to her!' David smiled and continued,

'I was going to say, you've got to hand it to her that she's not put off easily, is she? I would have given up by now especially after what happened at the home and, well, poor Brenda.' Trudie was quiet for a second and then announced,

'I think you'll have to take it over to Aggie.' That brought an immediate response,

'Hold on! I'm not going over there. She'll probably try to recruit me for her dramatics group. Gary calls it DamnDram instead of AmDram. I don't want to be pulled into that.' Trudie listened intently and shook her head.

'Just say no then. Are you a man or a mouse?'

'Squeak, squeak!' said David. 'You'll need to take it over. Why didn't you take it over earlier? Not worried, are you?'

'Stupid postie!' Trudie moaned. 'We could just put it by her front door step, ring the bell and run.'

'What if she's not in and it rains? We can squeeze it through her letterbox like the postie did here,' said David, who was creating a lot of ideas but no proper plan of action.

'It'll be hard to get it through the letterbox,' said Trudie, 'which will give us less time to escape back across the road.' Suddenly David had had enough.

'This is stupid!' he declared. He picked up the envelope, opened the front door and walked across the road to Aggie's house. Trudie watched through the window as he pushed the envelope through the letterbox but as he did, Aggie opened the door. Trudie looked on with an equal feeling of fear and amusement.

'It's like a spider catching a fly,' she said to herself. 'Just say NO.' She watched Aggie talking to David. He was shaking his head as he walked away and came back into the house.

'Did she recruit you?' Trudie asked.

'She didn't ask. I think that might have hurt my feelings now,' David replied.

'So what were you shaking your head about?' asked a curious Trudie.

'We were agreeing on how bad the postal service has got,' he replied and after a moment's thought added, 'what an insult, she didn't want me for her production. I'd be good at biting people!'

Saturday had drawn to a close across most of the world and for Gary and Brenda it had been a relaxing evening. Both were tired and fell asleep watching the television straight after they had eaten their meals. In case you were wondering, both opted for fish and chips followed by a fruit crumble with custard. It was something they could have got in their local pub but it tasted better in a hotel room in Huddersfield, with a couple of glasses of wine.

After breakfast on Sunday morning, they checked out of the hotel and drove west on the M61 to Blackpool. It took about an hour and a half to get to their destination. They found a nice little café for a hot drink and then went for a walk along the sea front.

'Well this is nice but it isn't what I had originally planned for you,' Gary said. Brenda looked at him and smiled.

'This is lovely. It's good to see the sea but I'm intrigued now, so what were your original plans?' she asked.

'I was going to take you somewhere where we could see the Northern Lights but the forecast is for cloud all over the country so the chances of seeing anything are very low,' Gary replied, unable to hide the disappointment in his voice. 'So instead I diverted us to Blackpool where you'll see another form of northern lights! We've never been here before to see the illuminations, so it'll be a new experience for both of us. It's not quite as spectacular as I'd been hoping for though.' Brenda grabbed his arm and spoke into his ear. He could feel her warm breath as she said,

'Ah, my love, it's the thought that counts and Blackpool lights . . well what more could I ask for?'

'Something that isn't reliant on our weather perhaps?' he answered, 'I should have whisked you off to Paris for a weekend or even better, somewhere hotter than here.'

'Then we couldn't have popped in on Mary, could we?' she replied. 'Who needs the Eiffel Tower when there's Blackpool Tower? We are away together and that's just lovely!' Gary smiled and as they continued to walk, he looked thoughtful.

'Do the illuminations come on this time of year?' he asked.

'I don't think so but I didn't like to mention that,' Brenda replied.

They both started to laugh as they continued to walk holding hands.

After a romantic candlelit meal in a restaurant not far from Blackpool Tower and another overnight stay in a pleasant hotel, it was soon Monday morning and time to make the journey home. Brenda had managed to survive wearing the same underwear for more than a day without mental scarring. However, the vision in her mind of underwear stuck to a wall was proving traumatic and it would take longer to recover from that.

By mid-afternoon on Monday, Gary and Brenda were home and walking into their lounge.

'It's lovely to get away but it's so nice to be home, isn't it?' Brenda sighed.

'Yes it is, and it's so nice that this house now feels like home,' Gary replied. 'I told you everything would be alright, didn't I? I'll put the kettle on.'

'That'll be lovely,' Brenda said. Gary left the room leaving Brenda taking her jacket off and walking to the sofa where she sat down. She looked at the photo of her parents.

'Well, Mum and Dad, I've had a great couple of days. I didn't get the Eiffel Tower but I got Blackpool Tower. I didn't get the Northern Lights but I got the Blackpool illuminations, without the illuminations. Best of all was the company and entertainment my Gary provided. I laughed so much when he was stuck in a lift. Remind me to tell you about it soon.' Gary walked back into the room.

'I've put the suitcase upstairs for now and the kettle won't be long, actually it's tall and thin and hurts if it lands on your head,' he joked. They both smiled. 'Who were you talking to?'

'Just to myself and the photos,' Brenda replied.

'You are funny,' Gary remarked. 'Well that's another year of marriage!'

'Yes, and I hope you are already planning for next year,' Brenda said, then she suddenly remembered something. 'Oh goodness, I almost forgot, I've got you a present. I meant to take it with us at the weekend but I forgot to pack it. It's really appropriate now too after what happened at Mary's.' Brenda laughed as she walked to the cupboard where she pulled out a small package. 'Here you go,' she said, passing it to Gary. 'Happy Anniversary, Gary.'

'Ah thanks, love.' Gary smiled and opened the box. Inside he found a silver chain with oblong pendant. Engraved on one side it read, "Gary, your love lifts me" and on the other, "Love always Brenda x". They both laughed and Gary kissed Brenda.

'Bloody lifts!' he said.

The rest of Monday passed by in a flash. They, well Brenda, rang Mary to report their safe return home, sorted out the clothes for washing and cooked the dinner! By 9 o'clock she was exhausted. She always wondered why she got so tired from travelling when she was only a passenger, Gary had done all the driving. It was another of life's mysteries.

By 9:30 they were both in bed resting in the darkness. They had been there for just a couple of minutes when Gary said,

'Brenda?'

'What?' she replied, in a drowsy voice.

'How dirty do you think pants have to be before they stick to the wall?'

'DON'T GO THERE GARY!' she said, with great anger in her voice as she whacked him with her pillow.

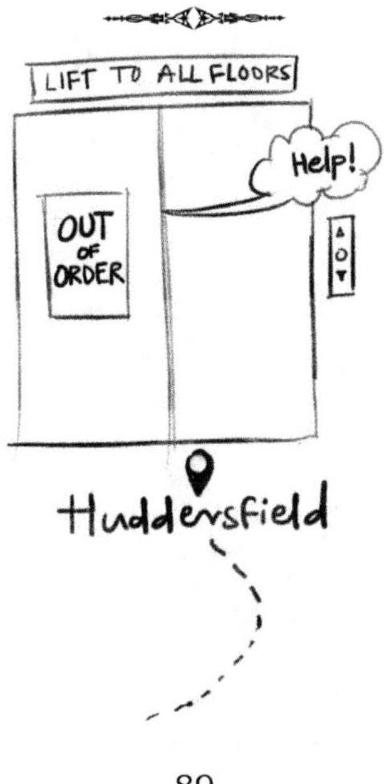

Chapter Five

May
A Handbag!

May started well with a lot of sunshine and ample opportunity to get the garden looking lovely. Brenda had spent the first two weeks putting in bedding plants and was pleased with how nice everything looked. She hoped there wouldn't be any late frosts to damage her hard work. There were just a couple of shrubs still to be planted. She spent many a happy time talking with both Trudie and Izzy over the garden fence. Izzy's bump was getting bigger now.

On this particular May evening some members of the WI were meeting for an social drink. Present were Amy Saunders (19), Marianne Pickles (26), Vera, Violet, Lucy, Susan and Brenda.

'It's lovely to see that some of the younger members have made it out this evening. We tend to be a bit top heavy with us oldies, don't we?' Susan said to Brenda.

'Watch it Susan! Who are you calling an oldie?' Brenda replied, with a smile. 'I've been told you are as old as you feel.'

'Or as old as the man you feel!' laughed Susan.

'I love my Gary but there's not much hope for me there then,' Brenda joked. She leant across to the next table to talk to Amy and Marianne. 'We have just been saying, young ladies, that it's nice to have young blood in the WI.'

'To be honest,' Amy replied, 'I only joined for a laugh and I knew Marianne was a member already so I'd have a friend here. I'm enjoying it though, with you old people.'

'What?' exclaimed Brenda, pretending to sound and look offended.

'Anyone over 30 is old when you are 19, Brenda,' Susan said reassuringly.

'I suppose so,' Brenda conceded. 'What sort of things are you into Amy? How can we make the WI more interesting to younger people?'

'Anything like that, Brenda,' she replied, with her gaze firmly fixed on the young men standing at the bar. They were members of the Young Farmers' Club who were also meeting.

'Well, I can understand that and if I were single and a few years younger . . .' Brenda started, but was interrupted.

'About two generations younger!' said Sarah. Brenda couldn't make out what was going on this evening, why was everyone picking on her age?

'Thanks for that, Sarah,' Brenda sighed, 'it's a good job I'm happy with my Gary then.'

'I think the one on the left fancies me, he keeps staring at me,' Sarah said.

'Perhaps that's because you are staring at him,' Brenda remarked.

'Oh no, don't start Sarah,' said Susan. Marianne had ignored Sarah as she was thinking. She was another younger member at just a mere 26 years old. She had been thinking about Brenda's original question.

'I'm interested in planets and things,' she started, 'Susan, have you ever thought of getting a speaker to talk about the science behind the stars and planets? Personally, that would interest me more than some of our recent speakers.' Vera suddenly became interested,

'What, like UFOs?' she said.

'No Vera, not UFOs,' Marianne replied, 'they don't exist, do they? No, I love reading my horoscope and often wonder what it really means and how they work them out.'

'Made up, I bet,' started Vera, 'like the UFOs.'

'What does it mean,' Marianne started to enquire, 'when it says Uranus is rising in your star sign which will help you gain courage to assert your independence and rise up against those factors holding you back?'

'In my case,' said a smiling Vera, 'it's more like my breasts are descending in the direction of Uranus helping me to assert my respectful hatred of gravity!' All those over fifty laughed in sympathy.

'That's interesting, urrr, the wish for other topics to be explored that is, not Vera's gravitating um, never mind,' Susan said, becoming more embarrassed by the second.

'What birth sign are you, Brenda?' asked Amy.

'It will be my birthday next month Amy, my birth sign is Gemini,' she replied. Marianne looked interested in this news.

'Oh really? The twins, so a split personality with a psycho tendency!' Marianne piped up. 'You don't strike me as a Gemini.' Brenda looked a bit puzzled by this.

'Well thanks, I think?' she replied. Marianne was in full swing now as she had found her favourite topic to talk about.

'They say certain star signs don't mix in love,' she continued. 'I always ask potential boyfriends what star sign they are before I agree to go out with them.'

'What sign is Gary?' asked Amy.

'Pisces,' Brenda said. Amy and Marianne looked at each other and raised their eyebrows, displaying large shocked eyes.

'And are you good with Gary, things alright, are they?' Marianne asked.

'Yes, you take care Brenda!' said a shocked Amy. 'Gemini and Pisces, wow!' Brenda laughed it off but couldn't hide her worried expression. She'd been married to Gary for forty years and she knew they were solid but this revelation of Marianne's had chinked her armour. Marianne was tired with that subject so decided to pick another. To Brenda it almost felt like Marianne had hunted her down, shot her and then moved on to the next target.

'Perhaps WI could have a social night at the theatre. That might be fun as I've never seen a play performed live,' Marianne said. 'I've seen a few groups and musicals but I've never seen a play.'

'Neither have I,' said Amy, 'but I'm happy to leave it that way.'

'Why is that?' asked Lucy, whose need to educate people came to life.

'I'll probably get bored,' Amy replied.

'Unbelievable!' Lucy replied, 'Why not give it a try?'

'How do you know you'd get bored? You might like it,' remarked Marianne. 'You won't know unless you try.'

'I'm happy to accompany you to the theatre, ladies,' said Brenda, after coming out of her two minute depression caused by being married to a Piscean bloke. 'The Importance of being Earnest is on at the Oxford Playhouse at the moment. I'd be happy to go with those who are interested. It will give you youngsters a chance to see actors and actresses performing live.'

'That's better than performing dead, I suppose,' joked Sarah.

'Brenda, I think you'll find they are all actors now,' Lucy said after deciding to educate everyone with her extensive knowledge.

'No, really?' Vera butted in. 'No women or are all the men trans?'

'No, of course not. I'm saying that as an equality measure, everyone who acts is an actor,' Lucy replied. Vera looked a bit confused by this gem of knowledge from Lucy's brain and said,

'Well call me old-fashioned . . .'

'Old-fashioned!' Amy and Marianne shouted with perfect timing and subsequently high fived.

'Call me old fashioned,' Vera started again, ignoring the high spirits of the youngsters, 'but, if I was an actress I'd be proud to be a female actor. Like if I was an actor I'd be proud to be a male actress.' The others fell silent and looked confused turning that sentence around in their heads, did it make sense? Finally, Violet came to the conclusion that it did not make sense.

'That's amazing,' she started sarcastically, 'are you sure you went to school, Vera?'

'You cheeky mare!' replied Vera.

'That's a bit rude, Violet,' said Brenda. 'I've known Vera for years and she amazes me at times with her knowledge. It wouldn't have surprised me if she went to Oxford.'

'I did go to Oxford,' Vera responded. Again, Vera had managed to stun everyone into silence.

'You went to Oxford?' queried Brenda.

'Sure did, Brenda,' she replied, 'yes, only last week to the Westgate shopping Centre. I do shop in Swindon and Newbury too, but rarely Reading. Anything else you'd like to know?' That statement warranted another 'unbelievable' from the mouth of Lucy to which Vera replied,

'Yes Lucy, I know, the car parking charges are disgusting. It's enough to put anyone off.'

'I hope you bought something nice,' Brenda replied and then changed the subject back to the theatre. Perhaps sticking to theatres rather than university was best. 'So does anyone want to see The Importance of being Earnest? I'll see if I can get tickets for tomorrow evening if you do.'

'What's it about?' asked Amy.

'Oh, Amy, you must have studied it at school?' said Lucy. 'Don't you remember the famous Lady Bracknell line *a handbag*!?'

'I think I missed that one. It must have been when I was having a smoke behind the boiler house. Handbag though? Well I'll give it a go, Brenda.'

'I'd love to try it,' Marianne said.

'Me too,' Vera replied. The others all declined politely.

'Not for me thanks, Brenda,' said Lucy, 'I've seen it before and I've got Breakfast Club at school so it'll be an early start.' Amy's ears picked up this news.

'Breakfast Club?' she said, 'Can I come?'

'If you are between five and eight years old, yes; that's physical age not mental age,' Lucy replied, abruptly.

Sarah looked distracted as she eyed up the young men from the Young Farmers' group who were still standing at the bar.

'If you'll excuse me ladies,' she began, 'I'm off to the bar to talk to the bloke looking at me. Thanks for a nice evening though.' Marianne and Amy also got up with Sarah.

'Wait for us,' Marianne said, 'and if the one on the right is a Virgo, he's mine.' The remaining women decided to call it a night and go home. They'd enjoyed a couple of drinks.

'I think we've lost their interest,' Susan observed. 'They've had a better offer or they hope they have.'

'They are like moths to a flame,' Brenda said.

'Very true! Or lambs to the slaughter if you are talking about the young men!' she smiled. 'I hope you get the tickets and have a lovely time tomorrow at the Playhouse.'

Brenda's walk home was a wet one. Although May had started promisingly it had now turned very wet. The rain just kept on and on but luckily she had her umbrella with her. After ten minutes she reached her front door and could see the welcoming glow of the light on in the lounge. She walked in to find Gary at the table looking at his computer screen.

'Hi love, you had a good evening?' he said. Brenda had left her umbrella outside, leaving her only her mac to hang up. Gary continued to speak, 'You haven't missed anything good on the box, all rubbish tonight. I hope you didn't get too wet. They reckon we've had the whole of May's rain in one day. There are floods everywhere.' Brenda moved up behind Gary and put her arms around his neck and kissed his cheek.

'I love you, even if you are a Pisces!' she whispered in his ear.

'I'm glad to hear it, but it all sounds a bit fishy to me,' Gary joked and turned round to face her.

'The youngsters were talking about stars, horoscopes and birth signs this evening and apparently, I'm a psycho with a split personality,' she informed him.

'Well, I could have told you that, but a lovely psycho.' He laughed and pulled Brenda towards his chair.

'Where does all this rubbish come from?' she asked, 'And why do we seem to be glued to horoscopes when we are young? Why doesn't Gemini fit with Pisces?' Gary listened patiently as she continued, 'The two youngsters seem to follow it all, Uranus rising and so on.'

'I beg your pardon,' Gary remarked, 'sounds like you need to see a doctor about Uranus!' He smiled at Brenda.

'I probably do!' she admitted, with a big smile back. 'By the way, if I can get tickets I'm going to be out again tomorrow evening. Four of us are going to the Playhouse.'

'What are you going to see?' Gary asked.

'The Importance of being Earnest,' she replied.

'Gosh,' began Gary, 'that takes me back to my school days and I didn't like it then. I hope you ladies enjoy it more.' Brenda started to smile as she reminisced and explained,

'I have fond memories of seeing it years ago. I can't remember the name of the date that took me, but I obviously dated a better class of boyfriend then.'

'What!' Gary said feeling slightly hurt. 'I took you to the cinema, what more could you ask for?'

'I remember! We saw The Jungle Book,' Brenda recalled. 'It is funny how we make different memories though, isn't it? Lucy remembers the booming voice saying *a handbag* too, just like me.'

'Oh well, I don't remember that. Was that Baloo or Mowgli?' asked a confused Gary.

'No, not The Jungle Book,' laughed Brenda, 'Lady Bracknell in The Importance of being Earnest, oh never mind. We're alright though, aren't we, Gary? I got the impression that the girls thought Gemini and Pisces aren't a good romantic mix.' Gary could see that Brenda was genuinely worried. It seemed odd that some women who had only just graduated from being children could worry her like this. They have been, and still are, a happy couple who had celebrated their fortieth wedding anniversary just last month. Surely she must realise any serious problems in their relationship would have shown themselves by now?

'Hey, what's up with you?' he said, in a soft soothing voice. 'You aren't letting two youngsters, who think the world's coming to an end if they break a finger nail, get you down, are you? I love my psycho even if she remembers a quote about handbags above one from The Jungle Book.' Brenda smiled and started to sing,

'I wan'na be like you ou ou,'

'That's better than handbags,' Gary declared.

'What do you mean?' Brenda asked. 'A woman can never have too many handbags.'

'Yes, but they aren't any good if you find babies in them, are they?' Gary replied.

'Oh, so you do remember the story then!' Brenda said. 'How about you go and make us a nice mug of hot chocolate.'

'I've noticed that psychos are always bossy,' he joked and walked towards the kitchen. 'You haven't forgotten that I'm out tomorrow, have you?' he said, changing the subject. 'Remember? I'm fishing.'

'Forgotten? How can I forget! You had maggots in the fridge, you disgusting man!' she said.

'And she's back in the room. Welcome back love,' Gary called from the kitchen.

The next morning was brighter with a good amount of sunshine. It was mid-morning when Trudie walked into DDs.

'Hi Dolly. Can I have a tea please?' she requested.

'Coming up. Not working today then?' Dolly asked.

'No, I was on the late shift yesterday and David's working today so I'm meeting up with Sarah. She'll be here soon so could you get an Americano ready for her?'

'Yes, of course,' Dolly said and started to prepare the hot drinks as Sarah walked in.

'And here she is!' Trudie announced.

'Hi ladies,' said a smiling Sarah, 'it's not very warm out there is it? Still at least it's stopped raining. Didn't it come down last night? Can I have an Americano please, Dolly?'

'Already in hand, thanks to Trudie,' Dolly confirmed.

'Brilliant, thank you.' Dolly carried the drinks over to the two women.

'Did you make it to the WI meet-up last night?' she asked Sarah.

'Yes, I did and you'll never guess who was in the pub at the same time?'

'Not George Clooney again?' Dolly asked, with a smile.

'Ha, ha! You've got George Clooney on the brain, Dolly,' Sarah replied.

'I can't think of anyone better to have on your brain,' Trudie said and winked at Dolly.

'So, who was it then?' Dolly asked.

'The Young Farmers' Club,' Sarah announced excitedly.

'Excuse me if I don't faint with excitement,' Trudie said, smiling at Dolly.

'They are all fit young men, I tell you,' Sarah insisted. 'One kept staring at me. Brenda said it was probably because I kept staring at him, but I could tell he fancied me.' Dolly and Trudie looked at each other and rolled their eyes. It seemed like Sarah would never change.

'Brenda is a wise woman and is probably right, Sarah,' Dolly said.

'Not that wise as she ended up with Gary,' Sarah pointed out.

'That's a bit harsh! I know I've only known Gary a few months but he seems like a nice chap,' Trudie said, defending her neighbour.

'Yes, I suppose so but I know when someone fancies me,' Sarah insisted.

'Are we talking about the young farmer or Gary now?' Dolly laughed.

'The young farmer, although Gary fancied me at one time,' Sarah insisted.

Dolly and Trudie tried not to make eye contact to avoid making each other laugh, but it didn't work and the laughter could be heard outside.

'You are funny, Sarah!' Dolly said, still laughing.

'Ah, shut up you two!' Sarah protested.

'So what happened anyway?' Trudie asked trying not to laugh again.

'With Gary?' asked Sarah. 'Nothing. He never did anything I just . . .'

'I know that,' Trudie interrupted, 'what happened with the young farmer bloke? Did he sweep you off your feet and take you to paradise?'

'But she's here,' observed Dolly, 'and I've never heard this place described as paradise.'

'I went over to him,' Sarah continued, 'at the bar and he was lovely but it turned out he's only twenty years old.' A huge smile appeared on Trudie's face.

'What?' she said. 'Did he have his age sewn into the back of his t-shirt along with his name and class?'

'No, he told me!' Sarah continued. 'He thought I was lovely but a little too old for him. I told him I was thirty-two.'

'You are forty, aren't you?' Dolly asked.

'She's forty-two! We were at school together,' Trudie said, spilling Sarah's secret. 'Oh my goodness Sarah, you must have scared the poor boy half to death.'

'He realised he'd bitten off more than he could chew,' Dolly added.

'Yes, as he's still only got baby teeth!' Trudie said. Both ladies were trying so hard to hold it together as it seemed cruel to laugh at their friend, but oh, it was hard not to giggle.

'I'm sorry, Sarah, really I am,' said an ashamed Dolly, 'we shouldn't laugh but you are your own worst enemy. I'd listen to Brenda in future as . . .'

'At least Gary is in long trousers,' Trudie said, finishing off Dolly's sentence for her. That was enough to have both Dolly and Trudie laughing uncontrollably. Sarah was not amused.

'I'm pleased I amuse you both,' she said very insincerely.

'Let's change the subject, lass,' said Dolly, sensing that they were bordering on being cruel now. 'By heck, I haven't had such a good laugh for ages though. So did anything else exciting happen at the WI social? Did I miss much?'

'Amy and Marianne were going on about horoscopes and the theatre,' Sarah said, 'and four of them are going to the theatre tonight, if Brenda can get the tickets.'

'What are they going to see?' Dolly enquired.

'I can't remember really,' Sarah said, looking thoughtful as she tried to recall. 'I wasn't paying a lot of attention as I was staring at the blokes at the bar. Erm, the importance, the importance of, something, being Edward, I think.'

'What? Are you sure that wasn't the name of the child at the bar? I know The Importance of Being Earnest is on at the Playhouse,' Trudie said.

'Yes, that's it! I don't like plays so I'm not going.' Dolly started to smile again and all her good intentions of being nice to Sarah went out the window.

'What?' she said. 'You don't think old Ernie Earnest might fancy you then? He might be staring at you from the stage.' And that started Trudie laughing again too.

'You are both so mean,' Sarah moaned, but this time she was smiling back at them.

It was now early afternoon and Gary was about to leave home for his fishing trip. He called upstairs to Brenda who had just finished cleaning the bathroom,

'I'm off now! Going to drive round to pick up Anthony and then Cyril.' Brenda started to come down the stairs.

'Don't you dare leave without giving me a kiss first,' she demanded.

'As if I would,' Gary said, 'psychos make good kissers.' Brenda reached the bottom of the stairs and collected her kiss.

'Go on then Mr Pisces, your gills are showing!' Brenda declared. 'Go and catch fish and make sure you've taken all those maggots with you.'

'I've got them!' he shouted as he walked down the path to the road.

Brenda closed the door, walked into the lounge and started dusting around the photo of her parents. She stopped for a moment holding the photo to look at it.

'Well Mum,' she said, 'it's a good job he doesn't remember that you were a psycho too. Or perhaps he does . . . poor Dad!' She smiled and placed the photo back on the shelf. She carried on with her boring chores as it was always good to get the jobs done while Gary was out of the way.

Gary picked up both his fishing companions and started to drive to the river. The Roadeteers were working on a road just outside Wancott. They were removing overhanging hedging so they could dig a hole next to the bank. The ditch next to the road was full of rain water from the previous day's downpour. The road rose slightly at the edge meaning the tarmac and slope were a barrier stopping the water from the ditch spilling into the road. They had successfully cut the hedging so could move on to the second stage.

'I'll bring the digger in then Frank, to get started on the edge of the road,' Steve said eagerly. His favourite plant machinery was the roller but the digger came a close second.

'Yes, good one,' said Frank, 'but remember not to dig the road out too close to the hedgerow because there is a full ditch directly behind. The higher road edge is holding that water back.'

'No problemo, boss!' announced a confident Steve. He plunged the digger into the road surface about ten inches from the edge. The tarmac was old and quite soft. As the first large lump was lifted it pulled out hedge roots which ran under the road from the side. The tarmac crumbled and the barrier holding back the ditch water sank disappearing into the ditch itself. The water rushed through into the road and was about eighteen inches deep in the middle. Steve looked bemused.

'No problemo, hey? You f**king idiot!' shouted Frank.

Gary's car appeared from around the corner and approached the flooded road. He stopped and brought down his window to speak to Steve.

'Is it safe to drive through that?' he enquired. 'How deep is it?'

'It's up to you but it's fairly deep,' Steve replied. 'I'm gonna deal with it though. I'm gonna use the scoop to collect the water and tip it off the road.'

'Will that take long?' asked Gary.

'As long as it takes, Sir,' Steve replied unhelpfully and climbed back into the digger. He plunged the scoop into the water and lifted it up. Some water was escaping out of the sides but a fair amount had been collected. He then emptied it in the ditch resulting in it pouring straight back into the road. He did this a couple of times before Frank shouted,

'Stop, you wally! It's not draining away. You are just throwing it back into the road.'

'We are trying to get to the river to do some fishing,' Gary said to Frank. 'I think I'll take another route.'

'I reckon you might as well fish here, look at it, more water than in the toilets at a music festival,' Frank replied. Gary thought to himself that he wouldn't tell Brenda that comment as it would make her feel sick like the dirty pants sticking to walls scenario.

'Right, on that nice thought I'll turn round,' Gary said. Frank and Steve both replied in unison with 'Right you are!'

Gary and his two friends made it to the river by taking a fifteen minute detour. They chose their spot and sat on the riverbank with their fishing lines cast out on to the water ready for action.

'We've been here well over an hour now, do you think we'll catch anything today?' Anthony asked.

'Just catch a cold I expect, it's not very warm, is it, for May? Brenda always says I'll only catch a cold,' Gary recalled.

'It's a bit of a long shot this time of day,' said Cyril, 'you've got more chance at dawn or dusk of catching something. I don't fancy getting up that early though or sitting in the dark later.'

'Perhaps we should have tried the flooded road first,' Gary joked.

'Do you think the river's well stocked?' Anthony asked.

'Who knows these days?' replied Cyril. 'I expect the numbers are down due to the raw sewage they are pumping into the river. With all that rain yesterday, well.'

'Terrible isn't it?' Gary said, looking serious. 'It's annoying that they can get away with it.'

'Yes, it's terripoo!' Anthony remarked jokingly. The others cringed and there was five minutes of silence as the men concentrated on watching their fishing lines. Silences never lasted long though as these fishing trips were more about socialising than catching fish. Sure enough, after those quiet five minutes Cyril broke the silence.

'How's everything with you, Gary? Has the dust settled after your cooking mishap?'

'Yes, all's fine now. Mind you, it cost me the price of a new microwave. Poor Dolly couldn't use the old one again, so I had to replace it,' Gary replied.

'You weren't supposed to blow the bloody doors off!' Anthony chipped in using his best Michael Caine impersonation. The others smiled and Gary said,

'I didn't know Danny Dyer was in The Italian Job.'

'Cheek,' said Anthony, 'that was nothing like Danny Dyer.'

'Not a lot of people know that!' joked Cyril.

'Look on the bright side Gary, I'm sure you won't be asked to cook again,' Cyril was quick to point out. 'I hope Brenda got over the shame quickly.'

'Ah, she's fine, thanks,' Gary replied, 'to tell you the truth I think the WI has a lot to answer for. When we come fishing we don't take stupid challenges home for our other halves, do we? It's like us going home today and saying we've decided to see which partner can cast out the farthest.'

'Yes, but Brenda would have told you to get lost,' said Cyril. 'Men are too accommodating.'

'Walked over you mean,' Anthony said.

'Yes, WI is a pain!' Gary protested. 'It's more trouble than it's worth. First cookery competitions and now the younger ones are into horoscopes and unsettling my Brenda with star sign rubbish. They implied Brenda's star sign doesn't match well with mine apparently, and it's left her insecure.'

'They are funny things women with their insecurities,' acknowledged Anthony. 'My Tess gets unsettled and thinks I'm seeing someone else.'

'Yes, but you were seeing someone else!' Gary was quick to point out.

'Yes, but it wasn't anything serious, nothing for her to worry about,' Anthony insisted.

'Oh that's alright then!' Gary said, sarcastically. 'Silly Tess! I don't know how you could do that. Anyway, that's completely different to me and Brenda, I'd never cheat on her.'

'It was ages ago and we went to mediation and everything,' Anthony said, trying to protest his innocence.

'So what is worrying your Brenda, what's she doing?' asked Cyril. At this point Gary's fishing rod started to move as the float bobbed up and down; something pulled on the fishing line.

'I've got a nibble,' Gary said, excitedly.

'She got a bit violent, then?' Cyril said and Anthony laughed.

'No, there's a fish nibbling, not Brenda. Actually just between us, I like it when Brenda nibbles my ear,' Gary said, even more excitedly.

'Spare us the details, please.' Anthony said. Cyril smiled at Gary and remarked,

'He's jealous. You'd better keep your eye on him or he'll be after your Brenda. He might be the right star sign too.' Gary reeled in his line and there was nothing there.

'There's no likelihood of that,' Gary said, 'Brenda is as loyal to me as I am to her, whatever the star signs!'

'I've had enough of this,' Anthony said. Gary looked across at him.

'Sorry if my happiness bores you,' he said.

'No,' moaned Anthony, 'I'm talking about the fishing and lack of fish. I'm very happy you are getting nibbled at home Gary, if that floats your boat.' Cyril laughed and said,

'Let's call it a day and have a pint in the pub on the way home. What do you think? What did your horoscope say about that Gary?' Gary started to pack up.

'Funnily enough,' he started, 'I didn't check it, but personally I think that's the best thing you've said all afternoon. Let's call it a day here.'

'A day here!' yelled Anthony, as he started to get his things together to leave.

Back in Seymour Rise, Brenda was making arrangements for the evening. She was on the phone.

'Hello Vera. It's me . . . I'm fine thanks. I've got the tickets for the theatre tonight. The doors open at 7:30. I've spoken to Amy and Marianne and they will make their own way there. How about you, would you like a lift? . . . That's fine, I'll pick you up at 6:45. That will give us plenty of time to park and walk through. The other two will see us outside at 7:25ish, . . . great, no problem, I'll see you later. Bye.'

Having ended the call she walked over to her 'parents'. In Brenda's mind her parents were very much alive inside the photographs and she always felt their presence around her. She had never discussed this with Gary as she didn't want to freak him out.

'Hey, Mum and Dad. I'm going to the theatre tonight, you'd be proud. Only posh people go to the theatre, you said! But then you thought we'd climbed the social ladder when we bought our first television instead of renting it from Wigfalls! Do you remember?'

Gary, Anthony and Cyril made it safely to the pub. Gary took the same route back as going as he feared the Roadeteers would still be attempting to mop up their mishap. They sat drinking their beer when Tim, a bowling mate, walked in.

'Hey Tim, come and join us,' said Cyril, 'we've been fishing but didn't catch a single thing. Gary thought he had a nibble but it was just Brenda.'

'Boom, boom!' Gary shouted. 'What are you doing here then, Tim? Have you escaped from Belle?'

'She's at the hairdressers and I've got an hour still to spare before I've got to pick her up,' Tim replied. He sat down next to Cyril. Gary noticed a yellow post-it-note on his sleeve.

'What's that?' Gary asked, while pointing at it.

'Oh that?' Tim said, 'that's to remind me to say how good her hair looks when I pick her up. There'll be hell to pay if I don't. Can I get you gents another drink while I'm getting mine?' He turned to go to the bar.

'No thanks, not for me, mate,' Gary replied. 'I've got to get home soon and I'm driving so a half's my limit. These two can have another if they want to stay and make their own way home.'

'No ta, mate,' Anthony said. 'If I go home smelling of beer Tess won't be pleased.'

'Go on, I'll have one and keep you company,' Cyril said. 'I can walk home from here. I'll pick my rod up from you tomorrow, Gary.'

'Great, that's fine, see you tomorrow,' Gary replied and addressing Anthony continued, 'right let's make a move then.'

It was almost 6 o'clock when Gary got home.

'That's what I call perfect timing, love,' Brenda called out, 'I've just dished up your dinner.'

'Ah, that's nice. I wasn't expecting you to cook for me today with you going out.'

'Well I didn't want you trying to cook anything, I love my microwave,' Brenda said.

'Very witty,' Gary replied.

'Did you catch anything?' Brenda asked, trying to sound interested although she really didn't care that much.

'Sadly not, I had a very large one hooked but it escaped before I could reel it in. Well that's what I'm saying anyway,' Gary said and winked at her.

'Oh well, never mind. Did you get rid of those maggots? I don't want them in here.'

'Yes, they have gone,' Gary confirmed.

'And the car is in a decent state inside?' she queried, 'I don't want to be shown up when Vera gets in it this evening.'

'Relax! Everything is fine,' he confirmed. 'When are you leaving?'

'In about thirty minutes, so I'll start getting ready now,' Brenda said.

'You'll never be ready in thirty minutes!' Gary laughed.

'What are you implying, that I need a lot of work to look attractive?' Brenda moaned.

'No, it takes a long time for you to look half decent, just kidding,' Gary joked. 'You always look lovely but you'll have six different things on and off before you decide what to wear.'

'I've already decided . . I think,' she said, smiling at Gary.

'Well whatever it is it'll look great' Gary began, 'and, before you ask, your bum won't look fat in it.'

'Aw, shut up and eat your dinner oh Fisherman's friend,' she said and headed upstairs.

'You what?' Gary muttered to himself, 'I'm a cough sweet now!'

Brenda drove to Vera's house and they headed into Oxford. The journey went without a hitch and parking was easy too, although Brenda thought parking charges were excessive. Perhaps that's why there are so many available spaces, she thought to herself. Marianne and Amy were waiting for them and they all entered the Playhouse. Vera sat next to Brenda who had Marianne to her left. Amy was next to Marianne.

It was a nice production and performed very professionally. By the end Vera had fallen asleep and had her head on Brenda's shoulder. Marianne was looking at her watch every now and then and Amy was staring intently at the stage. The play ended and the applause of the audience woke up Vera. Marianne clapped politely and Amy got up onto her feet appearing to offer a standing ovation, her focus never left the stage. They got up and left the theatre along with the rest of the audience and were reunited on Beaumont Street outside.

'I'm sorry Brenda,' said an embarrassed Vera. 'I enjoyed half of it but I was so tired I couldn't keep my eyes open. How embarrassing.'

'Don't worry,' Brenda replied, 'it was quite hot in there and that would make you feel more tired. At least you didn't snore. It's funny you know, I saw this play years ago when I was in my late teens.'

'Wow!' exclaimed Amy, 'These actors must be ancient.'

'Not the same cast, obviously,' explained Brenda, 'but I have, or had, fond memories of it and of the man who took me.'

'Oh yes, you devil Brenda!' Marianne said, 'what star sign was he?'

'I don't know Marianne but it's all coming back to me now,' Brenda said. 'The reason I didn't see him again was because he fell asleep and dribbled over my shoulder. I was much better off going to see The Jungle Book later on with my Gary. He was interested in me enough to stay awake.'

'Ahhh, that's romantic!' cooed Vera. 'And you are still with Gary.'

'I thought the play was a little long but . . .' Marianne started but was suddenly interrupted by Vera.

'Well a little long is better than a big short!' she said. Marianne winced at that and continued,

'But, I'm pleased I've experienced the theatre. Thank you Brenda for accompanying me and to you other ladies.'

'You are welcome,' Brenda replied. 'And what about you Amy? You must have liked it as you were watching intently all evening.'

'To be honest Brenda, I was very confused,' admitted Amy. 'Yesterday Lucy said there were going to be handbags. I didn't see many. I watched every inch of the stage all night even standing at the end to get a better view. There's a mention of a handbag, and an ordinary one at that, but that's all. If I were to be found in a handbag it'd have to be inside a Cartier, not an ordinary one.' The others laughed.

'How about a carrier bag?' Marianne asked. 'We could make it a Harrod's one!'

'I'd rename that play - The Importance of being Honest. THERE ARE NO HANDBAGS!' Amy declared. The others were still laughing. 'What? What's so funny?' Brenda found her best Lady Bracknell voice to boom,

'No handbag!' The women laughed and said goodbye, Brenda dropped the sleepy Vera home and got home herself around 11 o'clock.

Gary was already preparing to turn in for the night when Brenda got in and by 11:30 the pair were safely tucked up in bed. Brenda cuddled up to Gary. She felt safe and secure with her man. Her memories of watching The Jungle Book suddenly seemed more important than those of watching any other film or play.

'How's the bedroom feeling tonight, love?' Gary whispered. 'Is it soothing?'

'It's lovely,' Brenda whispered back.

'That's good,' Gary said. 'And what about passionate? Are you feeling passionate? How about some passion? Brenda? Love?' Brenda was now fast asleep. 'Just my luck,' Gary moaned, 'it's too bloody soothing!'

Chapter Six

June
Oh Bronwyn, ti diawl bach!

(you little devil)

So, here they were in June. Gary and Brenda had almost made it to half a year in their new home. They had settled in so well and ironically Gary, having given Brenda all the reassurance earlier, was the one now finding more faults with their smaller house. Oh, he missed his garage, oh, he missed his larger man cave, oh, shut up, Gary!

June is probably Brenda's favourite month. I say probably because she used to have to toss a coin between May and June, but the last two Mays had been washouts, so for now the favourite was June. She recalled many birthdays in early June that were cold and wet, but at least the daylight hours were longer. This month promised to be a good one.

It was early in the morning, just 5 o'clock, the sun was rising and it looked like it was going to be a beautiful day. The birds were singing the dawn chorus and Brenda was up, looking out of the bedroom window. Gary awoke to see her standing there. He was only half awake but could see a blurred image of his wife at the window.

'What are you doing? Are you okay?' he asked.

'Isn't that a beautiful sound? I love hearing the dawn chorus. It's remarkable, so many birds welcoming in the new day,' she said, so enthusiastically she hardly stopped to draw breath. 'The blackbirds are the loudest. Can you hear them?' Gary yawned, he rubbed his eyes and turned to read the clock.

'What?' he replied, 'Oh, yes but it's early, come back to bed.'

'Well dawn is usually early in June,' Brenda continued, 'it gets earlier each day right up to the middle of this month.'

'Can't you listen to it while lying in bed?' Gary asked, almost pleading.

'Not when you are snoring, I can't,' Brenda answered. 'Anyway, it is lovely to look out of the window and spot where the sounds are coming from. It's beautiful, isn't it?' Gary had turned over and appeared to be snoring again. 'Typical,' she continued, 'I've now got the snore chorus.'

'I heard that and I'm not snoring,' Gary insisted, 'I'm not really asleep because some mad bird woman is trying her best to wake me up.'

'Oh, there's Bronwyn over there,' Brenda said, she was so excited.

'This time of the morning?' asked a confused Gary, 'Bronwyn who?' Brenda pointed at a tree in a garden two houses down from theirs.

'Bronwyn, the Welsh blackbird,' she replied, 'I've heard her all this week.' Gary sat up in bed; he was trying to wake up enough to make some sense of what his wife was saying.

'What?' he queried. 'Can you get Welsh blackbirds?'

'Can't you hear her?' Brenda asked. 'She sings in a Welsh accent. She's definitely Welsh. All the best voices come from Wales and I'm sure that is true of birds too.' Gary was beginning to think he was still asleep and this was a peculiar dream. All he needed now was for Aggie to appear hovering outside the upstairs window.

'I can't believe this,' he said.

'Listen! Can't you hear that?' Brenda said, unable to hide her excitement. Gary thought he ought to play along so he listened intently for a few seconds.

'Oh yes,' he joked, 'she's tweeting, *hey big spender*. Yes, she must be Welsh.' Brenda looked annoyed.

'Well, if you are going to be silly!' she complained.

'Me be silly?' Gary laughed. 'You are the one talking about Welsh blackbirds. Sometimes Brenda! Whatever next?'

'I'm getting up, are you getting up?' she asked.

'No, not for at least another three hours, I'm not,' Gary replied, as he lay back down and turned over.

'Suit yourself!' Brenda replied and walked over to a washing basket she had left in the corner of the room. She carried it downstairs and emptied the clothes into the washing machine. Talking to herself she said, 'I appreciate you Bronwyn, you sing girl!'

It was now 5:30 and over in Turnpike Road, Kai was getting dressed ready for his 6 o'clock start at Royal Mail. As he combed his hair Izzy sat up in bed.

'Do you think you'll have to work later today?' she asked.

'Not sure,' he replied, 'it depends on the volume of mail I've got to shift. I might be asked to work beyond 2 o'clock, why? Are you wanting to do something?'

'We've got to choose things for the baby and I thought we could have a look this afternoon. My last cleaning job finishes at 2 o'clock. What do you think?'

'You finishing at 2? That's early,' Kai replied.

'Not about the time I finish, what do you think about looking online for baby things? It'll be nice to get some things for Goofna.'

'Daniel you mean!' said a determined Kai. 'He's not being called Goofy Goofna!' Izzy stroked her bump gently with her right hand.

'We'll see. It's okay Goofna, Daddy doesn't mean it,' she said. Kai didn't have time for a pointless argument, after all the baby might be a girl. They had chosen not to be told the baby's sex at the scan.

'I'll try to get home as quickly as I can,' he said, 'Bye Daniel!'

'Goofna!' Izzy shouted back immediately.

It was now nearly 10 o'clock and Gary was eating toast and drinking tea as Brenda was unloading the washing machine. He couldn't help himself, he had to pull Brenda's leg.

'Has Bronwyn finished belting out *gold finger* now?' he said. 'You are nuts, a Welsh blackbird, what next?'

'Very funny,' Brenda replied. 'You can take the mickey but at least I appreciate nature. You just snore through the nicest part of the day.'

'Well, I would do if mad bird lady didn't wake me up,' Gary moaned, 'I would have stayed in bed a bit longer but that washing machine vibrates through the whole house. I only got back to sleep again at 8 o'clock.'

'I didn't start the washing machine until 7:30 because I knew you'd moan,' she said. Then she looked thoughtful as she folded a wet skirt.

'Do you think birds have conversations like this? You know, Mr and Mrs Blackbird? I know they can't talk but they communicate, don't they?' she asked.

'Have you eaten too much dark chocolate again?' Gary replied.

'No, I'm serious,' she said. 'Do you think when Mr Blackbird sings across the garden to Mrs Bronwyn Blackbird he is saying something meaningful?' Gary looked puzzled.

'Oh yes, for sure love,' he joked. 'He's saying, can't you sing something else? I'm sick of *big spender* but I'm looking forward to having *fun, fun, fun* when you *show me a good time*.' Brenda threw the last bit of washing into the basket to let Gary know she was annoyed.

'It's no good talking to you sometimes!' she declared. Gary smiled and couldn't let it go.

'Why didn't you call her Shirley B? B for Bassey not blackbird,' he laughed.

'You are being stupid now!' she said in a way that told Gary he ought to stop this for his own good. He took the hint and turned more serious.

'They obviously do communicate,' he said, trying to calm Brenda down, 'but it's probably to establish where each of them is, where the dangers are, where the babies are and so on. It's not whether they want jam or marmalade on their toast.'

'I know that!' she insisted. 'I'm going to hang the washing out.' She opened the door and walked into the garden.

'Amazing!' Gary muttered to himself. 'From the Importance of being Earnest a little while ago to Mr and Mrs Blackbird's Welsh musical now!' His thoughts were interrupted by the sound of post dropping through the letterbox. He walked out to collect it carrying his mug of tea with him. He took the mail back to the kitchen and was holding it in one hand when Brenda came back in from the garden.

'The post is early today,' Gary remarked.

'It's gone 10 o'clock so it's not that early. It's you getting up late that's made it seem early,' Brenda replied.

'I was tired having been woken up by you and the Bronwyn choir,' Gary complained.

'What's that?' Brenda asked.

'Your blessed dawn chorus!' Gary tried to explain.

'No,' said Brenda, and pointing at the envelope she continued, 'what's that letter?' Gary passed it over to her.

'You look, I'm drinking my tea,' he said.

'And men can't multi-task, can they?' Brenda snarled back. She opened the letter and started to read it to herself.

'Oh, it's one of those keep this day free cards. There's a letter from Mary too.' Gary looked puzzled and swallowed another gulp of tea.

'What do you mean, a keep this day free card?' he asked.

'Great-niece Verity is getting married!' Brenda said. 'A formal invitation will follow but this is just giving us notice of the date, so we can keep the day free. Mary says she can't believe her little granddaughter is getting married. Ah, that's lovely, isn't it?'

'Whatever next? Keep this day free cards!' Gary groaned.

'Isn't it nice, Gary?' Brenda repeated.

'Why don't they just ring and tell you the date so you can put it in your diary? Keep this day free cards . . . what a . . .' Gary was unable to complete his sentence because Brenda asked again, this time with an air of anger and urgency about it.

'Gary! Aren't you happy for Verity?'

'Yes, of course I am,' he replied. 'It only seems like last summer she and her sister Tammy were staying with us for a couple of weeks. They were only little girls, eight and six years old. Now she's getting married.'

'That wasn't last summer, that was years ago. Verity is 22 now and Tammy is 20,' Brenda said. 'Mary says she is marrying Paul. Who's Paul? I thought she was going out with Greg. I thought they'd been going out for a while.'

'Obviously she thinks Paul is better. Youngsters don't have any staying power like us,' Gary said proudly. Sadly, Brenda didn't take that well.

'Staying power?' she questioned. 'What do you mean by that? It sounds like staying with me has been a challenge.'

'I didn't mean it like that,' Gary pleaded.

'What did you mean then?' Brenda asked looking a little upset.

'If you must know, I was referring to your staying power,' Gary said, looking a little subdued. 'Remember when we were in our first house? We'd been married four years and I lost my job and we worried about losing our home. The mortgage was so expensive. We had a hard time but it all worked out because I got the job at Brookes. I bet there were times during those six months that you wished you'd married Tommy Thacker. You know the one who went into banking in the city and had made millions by then. So perhaps it was a chore for you to stay with me!' Brenda listened intently and smiled. She hadn't heard the name Tommy Thacker for many years.

'Oh sometimes, Gary! You are an idiot,' she sighed. Gary looked depressed, like the air had been let out of his balloon.

'Kind of you to mention that!' he said.

'You can be a real worrier when you start thinking too deeply about things,' she said. 'I've never regretted marrying you. You are the most important thing in my life; I'd die without you.' Gary put his mug down and put his arms around her.

'We are stupid sometimes, aren't we?' he said. 'With my love close to me, I've got everything I need.'

'That's good to know, what's her name?' Brenda joked.

'Oh her? I can't remember but you will do,' Gary replied.

'By the way,' Brenda went on, 'Tommy Thacker only took me out once and never contacted me again so I didn't have the option of a future with him.' Gary released her from his hug and smiled as he said,

'Oh you've just spoilt the moment.' They laughed and he continued, 'so when is this date we've got to keep free?'

'23rd November. I'll have to look for a good hat. Then I'll match it to a good outfit. I'll go shopping this week,' Brenda said excitedly.

'But it's months away, anything can happen. She might be back with Greg next month. And buy wisely and keep the receipts so you can get a refund if you need to.' Brenda smiled as silently she had managed to mouth the words 'keep the receipts' in sync with Gary saying them. The phrase had been used so often during their marriage!

'It's stupid to leave everything to the last minute,' she said. 'You'll need to start thinking about what you're going to wear too.'

'Great,' Gary said submissively.

'I'm going to go for a walk to think about it all. Oh, this is so exciting!' she said.

'Isn't it just,' Gary said sarcastically.

It was 11 o'clock and in DDs Aggie was sitting at a table reading a script while drinking coffee. Dolly approached her.

'Are you okay there? Do you need anything else as I'm about to pop out the back for a couple of minutes?'

'I'm fine, thank you,' replied Aggie, but then changed her mind, 'well actually could I have another coffee, please?'

'Of course you can,' Dolly replied and walked to the counter to pour a coffee. 'Are you planning another production then?'

'Yes. It's early stages though,' Aggie replied.

'Early stages! Very good,' Dolly laughed.

'Oh yes, excuse the pun,' Aggie said, with a smile.

'A bun? Would you like one with your coffee?' Dolly asked.

'No, pun,' Aggie said in a louder voice, trying to clarify what she had said.

'Okay, don't shout, no bun then,' Dolly said, slightly annoyed at being messed around.

Aggie looked bewildered as the coffee was delivered and she continued to read her script. Dolly went out the back and a few seconds later Sarah walked in and went to the counter.

'Dolly has popped out for a couple of minutes,' Aggie shouted across to Sarah.

'Right, no worries,' Sarah replied. Brenda then walked in. She noticed Aggie and waved to her.

'Hello Aggie!' she said. Aggie raised her hand as Brenda continued to the counter.

'Hi Sarah, how are you?' she enquired.

'Hiya, I'm great thanks, Brenda,' Sarah replied, 'I've got today off work so that is definitely great. I thought I might pop into Oxford this afternoon and do a bit of shopping.'

'I was thinking of doing the same. Do you feel like going together?' Brenda asked, 'I'm going to look for a wedding outfit starting with the hat. But right now I'm going to buy a piece of Dolly's chocolate cake for Gary. I feel guilty because I woke him up early.'

'Aye, aye, wink, wink, say no more,' Sarah said, in a saucy voice.

'Nothing like that, we aren't as young as we used to be,' Brenda admitted. 'You know the saying, run like the wind? Well we run like the winded!'

'Ah,' Sarah replied sympathetically, 'I liked your Gary when I worked with him.'

'Yes I know. Didn't you think he fancied you?' Brenda asked.

'Wow, he told you he fancied me then?' Sarah replied.

'No, he told me that you thought he fancied you, not that he fancied you,' Brenda said, trying to clear up that misunderstanding.

'I suppose he wouldn't tell you,' Sarah said.

'No, he wouldn't tell me that he fancied you because he didn't fancy you, but he knew you thought he fancied you,' Brenda said, again trying to get through to Sarah.

'I swore he fancied me, that's a shame,' Sarah said.

'Why is it a shame?' asked a confused Brenda. 'Did you fancy Gary?'

'OMG no!' protested Sarah.

'That's all okay then, isn't it?' Brenda stated, hoping that would put an end to this line of conversation. Meanwhile, Aggie had overheard the whole thing and she looked up, her mouth open in amazement at what she had just heard. At this point Dolly reappeared from the back of the café.

'Hello you two. I'm sorry to keep you waiting. What can I get you?' Dolly enquired.

'A hot chocolate please,' Sarah requested.

'Just a piece of chocolate cake to take out, please,' Brenda said. Then she turned to Sarah and asked, 'so Sarah are you on for going shopping this afternoon? I can pick you up from here in forty-five minutes, if you like.'

'I like!' Sarah said. 'And it's very kind of you to be so understanding.'

'Understanding?' Brenda said, looking very confused. 'Understanding about what?'

'About your Gary fancying me, but it was years ago I suppose,' Sarah replied.

'I give up!' Brenda declared.

'Are you still on that one, Sarah? Give it a rest!' Dolly said. Aggie looked up again and felt obliged to intervene.

'Yes, please give it a rest!' she said. Sarah looked at Aggie and then whispered to Brenda, 'Who asked Judi Dench over there?' Brenda thought that was funny and left with a large smile on her face.

When Brenda got home she found Gary on the sofa looking at something interesting on his laptop, well interesting to him anyway. He was always on that laptop!

'Hi love, did you have a nice walk?' he asked.

'Yes, I did and I stopped off at DDs and bought you a piece of Dolly's chocolate cake.' Brenda passed the box to him.

'Ah, that's nice. What have I done to deserve this?' he asked.

'It's for putting up with me and my Welsh choir first thing this morning,' she said, 'and also I'm off shopping this afternoon with someone you used to fancy.'

'Me?' Gary looked puzzled and guilty, although he knew he'd done nothing wrong.

'Yes, Sarah,' Brenda said, with a smile.

'Oh no, don't you encourage her,' Gary begged.

'I'm not. I'm going to find my wedding hat.'

'You are quick out of the blocks. The wedding isn't for ages,' Gary said. 'While you are out I'll work on sorting through the stuff in the shed.'

'You mean you will be sitting on the chair daydreaming!' Brenda joked.

'Cheeky!' he replied.

'I'll leave the washing on the line until I get back,' Brenda said, 'it'll air well out there in the warmer breeze. Right I'll get ready to leave shortly.'

'Who is this shortly?' joked Gary.

'Very funny,' Brenda groaned, 'it gets better every time you ask it.'

Kai arrived home from work at 2:30 to find Izzy was already using the laptop. He went into the kitchen to grab a hot drink and then sat down next to her.

'Okay then, what are we looking for?' he asked.

'We are looking for the essential things we need to have when the baby arrives,' Izzy explained. 'The NHS website has a page about it. So first of all we need nappies. Should we go for disposable or reusable?'

'What is a reusable nappy? If it's dirty you can't reuse it, can you?' Kai asked.

'It is material and you wash it, like your clothes,' Izzy replied.

'I don't poo my clothes, although I come close to wetting myself when the Doberman gets out at number 29!' Kai continued, 'I know what you mean now though. It's like the old days with nappies. Perhaps you could wash them in with one of the washes you do for your clients?'

'I can't do that!' Izzy said, looking horrified. 'Actually I don't fancy soiled nappies in the washing machine and disposable will be easiest. Let's leave that for now as we can buy those at the supermarket. I can buy baby clothes from there too. Let's concentrate on the online stuff. We'll need a Moses basket.'

'What's Moses got to do with it? Isn't he the commandments man?'

'It's just a name, it's like the basket Moses was found in on the river. Let's go for a carrycot then. I hope you know what a carrycot is? Also, we'll need a mattress, waterproof mattress cover and sheets,' Izzy continued.

'There's quite a lot to this baby lark isn't there?' Kai said, looking worried.

'Baby bath, car seat, pushchair or buggy,' she continued.

'You are frightening me. This is going to be expensive,' Kai said.

'Well babies don't grow on trees,' Izzy stated, which Kai found amusing,

'I think it's money doesn't grow on trees, not babies, and it's a shame we can't grow a money tree,' Kai replied. Izzy didn't react at all to Kai's comments.

'It's also very important to get the feeding right,' said Izzy.

'Well yes, no food, no grow,' Kai said.

'Shall I breast feed or do I get formula?' Izzy asked.

'Formula what?' asked Kai who went on to joke, 'Does formula one mean they can run around a track at just six months old.' Izzy was listening but didn't understand.

'Formula milk, you just make it up by adding water,' she informed Kai who looked bemused.

'I think you are just making this up!' he said.

'No I'm not,' Izzy said, 'I'm going to need a nursing bra too.' Izzy was now getting annoyed.

'Are you going to be a nurse?' Kai said jokingly.

'You are useless!' Izzy shouted.

'Sorry Izzy!'

'I'll need nipple cream,' Izzy continued.

'Whipped?' Kai replied. He was getting worried about it all and found joking relieved his anxiety. Sadly it only wound Izzy up.

'You are more than useless. You know what I mean so stop messing around. Oh yes, I'll need a breast pump too.' This time Kai looked genuinely confused.

'Well joking apart, you've got me there. What is that? I've got an old foot pump for inflating tyres in the back of the car, any use?' he asked.

'It's to express my milk, not inflate my boobs. Perhaps you should have stayed at work,' Izzy insisted. 'Are you really this stupid or are you making it up?'

'Sorry, the worry of the cost is affecting my brain,' Kai replied.

'It's going to be expensive and we'll lose my wage for a short time,' Izzy said, 'but it will be worth it. At least it's not twins, although that wouldn't be too bad, would it? We could have a Goofna and Daniel or Goofna and Camille. What do you think?'

'I think we should have used contraception!' replied a worried Kai.

'Kai!' Izzy said in a raised voice. She looked upset.

'Sorry, only kidding. Honestly I'm really happy and excited,' Kai replied, with his fingers crossed behind his back.

Brenda picked up Sarah from DDs and they started their journey to Oxford. On the way they found the Roadeteers digging a hole which took up half the road. Brenda was at the back of the short queue on one side and Steve was controlling the traffic. When it was time to go Brenda stalled her car.

'Oh dear,' she said, 'that was clever of me.' She started the car as Steve walked over.

'Is everything okay, love?' Steve enquired. Brenda brought down her window to speak.

'Yes thank you, I just stalled, all okay now,' Brenda confirmed. Steve looked through the window at Sarah and smiled. He looked flustered and dropped the stop/go board. He hurriedly picked it up again as Brenda drove off.

'Well, there you are,' she said smiling at Sarah, 'he wasn't interested in me!'

'What?' asked Sarah, she seemed to be oblivious of the distraction she had just been for Steve.

'You can't say you didn't notice?' Brenda asked in disbelief.

'Notice what?' she replied.

'That's unbelievable,' Brenda went on, 'he's obviously attracted to you. That's someone who fancies you and you didn't even notice him.' Sarah suddenly became interested in what Brenda was saying.

'Do you think so? Do you think he's good looking? Do you think he'll be there on the way back?' Sarah blurted out excitedly.

'That's a lot of *do you thinks*,' Brenda continued, 'but that'll be me once we start shopping. Do you think this looks right? Do you think the colour is right?' The two laughed and continued into Oxford.

At the same time, in Seymour Rise Gary was sitting on the picnic chair in the shed with a mug of coffee. He looked out of the window and spotted a blackbird pecking amongst the grass.

'Hello, Bronwyn. Are you Bronwyn?' he asked. 'If you are do you think you could have a word with your mates to turn down the noise a bit at dawn, please? Dawn is very early and I'd prefer to get some sleep.' He smiled and continued to mutter to himself, 'what am I doing talking to a bird? I'm as mad as her.' As he sat there relaxing in his daydreams he noticed some wood in the corner of the shed. So going back into madman mode he started to talk to Bronwyn again.

'Hey Bronwyn,' he started, 'would you like me to make you a bird table? I could hang it in the tree and Brenda could put some bread and seed on it for you.' He started to smile as he thought the birds might not be able to sing so loud with their beaks full of seeds. He took a square piece of wood about 8" x 8" and drilled holes in the four corners.

He then took some string and fed a piece through each hole and tied them together in the middle above the wood. He walked over to the small lilac tree in the garden and placed it in the branches hanging it by the string. It was a bit wobbly but if he altered the string a little he soon found the centre of gravity. All was now fine.

'That's not bad is it, Bronwyn?' he said out loud. 'You can thank me later. You might need to bring a friend to stand on the other end when you are on it. Umm, it might have a see-saw property to it. I'm sure bird lady Brenda will put some food on it for you.' David came up to the fence from his side of the garden.

'Howdy Gary!' David started. 'First sign of madness, talking to yourself.'

'It's worse than that!' Gary replied, 'I'm not talking to myself but a bird and even worse, it's a bird Brenda's named. Still never mind. How are you? No work today?'

'I've got today off which is nice,' David replied, 'Trouble is a day off usually results in Trude finding me work to do at home! I don't think she likes it if I'm off and she's not. So I'm officially gardening.'

'And unofficially?' asked Gary.

'Listening to the cricket on my head phones. I'm weeding too but only slowly, about five weeds per over,' David proudly announced. 'I can speed up, I pulled up three weeds in one go when England hit a six. It's amazing how a good batsman can increase my productivity. Looks like you're being productive too. What's that in the tree?' David pointed to Gary's new creation.

'What that? That's nothing really,' he replied modestly. 'Brenda has a thing about the birds at the moment. So I've made a bird table, well it's more like a shelf really. I'm supposed to be tidying the shed but like you my productivity is on the low side.'

'Join the club, mate,' David said, 'where is Brenda?'

'She's out with Sarah,' Gary replied.

'You mean the Sarah you used to fancy?' David said, his face breaking out into a big smile.

'Not you too?' moaned Gary, 'You know it's not true, don't you?'

'Oh, mate,' said a reassuring David, 'don't worry, I know what she's like.'

'Well she's shopping with Brenda now. Brenda is looking for a wedding outfit which will hurt the bank balance.'

'So sorry, yes that is a stressful time for you. Not only costly but you'll have to use your best acting skills if you don't like what she buys,' David said. 'Let me get you in training for this. Say after me, it looks lovely darling.'

'No, no, she'd know that was wrong as I never call her darling,' Gary said. 'How about, it looks lovely, love?'

'Oh no, no, no!' said David, shaking his head. 'You'll need to put a bit more effort in than that.'

'Don't worry, I've had lots of experience of this and I've got it just right now,' Gary said confidently. 'She's not a bad shopper, she's got nice taste but nine times out of ten it goes back anyway. I believe the female of our species just treats shopping as a hobby. It's a way to avoid boredom. The clothes are borrowed for a day or two, remain in the bag and then go back to the shop. The other option, which also occurs frequently, is the garment is neatly placed on a hanger and put in the wardrobe. Then two years later, Brenda will pull it out and say, when did I buy that and why did you let me buy something that awful?'

'Yes, I completely understand that,' said David, 'Trude is the same. We blokes know what we want, buy it, keep it and wear it. Even if it's bloody awful we just wear it as only fairies take things back for a refund.'

'You've got me there,' sighed Gary. 'I can only buy things Brenda likes me to wear.'

It was 4:30 when Brenda arrived home from her shopping expedition and by then Gary was on the sofa in the lounge. He heard Brenda open the front door.

'I'm home! Gary, are you in there or still daydreaming in the shed?' she shouted.

'I'm in here,' Gary replied. Brenda entered the room carrying a large hat box. 'Hi love, how did you get on?' he continued. 'Is that a hat in that box or have you bought me another big cake?'

'It's a hat, silly!' she replied. 'I've had a great afternoon. I've not only found a great hat but also a boyfriend for Sarah.'

'Crikey, do they have a shop for that now?' Gary questioned.

'No, not a shop. You're in a right silly mood. It's one of the Roadeteers; he is smitten,' Brenda said.

'You are kidding! Really? Well that's a turn up for the books,' Gary said, with a smile.

'Yes, he dropped his stick!' Brenda announced.

'His stick?' Gary asked. 'Is that a euphemism or something?'

'His stop/go stick thing. He got quite flustered,' Brenda explained.

'And the best news is that I found a hat,' Brenda said, excitedly holding up the hat box. 'It's a beautiful pale pink.'

'Not Pink Passion like the bedroom paint?' he asked.

'No Gary, and you don't need to keep reminding me of that mistake.'

'Sorry,' Gary said.

'It's a beautiful pink with lace and, oh let me show you.' Brenda pulled the hat out of the box and placed it on her head.

'What do you think?' she asked.

'It's lovely but what are you going to wear with it?' Gary said.

'Nothing yet, I've got to find the outfit,' Brenda replied.

'Go to the wedding in the nude but with a great hat,' Gary joked.

'Well, it's such a nice hat no one would notice if I were nude. They'd be looking at the hat,' announced Brenda, confidently.

'Really? I doubt that,' Gary said.

'You're right,' Brenda agreed, 'I'd better find an outfit as otherwise I could be the cause of major mental health problems if I'm seen in the nude.'

'Yes,' Gary laughed.

'You aren't supposed to agree with me!' said an annoyed Brenda. 'You should be saying, oh no love, everyone appreciates beauty.'

'And the beast!' said Gary, who was obviously a very brave, if not stupid, man. Luckily Brenda was in a good mood because she loved the hat and she laughed.

'Gary!' she said, 'that makes you the beast then.'

'Of course it would save us money if you didn't buy an outfit,' Gary continued.

'You're a tight beast!' she insisted, the smile having left her face. She changed the subject to avoid getting angry as she needed to control her blood pressure.

'Did you get much done in the shed?' she enquired.

'I did and you'll be pleased with me,' Gary replied.

'You've cleared the rubbish?' she said, in hope rather than belief.

'No,' he said, 'but I did something productive. I made something for Bronwyn and her friends.'

'Really, what?' Brenda asked.

'I used a bit of wood from inside the shed to make a hanging bird table thingy. It's hanging in the lilac tree. You can put some food out for her tomorrow,' Gary said, looking proud of himself.

'Ahhh, there's lovely,' she said in her best Welsh accent. They smiled, then Brenda continued, 'Right let me start dinner. Are you hungry?'

'Starving,' Gary said, 'this being productive lark makes you hungry.'

'Oh, I'd better get the washing in first,' Brenda said, suddenly remembering it was still on the washing line.

'That reminds me,' Gary remarked, remembering an event he witnessed while looking out of the shed window. 'I'm sorry I took the mickey out of you for saying Bronwyn is Welsh, she obviously is.' Brenda smiled at the fact he was coming around to her way of thinking.

'Yes, I told you. What's persuaded you she is?' she asked.

'I haven't heard a Welsh accent myself,' Gary explained, 'but the leek is a symbol of Wales, isn't it?'

'Yes, but what has that got to do with it?' Brenda asked.

'Well this afternoon Bronwyn 'leeked' all down your washing.'

'No. I'll have to wash it again now,' Brenda sighed. 'Oh Bronwyn, you little devil!'

After eating dinner, watching television and washing certain things again, the couple made it to bed. As they lay in the darkness there was a loud crashing noise outside which made them jump.

'What was that?' Brenda said, grabbing Gary to be as close to him as she could.

'No idea,' Gary replied. 'It's probably First Class jumping over the fence.'

Gary went straight to sleep but Brenda stayed awake for a long time frightened by the thought that someone was in the garden. In the morning Gary discovered that his bird table had fallen to the ground hitting the metal composter bin on the way down. Brenda was not pleased that Gary's productivity had resulted in her sleepless night and kept reminding him of this all of the day! Hey, Happy June!

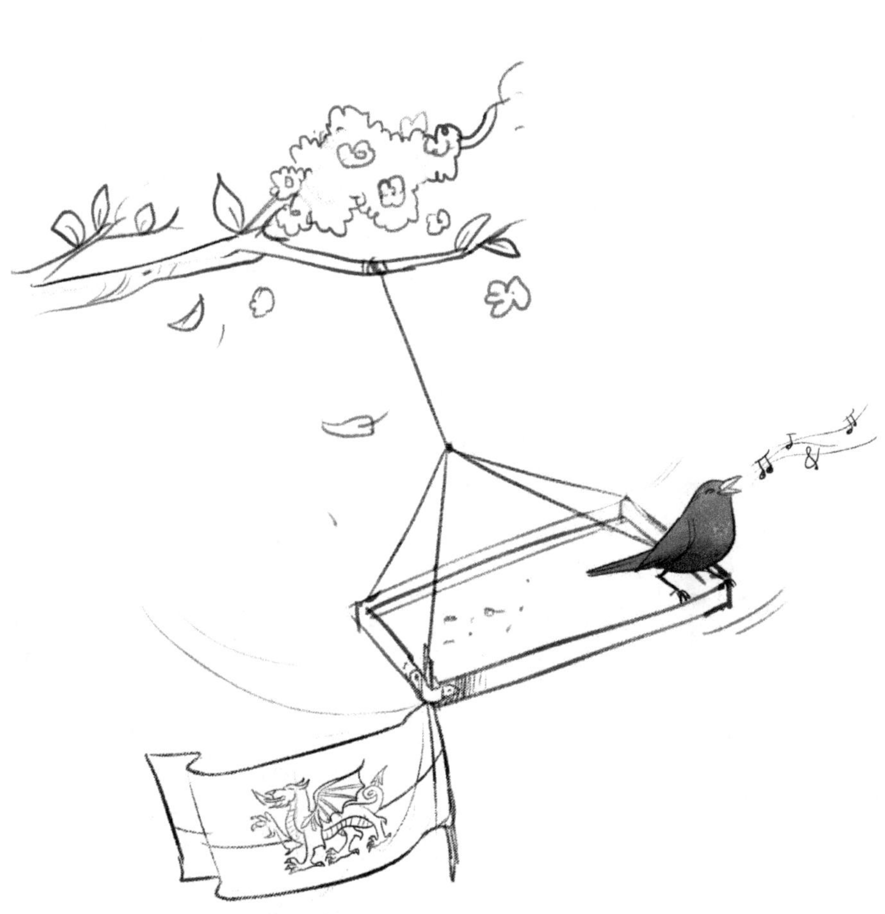

Chapter Seven

July
Ah, her beautiful eyes and smile

July had started hot, hot, hot! Glorious sunny summer days were filled with walks, picnics, a day out in Bournemouth and decorating! As we know, Gary had already painted, repainted and rerepainted the bedroom. Does the word rerepaint exist? Apparently so, just ask Gary! Since April he'd also decorated the kitchen, bathroom and the spare bedroom, the latter also being known as the guest room. There were only the hall, stairs/landing and lounge to go.

With the weather being hot, paint dried quickly and Brenda didn't want to waste this opportunity. She had started making plans for the other areas. Gary kept his head low hoping he wouldn't be called upon to bring out his paint brush and roller again too soon. It was now the middle of July and Brenda's attention was drawn to the lounge. Gary, on the other hand was thinking about his neighbours.

'We've been lucky with our neighbours, haven't we?' he said. 'Moving here and finding them to be friendly was a bonus.'

'Yes, but I was sad to leave our old neighbours behind as they were lovely,' she said. 'I saw Joyce from number 6 in town just the other day. She looked great.'

'That's nice,' Gary replied. 'The only new neighbours who are a bit odd are Aggie, who frightens me, and Izzy, who is just strange.'

'You have just insulted two of our neighbours!' Brenda exclaimed.

'I suppose I have, but they could be worse,' Gary admitted.

'Trudie and David are nice,' said Brenda, 'and we hardly see Kristian and Joshua.'

'That reminds me,' Gary said, suddenly remembering, 'Kristian and Joshua are getting a dog. Kai told me yesterday they are collecting one from the Rescue Centre tomorrow. What do you think they'll get? My money's on a miniature poodle called Tarquin.'

'Aren't they yappy?' Brenda asked.

'Kristian is a bit talkative but I wouldn't say yappy,' Gary replied.

'Poodles! Aren't poodles yappy?' she said.

'Right, I see,' Gary started, 'well I don't know. Do you think they'll put ribbons on its collar?'

'It'll be a camp dog if they do. You are just stereotyping again, Gary,' Brenda warned.

'Well, we'll see!' he said. 'What are you looking so serious about anyway?'

'I don't like the colour of these walls, do you?' she replied.

'Well . . .' Gary started to say, but was interrupted.

'And there are a few chips in the paint.'

'Well I think . . .' he started again but was interrupted again.

'And the ceiling needs painting too.' Gary's opinion didn't really matter so the effort he put into offering one had dwindled to nothing by now.

'I think the walls are dull and chipped and the ceiling needs painting,' he said, submissively. Brenda smiled.

'I'm glad you see it too and it's not just me,' she said.

'I've had a brilliant idea,' Gary continued, 'why don't I decorate this room?' He was proud of himself for managing to sound enthusiastic.

'Excellent idea Gary, and I think we should replace the sofa too, it's past it now,' Brenda replied. She had been encouraged to bring up the idea of a new sofa by how easy it had been to get Gary to agree to the decorating.

'The sofa is a bit like me then!' Gary said. Brenda smiled and then joked,

'Yes, but I'll put up with you for now.'

'Well, thank you very much,' Gary replied sharply, as he was feeling a little hurt, 'I suppose you don't have to sit on me. I'm more like a carpet, walked over.' Brenda ignored this comment, she wouldn't be distracted from her mission.

'What colour do you think for the walls?' she asked. Gary knew that his opinion wouldn't count for anything so didn't offer a colour.

'Oh no, this isn't going to be a repeat of the bedroom saga, is it?' he asked.

'That sounds like a cheap porn film, *The bedroom saga*,' Brenda said. She knew full well what he meant but didn't want it dragging up again.

'Okay, the bedroom WALL saga then!' he replied. Brenda again ignored Gary's pointed remark, after all the colour in the bedroom was only changed a few times. She didn't want an argument.

'The colour in here mustn't be restrictive but we don't want it to be too dull either,' Brenda continued.

'You don't require it to be soothing then, like in the bedroom?' Gary remarked.

'No, you don't have any trouble falling asleep on the sofa now,' she said. 'How about magnolia?'

'Isn't that the shade on there now?' Gary asked.

'Oh, yes you are probably right. It's hard to know what colour the previous owners used. It's a bit dull and too cold then,' she concluded.

'Cold? How can a colour be cold?' Gary said, looking puzzled.

'When it doesn't convey warmth and cosiness,' Brenda confirmed.

'What? Ah, like you if we go to bed on an argument. You certainly aren't warm or cosy then! I'm usually pillowed,' Gary said. His words were sharp and hurtful.

'It's got nothing to do with that,' she snapped. 'We've been married for forty years and decorated loads of times and you still don't understand the concept of cold and warm colours? Oh sometimes, Gary!'

'To be honest I've always just done as I've been told, haven't I?' Gary moaned, feeling sorry for himself. 'Or should I say I've had brilliant ideas which match your ideas after you've had them?' Brenda was getting annoyed now. Gary seemed to be throwing hurtful words her way.

'Are you saying you can't think for yourself, Gary?' she asked bitterly.

'No, I'm saying I think very wisely for myself and make sure my way of thinking matches yours, *love*.' Gary replied emphasising *love* in the most sarcastic way he could.

'I'm not sure I follow, but never mind,' Brenda replied and tried to steer away from the tension. 'How about a warm cream, a yellowy cream?' she asked.

'I've had an idea,' Gary piped up but couldn't continue as Brenda butted in straight away with,

'Don't start that! You've just said you only copy my ideas for a peaceful life.'

'Well actually I have had a great idea all of my own,' he insisted. 'Go ahead and choose your paint and make it a neutral colour. Then hopefully you won't be changing your mind like you did with luscious lime and pink passion in the bedroom. I still think Gun Powder grey would have been okay.'

'Shut up!' Brenda snapped. 'And it was passionate pink not pink passion!'

'Okay,' Gary submitted!

There was a short pause before Brenda revisited the subject of the new sofa. She thought now would be a good time to get agreement from Gary, as she'd already psychologically knocked him down, the count was at about 8 and he hadn't got back up yet.

'We need to look for the new sofa too,' she said, but Gary got up before the count reached 10!

'Oh my God. What colour does that need to be? A warm neutral that is soothing for the bum?' he retaliated half-heartedly with a smile that changed the mood from aggression to fun.

'You are stupid, but I do still love you!' Brenda declared as they smiled at each other. 'I'm going to look in on Izzy today to see how she's getting on.'

'Couldn't you have concentrated a little more on how much you love me before changing the subject to Izzy?' Gary said disappointedly.

'I love you, I love you, I love you,' Brenda declared and declared and declared until Gary stopped her.

'Right, thank you that's enough!' he said, 'I'll check the paint colour chart for a buttermilk shade. I can buy it this morning and make a start.'

'Thank you,' Brenda said with a smile, 'did I mention that I love you?'

'Okay, shut up now!' he said. 'Are you going round to Izzy's this morning? She's a bit of a funny one isn't she, oh Glenda?'

'I quite like being Glenda,' Brenda admitted. 'It's like having a second personality. Perhaps it's my Geminian twin! Izzy is a lovely young woman, just a little highly strung that's all. She takes everything literally. Do you remember my friend Martha?'

'Martha? Martha?' Gary couldn't remember this former work colleague of Brenda's.

'Well Martha,' Brenda continued, 'had the same traits as Izzy and was later diagnosed as being autistic. On a driving lesson the instructor told her to go straight across the roundabout so she did; straight over the bump and everything.'

'Perhaps that's why it is spelt out now. Sat nav would say take the third exit or whatever it is,' Gary said.

'Yes, I suppose so. Martha didn't understand jokes either and neither does Izzy. I still joke with her though as I forget, but she never understands and looks blank. Her world is black and white,' Brenda said.

'It must be a strange world to be living in,' Gary commented. 'I'll drive into town now to get some buttermilk paint.'

'Brilliant, you can give me a lift to DDs. I'll grab a piece of cake for Izzy,' Brenda announced. 'Then I'll walk back so I don't hold you up!' That sounded thoughtful but really Brenda just wanted Gary to get on with the painting.

'Yes, she'll like cake,' Gary acknowledged. 'You are the cake lady!'

'What, like tempting and very tasty?' she asked.

'No, more like sickly and full of fat,' he joked.

'Get out!' she laughed, 'Let's go!'

It was 10:15 when Brenda arrived at DDs. It wasn't busy so Dolly was pleased to see a friendly face walk through the door. Brenda bought a piece of the delicious chocolate cake for Izzy assuming that she would like that as everybody loved Dolly's chocolate cake!

'I hope Izzy enjoys it,' Dolly remarked as she handed Brenda the boxed cake. 'I don't know Izzy, she doesn't come in here. I know of her though as Kai often stops for a chat when he delivers the post. It's nice that they are a happy young couple. They need to appreciate these times before it all goes stale.'

'Before you get so used to each other everything becomes the norm, you mean?' Brenda asked.

'Aye, because things become challenging later on,' Dolly replied.

'But things are okay with you, aren't they?' Brenda asked.

'What with Ian?' Dolly replied. 'Yes, we've got our wedding anniversary coming up next week but it'll just be business as usual. When you've been married a while the passion leaves, doesn't it?'

'Don't you still feel that tingle when he kisses you?' Brenda enquired, with a romantic look in her eye.

'Only in the winter when my lips are chapped,' Dolly replied, with a wink. 'Do you with Gary?'

'Sometimes,' Brenda replied, 'it's after he's said something special. When he's made me feel good. I know it's only stupid talk but he managed to use his stupid talk to make me feel special. It doesn't happen every week but, sometimes. This morning he simply annoyed me!'

'Ian is still my best friend though and that's important,' Dolly acknowledged.

'Yes it is,' agreed Brenda, 'you can insult your best friends and they'll always understand. Do you and Ian have many arguments?'

'All the time but they are respectful arguments,' Dolly replied.

'Respectful? What are they?' Brenda asked, looking intrigued.

'We argue and he respects my right to win!' Dolly laughed. Brenda smiled realising that most of her arguments with Gary could be classed as respectful then.

'All couples argue, don't they?' Brenda remarked. 'Anyone who says they've never had an argument with their other half must be lying. I've heard a few arguments in the street and in the supermarket.'

'Aye, so have I,' Dolly said, 'I've heard a lot in here. I hate it when couples argue in public and I've missed the beginning so I don't know whose side I'm on!'

The café door opened and Sarah walked in with Steve.

'Hello Sarah love,' Dolly said cheerily.

'Hello Sarah and . . .' Brenda started.

'It's Steve, you know the stop/go man?' Sarah said. Steve smiled then proudly made the following announcement,

'That isn't a description of my performance in the bedroom. It's . . .' Sarah stopped him from saying anymore by talking over him.

'Okay, that's enough, it's the stop/go board, we all know that,' she said.

'Aren't you working today, stop/go man?' Brenda asked.

'Yes, I've just started my lunch hour, I get thirty minutes,' Steve replied. Hearing this Sarah pulled a funny face at Brenda. 'So I'm meeting up with Sarah,' he continued.

'Lovely!' Brenda replied, with a smile.

'Are you two an item then?' Dolly asked.

'An item?' Steve said, looking confused.

'Don't worry Steve,' Sarah said reassuringly, 'Dolly's not asking if you're an object. It's old-fashioned code for getting it on. We are enjoying getting to know each other.'

Dolly and Brenda both said, 'Lovely!' Brenda turned to Dolly so that she now had her back turned to Sarah and mouthed, '*getting it on*?' Dolly did well to keep it together as she asked, 'What can I get on, I mean get you?' Brenda worked hard on stifling a giggle.

'Two Americanos please,' Sarah replied.

'You already know what he drinks then! Two Americanos coming up!' she said.

Brenda looked at her watched and looked shocked.

'Is that the time?' she said. 'I'll leave you two lovebirds in peace. I'm off now, bye all.' She grabbed her box containing cake and headed for the door.

'Bye Brenda,' Dolly called after her as she was walking over to Sarah and Steve's table with their hot drinks. She deposited them and walked back to the counter and started to wash it down.

'Do you want to do something tonight then?' Steve asked Sarah.

'Yes, why not!' she replied, 'What have you got in mind?'

'How about an Oxford pub crawl?' he said, enthusiastically.

'Oh great. Really?' Sarah replied, sarcastically.

'Or,' he continued, 'we could stay in at my digs and watch footie?' By now Sarah was yawning.

'The excitement is killing me,' she lied but Steve hadn't realised.

'Right you are. Football it is, good one!' he said.

Sarah looked disappointed and took a sip of her coffee, as she did Trudie entered DDs.

'Hi Sarah,' Trudie shouted across to her.

'Hi Trude!' she replied. Trudie walked over to the counter where Dolly was standing and speaking quietly she said,

'Is that the new man?'

'Looks like it,' Dolly replied.

'First impressions?' asked Trudie.

'Good looking but thick as shite.' Dolly replied. 'Of course that's only my first impression.' Trudie tried not to laugh.

'Don't hold back, Dolly!' she said. 'I'll have a pot of tea please.'

'Okay lass. Are you going to join Sarah and TAS?' Dolly asked.

'TAS?' Trudie said. 'I thought he's called Steve.'

'Yes, TAS stands for Thick As Shite,' Dolly stated. Again, Trudie tried not to laugh.

'No, I won't be joining them,' Trudie said, 'three's a crowd so I'll leave the lovers alone. I'll sit over there by the window. TAS, that is funny.'

'Doug, his workmate, calls him that, I can't claim it as my description,' Dolly said. 'I asked him what it stood for and that's what I was told. I thought it was a bit harsh until he just announced he's on a thirty-minute lunch hour.'

'No!' Trudie said in disbelief. 'Still, if he's kind natured and makes Sarah happy then that's all that matters.'

'Absolutely. Do you want cake with your tea?' Dolly asked.

'Oh, go on then,' Trudie said, 'a piece of your carrot cake please. The carrot is one of my five-a-day. I suppose if I believe that you should start calling me TAS.' Dolly smiled.

'No, I'll start calling you wishful!' she said.

Meanwhile, Gary had bought the paint. It matched all of Brenda's criteria, smooth, non-restricting, warmish and neutral. The shade was called custard cream. He had driven home and was getting out of his car as Kristian was coming out of his front door. Kristian waved to Gary and walked over.

'Hello, how are you?' he asked Gary in a way which made it obvious he was going to want something from him.

'Very well thank you, and you?' Gary replied.

'I'm fine too, thanks,' replied Kristian. Then came that extra request Gary was expecting from the start . . 'I was wondering if I could ask a favour of you, Gary? It's nothing complicated, very simple.' Gary thought, well there's a surprise! But he responded politely and in a way that would have made Brenda proud.

'Of course,' he said. 'What is it?'

'It's for Joshua,' (that's Kristian's husband, just in case you had forgotten), 'he's in his final year at Oxford studying Psychology and Human Behaviour,' Kristian explained.

'Wow, that's impressive, a clever boy then?' Gary remarked.

'Yes, he's very gifted academically,' Kristian confirmed proudly. 'Part of his course is studying human connection and sexual chemistry.' At this point Gary's imagination was working overtime and he began to worry. The anxiety could be seen on his face.

'Don't look worried,' Kristian continued, 'it's really quite simply looking into sexual attraction and what attracts us to our partners. He's got a very simple question which he's got to ask as many people as possible. I can't remember what the question is now but would you be willing to help him out? It's all anonymous so your answer will be confidential.'

'Well if it's just one question then that's fine,' Gary replied looking relieved, after all what could possibly go wrong?

'Brilliant, I'll let him know. He's young and a little shy that's why I've asked you. He'll pop round later, thanks.' Kristian carried on to his car.

'That's fine,' Gary said, 'I hope.' Gary and his can of custard cream paint headed into the house. He planned to start painting almost immediately after washing down bits of the wall.

In Turnpike Road, Brenda knocked on Izzy's front door. She had come from DDs via the shops where she'd bought a few groceries she needed. Izzy opened the door and invited her in.

'I hope I haven't called at a bad time, Izzy?' Brenda said, as they walked to the lounge.

'No, just right really, Glenda,' she replied, 'I've just finished buying a new cot online. It's a bargain at £50 and it's new, I double checked.'

'It's nice to find a bargain, isn't it?' Brenda said. 'You are looking great Izzy, not too long to go now.' Izzy smiled but looked blank.

'Too long until what?' she asked.

'Until you give birth!' Brenda said.

'Oh yes!' Izzy replied. 'Of course, just over a couple of months.'

'I bought you a piece of chocolate cake, fresh from DDs in town.' Brenda handed the box to Izzy.

'That's kind of you, thank you Glenda!' Izzy said and took the cake. 'I'll enjoy that later with some tea.'

'It's lovely outside today, a beautiful day,' Brenda remarked. 'I saw a lovely big fluffy grey cat on the way over here.'

'How did you know it was on its way over here?' Izzy asked, 'Perhaps it's friends with First Class.' Brenda felt a little awkward and tried to explain.

'No, I was on the way over here. How is First Class?' she asked, trying to get away from the topic of the grey fluffy cat.

'He's fine,' Izzy confirmed.

'Great! And how are you Izzy?' asked Brenda. 'Is everything going well?'

'Ah, yes thank you,' she replied, 'but getting things sorted and the cost of everything is a bit of a worry. That's why I was so lucky to find that cot online!'

'Try not to worry too much,' Brenda said reassuringly, 'everything will work out.' Suddenly, the lounge door was pushed open by a furry paw and First Class walked into the room.

'Ah, hiya Classy!' Izzy said. 'You haven't got a grey fluffy friend with you then? Ah, Glenda, I think you got it wrong, that cat wasn't coming here.' Brenda smiled and stroked First Class, she'd already given up on that one.

By the time Brenda had walked home, Gary had already painted two walls in the lounge. He looked very hot as the temperature had now reached 28 degrees. Brenda was happy to see such good progress being made. She didn't want to hinder Gary in any way, so she put her shopping bag down on the kitchen floor, took him a cold drink and retreated upstairs with the laptop. An hour went by and then another half an hour. It was now 4 o'clock.

'Brenda, what are you doing?' Gary shouted, paint roller in hand.

'I'm in the bedroom on the laptop,' Brenda shouted back.

'Well get off, you'll break it!' Gary joked.

'Very funny, you haven't said that before, have you?' she said, having heard it dozens of times! 'I've just ordered our new sofa. It's in stock and next day delivery so it'll be here tomorrow. You'll be in, won't you, as I'm out with the WI? It's our trip to Waterperry Gardens!' Gary's smile faded into an anxious frown.

'Oh God!' he muttered. 'This is a costly week.'

'What? I can't hear you from up here,' Brenda shouted.

'Nothing love,' Gary shouted back. 'I'm going to take a break and sit in the garden for ten minutes. I've almost finished but I'm so hot I need a rest.'

'Okay love,' Brenda replied.

Gary headed into the garden and spotted David in his garden and went over to the fence for a chat. At the same time Joshua came around the side of the house and continued walking towards Gary.

'Hello Gary, David,' Joshua said.

'Hi Joshua,' Gary replied.

'Hello again,' David replied and turned to Gary and explained, 'Joshua is doing a survey and I took part earlier.'

'Ah yes, Kristian was telling me about that,' said Gary. 'Have you come to ask me a question?' Gary had left the back door open and Brenda was now in the kitchen unpacking the shopping bag she'd abandoned on the floor when she got home earlier. She could hear the conversation taking place in the garden.

'Right then,' started Joshua, 'I need to put you in an age bracket. Am I right in thinking you are between 65 and 75 years old?'

'Yes,' Gary said.

'And you've been in a relationship with Brenda for over ten years and you are still in love with her?'

'Yes and yes,' was the reply. Brenda was unpacking the fruit and vegetables and smiled as she heard Gary's replies.

'So there's just one question, Gary,' Joshua continued. 'Can you describe one thing that you find most attractive about Brenda?' Gary was silent for a moment as he was embarrassed by the question. He didn't know what to say on this personal issue especially with David listening in.

'Oh, err, umm, well, I suppose, well, let me think about this, umm.'

Brenda was annoyed and hurt by Gary's lack of response. Suddenly a tomato, thrown by her, flew through the open back door and hit Gary on the side of his head. He jolted sideways; it was a brilliant shot. David, who had spotted Brenda in the doorway, couldn't prevent himself from bursting into laughter. Joshua looked shocked and remained silent.

'Is it her impeccable aim with a tomato you're attracted to?' David said while still laughing. At this point Brenda walked across the garden towards them. She felt humiliated.

'Gary,' she started, 'why was it so very hard for you to think of one, just one thing that you find attractive about me?' David stopped laughing and tried to help his friend out.

'Ah Brenda,' David said, 'to be fair I expect there are so many things he was just having trouble narrowing it down to one thing in particular.' Joshua was so embarrassed he didn't know what to do or say. He felt guilty that his simple survey question had caused so much trouble.

'I'm sorry, I'll leave you alone,' he said. 'Sorry again, I didn't mean to cause any trouble.' He took off rapidly and exited the garden walking back around the side of the house.

'Yes, I'd better go too,' David said and started to walk away.

'No David, wait!' Brenda requested quite forcefully. 'Can I ask if you've taken part in this survey?'

'Em, yes I have,' David replied, a little concerned at what Brenda would do next. He had no idea if she was still holding tomatoes.

'If you don't mind me asking, what was your answer to that question?' Brenda asked.

'Oh that was easy,' David replied. 'It's Trude's beautiful eyes and smile. Right, sorry I must go.' David disappeared inside his house.

'Sorry love,' Gary said, 'but it's a personal question and I got embarrassed as I had David listening in too. There are loads of things I could have said.'

'Like what?' Brenda asked. Gary hadn't thought this through as he still couldn't think of anything by himself.

'Your beautiful eyes and smile?' he said, unconvincingly.

'Can't think of your own answer then!' she shouted.

'Only joking!' Gary said, smiling.

'So you don't like my eyes and smile?' she said, getting upset.

'I can't win,' Gary protested. 'How about I'm turned on by your feisty personality?' Brenda was now really annoyed. Her level of anger was far higher than any hurt she felt.

'It's too late now. And don't get any ideas later as we won't be getting it on tonight!' Gary was confused by this. What could that mean, he thought.

'Getting on what?' he asked.

'Oh, never mind,' she said, 'you are so old school!' Gary realised now that Brenda was talking about sex and replied,

'Oh, right, got what you mean now. Well I wasn't expecting to anyway as it isn't June or December, is it? We are about as frequent as the summer and winter solstice!' Brenda stormed back into the house shouting at the top of her voice,

'NOT EVEN A CUDDLE!'

Gary was left as a solitary figure in the garden. He felt sorry for himself and muttered,

'Well, that was a waste of a tomato! They aren't cheap either.' The rest of the day turned frosty for poor Gary, despite the temperature outside never falling below 26 degrees. After having his dinner thrown on his plate and a few doors slammed, he ended up sleeping in the spare room; that's the one also known as the guest room. That was the first time the guest room had been used since they'd moved in. Still, after all that painting he slept well, unlike Brenda who always found it hard to sleep without Gary next to her.

The next morning the sun rose and it promised to be another lovely day probably reaching 30 degrees, but sadly the temperature between Gary and Brenda didn't look like getting higher than -5 degrees. At about 10 o'clock Brenda was preparing to go out. She bumped around the house to make it clear to Gary that he hadn't been forgiven for the events of yesterday. She kept verbal communications with him to a minimum.

'I'm off on the WI outing now,' she said.

'Where is it you are visiting?' Gary asked, as he had genuinely forgotten.

'I told you before,' she replied abruptly, 'we are going to look around Waterperry Gardens.'

'Oh yes,' Gary replied. 'Have a nice time.'

'I intend to,' she snapped. 'Don't forget that the sofa will be delivered today. As I told you yesterday, it was in stock so on next day delivery.'

'Okay, I know,' Gary replied, 'but just as well you reminded me as I may be suffering memory loss after being hit on the head by a tomato!' Brenda left without kissing him goodbye. Gary knew he was in big trouble as he could count, on one hand, the number of times she had gone out without demanding a kiss goodbye. He knew she'd get over it and sat back on the sofa enjoying the peace and admiring his handywork. The room looked beautiful even though he hadn't painted the ceiling yet. He was hoping that Brenda wouldn't notice, yes, after forty years of marriage he still believed in miracles!

In Turnpike Road, Kai and Izzy were looking for more baby things online. It was Kai's day off. There was someone at the door so Izzy went to answer it and came back carrying a small box.

'Have you ordered anything?' she asked Kai. 'Are you expecting something?'

'No,' Kai replied.

'Well a courier has just delivered this. I wonder what it is?' Izzy said, looking puzzled. She went over to the drawer and pulled out a pair of scissors and used them to carefully open the small box.

'Oh!' she exclaimed, as she pulled out a miniature cot which was made as a speciality piece of doll's house furniture. Kai looked at it and shook his head.

'What's that then?' he asked of a rather embarrassed and upset Izzy.

'I think it's the cot I ordered!' she said.

'I don't think you checked the measurements, did you? That's for a doll's house.' Kai said, stating the obvious. 'Your labour should be a doddle if you give birth to a baby that will fit in that!'

'Bugger!' Izzy shouted.

'When did you start swearing?' asked a shocked Kai.

'About five seconds ago!' she said with a tear of frustration running down her cheek.

Gary hadn't filled his morning doing anything productive. He sat in the garden enjoying the sunshine and once looked in his shed but found it too hot to sit in his daydreaming chair. So he sat outside and daydreamed there instead. He was back in the lounge again admiring his decorating skills by 1 o'clock when the doorbell rang. He opened the door to find two delivery men standing there.

'Good afternoon,' said Delivery Man number 1, the older one of the pair who was obviously in charge. 'We've got your sofa here. Can we take a look at where it's going?'

'Yes, come in,' Gary replied and both men followed Gary into the lounge.

'My wife ordered it and she didn't tell me if you take the old thing away?' Gary said.

'Sorry no, I think you married her for better or worse,' he laughed.

'Very good,' Gary said, 'but what about the old sofa?'

'Sorry Sir, no, we don't take that either but we can help you get it outside.'

'Okay, thanks,' Gary said, he was grateful for any help.

The two delivery men removed it and left it outside on the footpath. They then unloaded the new sofa. Gary hadn't seen the sofa before but was surprised at the size of the one they had unloaded.

'Are you sure that is our one?' he asked.

'Yes, it says so on the delivery note,' Delivery man 1 replied.

'It looks big!' Gary noted.

'It does. You've only got a small room there and a small doorway and sharp angles to get it through, but we'll try,' Delivery Man 1 said. The sofa was about half the size again of the one it was replacing and despite their best efforts it wouldn't fit through the door, eventually they gave up.

'Did you check the measurements when you ordered it?' asked Delivery man 1.

'I didn't order it, as I said, my wife did,' Gary replied.

'Oh yes, that's right,' started Delivery Man 1 'What were you thinking letting her order it?'

'Clearly I wasn't thinking but she's crafty and orders things when I'm painting.' Delivery Man 2 had been present the whole time but had not uttered a word, this was about to change.

'That's the trouble with women,' he started, 'they always want everything bigger.' He ended his sentence with a wink.

'Shut it!' Delivery Man 1 said, demonstrating why Delivery Man 2 didn't say much. Gary looked worried. What was he to do with an oversized sofa?

'Can you take it back as it's no good here?' he asked.

'Yes, we can do that,' replied Delivery Man 1. 'The refund should go back into your account in three days. You'll need to sign here.' He passed the paperwork and a pen to Gary who duly signed in the appropriate box.

'Sorry for the trouble,' Gary said, as he passed the signed paperwork and pen back.

'No apology needed,' said Delivery Man 1, 'I'm married and I know what it's like.'

Both delivery men then got into their van and drove off. Gary turned to return to the house and realised the old sofa was still on the pavement. Luckily David drove up and parked outside his house. He got out of his car to be greeted by Gary.

'Hi mate,' he started, 'you couldn't help me get this inside, could you please? The new one's too big and on its way back to the shop. The love of my life may be a crack shot with a tomato but she's not so hot on measurements.' David smiled and picked up one end of the sofa.

'No problem, let's get it inside,' he said and they lifted it and carried it back into Gary's lounge.

'This sofa looks good, why are you replacing it?' asked David.

'Because the tomato tosser has spoken and always knows best,' Gary said, with real feeling.

'Oh yes, I've got one of those although mine doesn't throw tomatoes,' David replied, with a grin. They put the sofa down where it had been before and walked to the front door. Kristian was walking past with his new dog. It was not a small poodle called Tarquin with ribbons but a ribbon free German Shepherd. Both Gary and David stood there staring at them.

'Don't worry guys,' shouted Kristian reassuringly, 'this is Satan and he's very friendly.'

'Wow, that's a big poodle!' Gary said, looking shocked.

'What?' said a confused David.

The rest of the day was uneventful, well how much more excitement could anyone take? Brenda arrived back from her trip in a much better mood. Gary was very gentle in breaking the news to her about the sofa. He didn't want to make her feel small especially as her mood was so much better.

Later as they lay in bed in the darkness Brenda broke the silence with an apology.

'I'm sorry about the sofa,' she said.

'Don't worry, love,' Gary said.' How about a cuddle?'

'Okay then,' Brenda giggled and put her arms around Gary. He laughed and said,

'You have beautiful eyes and smile.'

'FORGET IT!' Brenda shouted so loudly the whole of Seymour Rise must have heard her.

'Is your sense of humour only available June and December too?' Gary asked as he was pushed back to his side of the bed, followed by Brenda's silhouette appearing to bash him with a pillow.

Chapter Eight

August
Paul's a bicycle

Despite their arguments and pillow fights, mainly Brenda hitting Gary, the couple had managed to make it successfully to August living in Seymour Rise. If you had asked either of them if they were happy both would have answered, yes very. Their marriage was built on constant bickering which was as normal to them as eating and sleeping. The truth was, when it really mattered both had proved themselves to be the most loyal, loving and supportive partner. It was fair to observe that at times they appeared to almost hate each other but neither would survive easily without the other.

Earlier in the month they had taken a five-day break in Paris. Gary had always wanted to make amends for not taking Brenda somewhere more romantic than Blackpool for their fortieth wedding anniversary. So he chose Paris in August. It was in peak season and busy but it was an organised coach trip and, all things considered, reasonably priced. The reasonably priced bit had appealed to Gary more than the prospect of seeing the Eiffel Tower. They felt at home on this trip as the coach was filled with, shall we say, senior citizens or at least people over the age of 65. Although Paris was full of families with noisy children, their travelling was childfree. That's not to say it was always peaceful on the coach, as often couples were having to raise their voices to be heard when hearing aids had been accidently left in hotel rooms. The trip went well with no rows between Gary and Brenda probably because Brenda had packed the right amount of clean underwear to cover the duration of the holiday! They arrived back late on 18th August and slept well. The next day was a Monday and Brenda popped next door to see Trudie who welcomed her into her home.

'Did you have a good time?' Trudie asked.

'Oooh la la oui, merci!' Brenda replied, with a smile. 'Yes, it was lovely, thank you. And the weather was great.'

'That's good,' Trudie replied, 'and have you got photos?'

'Of course, but I won't bore you with those now,' Brenda replied. Trudie was secretly pleased because although she was interested, it was only 9 o'clock on a Monday morning and she was due at work for a 10 o'clock shift. 'I can show you later though. I've popped round now to say thank you for watering the plants and give you this.' Brenda handed Trudie a little bag containing a bottle of perfume.

'Oh, thank you, but you shouldn't have,' Trudie said, 'you were only away for five nights and it was no trouble.'

'Don't be silly; I'm really grateful as the weather has been hot and you must have watered every evening,' said Brenda, 'and they would have died which would have been a shame after all my hard work putting them in.'

'Your garden is looking lovely, Brenda,' said Trudie, 'such lovely colours.'

'Thank you,' Brenda replied. 'It's a perk of being retired, you get time to garden properly. Well, I'll let you get on as you've probably got to get to work. I'll catch up properly later, but thanks again.'

'My pleasure,' Trudie said, 'and thank you for my present.' Brenda left Trudie and returned home to prepare some breakfast for Gary. She knew he'd been tired after yesterday's journey home so wouldn't be getting up in a hurry. Sure enough, he was still asleep in bed and hadn't realised she'd left the bed, let alone the house.

It was 10 o'clock and the Roadeteers were standing around a hole in the road they had come to fill in and resurface. They had arrived thirty minutes earlier and for the whole of that time Steve had said very little.

'You're quiet Steve,' Doug said, 'something bothering you?'

'He's in love, it's damaging his brain,' Frank said.

'What brain?' Doug joked.

'Very funny guys! Trouble is I think Sarah is about to dump me. I really like her too,' said an anxious Steve.

'Why do you think she's going to dump you?' Doug enquired.

'Because she said so,' Steve replied.

'Right you are then, can't argue with that. Why though?' Frank asked.

'She says she is tired of doing boring things and I've got to start treating her better or we're finished,' Steve explained.

'What does she mean by treat her better?' Doug asked.

'I don't know,' Steve said, proclaiming his ignorance, 'I take her to the pub once a week and buy her chips on the way home. I thought she liked that. What am I supposed to do, like?'

'You gotta make her feel special. Do something nice for her,' was Doug's advice.

'What, like buy her scampi and chips at the pub? Cut out the chips on the way home?' was the best Steve could come up with. Doug looked perplexed.

'No, mate. Forget the pub. Take her to a nice restaurant with candles and everything. Buy her chocolates and flowers,' Doug advised. Frank looked a little worried.

'There's no overtime mind, so you'd better have savings,' he said, thinking of his budgets. Steve just looked confused.

'Where do I buy candles to take?' he asked. 'Do they sell them in Sainsbury's?'

'The candles are already there, you muppet!' Doug replied. 'Oh dear, there's no hope! A good restaurant won't be cheap though.'

'Do you think that would work then?' Steve asked. Doug nodded and added,

'It'll show her you care.' There was a short pause and you could almost hear Steve's mind churning over ideas.

'I'll give it a go then, thanks fellas,' he said. During this mind blowing bit of male bonding and sharing of essential advice, the Roadeteers had taken their eye off the ball. Traffic was now gridlocked as nobody was in charge of controlling it.

'In the meantime I suggest you clear the traffic!' Frank bellowed.

'Right you are!' said Steve, grabbing his stop/go board.

Back in 19 Seymour Rise, Gary had managed to get out of bed and eat his breakfast. Brenda had left him eating toast when she went out for a short walk. She thought the beautiful morning would help clear her head and wake her up properly. She'd heard of jetlag which obviously didn't apply to her but thought there must be such a thing as Parislag! She walked around the town, waved to Dolly through the window of DDs and made her way back via Turnpike Road. Izzy was at her front door talking to Mark. It seemed it was Turnpike Road's turn to have their windows cleaned. Brenda waved to Izzy and Mark as she passed. She thought Izzy's bump had grown a lot since she last saw her.

When she made it home it was early afternoon and she felt refreshed and positive about collecting some vitamin D directly from the sunshine. She'd made it back just right as the sun was now at full strength and the heat was becoming unbearable to walk in. As they say, *mad dogs and Englishmen go out in the midday sun.* Brenda walked into the lounge and found Gary cleaning his fishing rod. He greeted her with a cheery,

'Hello love.' Brenda immediately felt annoyed by what she saw.

'Gary!' she said, 'Why have you got that smelly thing in here?' He smiled.

'I didn't have time for a shower so I'm wiping my rod down instead,' he replied. Brenda was not amused.

'Oh Gary, sometimes!' she declared. 'You are 72 years old with a mind of a 13-year old. Be careful of the furniture and the paintwork. Why can't you clean that in the shed?' Gary laughed his smutty laugh. 'Perhaps 13 years old was an exaggeration, you're younger,' Brenda said, reassessing the situation.

'If you say so, *dearest*!' Gary said sarcastically. 'Anyway, did you have a nice walk? See anyone?'

'I waved to a few people,' Brenda replied, 'I saw Izzy and she is very big now.'

'So SFI is getting a big bump then?' Gary said.

'I was talking about Izzy,' Brenda said. 'I've no idea who SFI is.'

'Izzy is SFI, Straight Faced Izzy,' Gary said. 'Well if Dolly is calling Steve TAS, I'm calling Izzy SFI.'

'I haven't heard about that. What is that then?' Brenda asked.

'Didn't you know?' Gary asked. 'Trudie told me that Dolly referred to Steve as TAS which is Thick As Shite.' Brenda pulled a face in disapproval.

'That's not nice, Gary!' she said.

'It's not me! Take it up with Dolly!' he protested. 'But I do think it's funny. That'll teach him to quote *them* rules at me!'

'Izzy is Izzy!' Brenda said. 'You'd better be careful or I'll think of an acronym for you!' she threatened. Gary smiled.

'That would have to be HAS for Handsome And Sexy,' he said.

'Almost, just add a B to the end, HASB standing for HAS Been!' she barked back.

'Rude!' said Gary, who was no longer smiling.

'What would mine be?' Brenda asked. 'No, don't bother to answer that. I don't want to know.' Gary's face lit up, he'd had a light bulb moment where he'd remembered something important.

'Oh, I forgot to tell you, Mary rang while you were out. Verity and Paul's wedding is off,' he said.

'What, off for good or just postponed?' Brenda asked.

'Off for good,' Gary replied. 'That's a waste of a good hat and dress!'

'I loved you in that dress too!' Brenda joked.

'Ha, ha very funny!' he replied, 'I told you to keep the receipts.'

'I bought them weeks ago,' she said, 'so it's too late for getting my money back. Anyway, that isn't important right now. What about poor Verity, is she okay? What happened?'

'Seems Paul is a bicycle so it's all off.' Gary replied. Brenda looked totally confused, Gary may have been speaking in Latin for all she understood.

'Paul's a what?' she asked.

'You remember Verity was going out with Greg for two years before she met Paul a year ago?' Gary started to explain.

'Yes,' said Brenda, listening intently.

'Well Paul was a friend of Greg's and it seems they were, and still are, more than friends. He must also be a bicycle and now the two are a tandem,' Gary explained. This explanation didn't make any sense to Brenda.

'What are you talking about?' she said.

'It's what Anthony at Bowls Club calls those who bat for both sides,' Gary went on. The meaning of Gary's peculiar riddle started to dawn on Brenda.

'Are you trying to say that Paul and Greg are bisexual and they are now in a relationship?' she asked.

'Yes, that's what I said, a tandem!' he exclaimed, as if Brenda was slow on the uptake.

'Grow up, Gary! Poor Verity, this is awful. Is she okay?' Brenda asked.

'Oh yes, she's not a bicycle,' Gary replied. Brenda started to get annoyed with Gary's insensitive attitude.

'I'm not talking about her sexuality, you fool,' she said. 'Is she okay? She must be heartbroken!'

'Mary thinks Verity's had a lucky escape,' Gary explained, 'she doesn't mind her granddaughter marrying a bicycle as long as he is faithful, but he used his pump . . .'

'Please stop this bicycle nonsense now,' Brenda interrupted. 'You continue to joke when poor Verity must be going through hell. This is a terrible experience for her.' Gary felt guilty, he knew Brenda was right.

'True,' he said, 'but she's young so she'll get over it. It is better she found out now rather than after they had got married.'

'That's true,' Brenda agreed. 'I'll ring Mary later to find out what's really happened minus all the references to bicycles!' There was a short pause before she continued with,

'So if Anthony calls bisexuals bicycles, what does he call heterosexuals?'

'Pickled onions!' Gary replied abruptly. 'Because they are quite happy to stay in the same vinegar all their life.' Brenda smiled at Gary.

'You are a twit!' she said. 'What about homosexuals?' she continued almost dreading the answer.

'Homosexuals?' Gary questioned. 'Well they are called gay, surely you knew that? Keep up, love!' Brenda looked stunned but she knew it was her own fault for asking. Gary's mind had already moved on and he changed the subject thinking ahead to later that day.

'You haven't forgotten you are driving me to bowls at 5 o'clock, have you?' he asked. 'I'd drive myself but that would mean I can't have a drink.'

'No, I haven't forgotten,' Brenda replied, 'although I'm not sure it is a good thing mixing with that lot, especially Anthony and all his bicycle rubbish.'

'Ah well, he can be annoying,' he replied, 'but he's okay really.'

'If you say so, now hurry up and take that fishing rod outside!' Brenda demanded.

'Alright, I've finished now,' Gary replied.

Outside in Seymour Rise, Aggie was walking, well marching really, across the road towards Kristian who had just got out of his car. Kristian had noticed her and stood waiting on the pavement.

'Hello, how are you?' he said cheerily to Aggie.

'Great thank you, have you got a day off work?' she asked.

'No, I'm just popping home in my lunch break to take Satan out,' Kristian said. Aggie looked intrigued as she hadn't heard the name Satan mentioned before.

'Satan?' she queried, 'Is that your nickname for Joshua?' Kristian smiled.

'Josh? Oh no, he's a real softie, hardly a devil. No, our rescue dog is called Satan. Mind you he's a softie too,' Kristian replied. That took Aggie by surprise.

'Oh!' she said but quickly recovered. 'Have you ever considered acting? I'm always on the lookout for new actors for my amateur dramatics group and . . .'

'No Aggie,' Kristian said interrupting her. 'Sorry, that's not for me.'

'Oh that's a shame!' she said. At this point Gary opened his front door carrying his fishing rod which he placed against the wall. He was taking it back to the shed the long way round as Brenda had banned it from passing through their kitchen.

'Hello Gary,' Aggie shouted across. Gary suddenly looked frightened.

'Hello Aggie, Kristian,' Gary replied. Kristian nodded his head.

'I'm trying to find some talent,' Aggie piped up.

'Really? Out here?' Gary said, and looking at Kristian he continued, 'I think you might be barking up the wrong tree there, Aggie.' Kristian laughed at Gary's suggestion. 'Have you tried one of those dating Apps?'

'I'm referring to acting talent, as well you know Gary!' Aggie said. At that point Joshua appeared from around the side of his house, riding a bike.

'I'm off Kris, got to get to today's last lecture,' he shouted to Kristian.

'Okay, see you later,' Kristian replied. Gary smiled to himself and couldn't resist a little joke.

'Kristian,' he shouted, 'you should be careful if he's a bicycle!'

'What's that?' asked Kristian. Brenda appeared in the doorway and pulled Gary inside with force. She appeared back in the doorway on her own.

'He means be careful on the roads,' she shouted, 'there's a lot of traffic about this time of day.' She went back inside and slammed the door. I think it was safe to assume that Gary was in trouble again.

The Roadeteers had finished their latest job and as it was nearly 3 o'clock, they decided to call it a day. Steve had disappeared for about fifteen minutes but was now walking back to Doug and Frank with his phone in hand and looking pleased with himself.

'Thanks for earlier,' he said. 'I've got it sorted. I'm taking Sarah to a really posh place. She'll love it.'

'Where's that then?' asked Doug.

'It's called, um it's called,' Steve was trying to recall the name, 'the Peter and Liz or something.'

'Never heard of it, have you heard of it Frank?' Doug asked.

'No,' said Frank, 'where's that?'

'It must be good, like,' Steve continued, 'because it's really booked up. I couldn't book a table until September. Anyway we are going in four weeks.'

'We've never heard of this Peter and Liz. Are you sure you're not taking her to a strip joint or something?' Frank asked, which made Doug laugh.

'No,' Steve replied, 'it's a posh place. I can't say it proper, 'ere have a look.' Steve pulled up the web page on his phone and showed it to Doug.

'Oh bleeding hell,' said a shocked Doug, 'That's Le Petale de Lys.'

'That's it. It looks great and it's got a dunlop star or two,' Steve boasted.

'You mean Michelin stars you muppet and that means it's very expensive!' warned Doug.

'Oh really?' asked Steve. 'But it'll be worth it if I keep Sarah though.'

'Check out the prices mate. I took the missus there for our Silver Wedding Anniversary and it cost about £500 then,' Frank warned.

'I can't back out now,' Steve explained, 'I've paid a deposit and I rang Sarah just now and told her that's where we are going. She's really excited.'

'You'd better ring her back,' Doug started, 'to say you're going dutch.'

'No mate, it's not there,' Steve said, 'it's just down the road and the bloke who owns it is French not Dutch.' Frank and Doug looked at each other and shook their heads.

'Okay, TAS mate,' Frank said, 'remember there's no overtime, mind.'

'Right you are!' Steve replied.

At 3:30 Sarah was found sitting at a table in DDs. After receiving the telephone call from Steve she couldn't concentrate on her work at Brookes University so had left early. She had got permission to take some flexi leave that was owing to her. Being so excited she had to share her news with someone or she'd burst. Trudie was still at work so Dolly would do.

'So when did he tell you this?' Dolly asked.

'He rang me about an hour ago and said he'd booked the table for next month. That's the soonest date he could get. I'm so excited. I've always wanted to go there!' Sarah said, fidgeting in her seat.

'Le Petale de Lys!' Dolly said. 'Wow lass, he's pulling out all the stops there. It'll cost him an arm and a leg! Still you deserve the treat.'

'Thanks Dolly, that's a nice thing to say,' Sarah replied, 'I can't get over the transformation. From chips in his digs watching football to Le Petale de Lys. I did tell him I was getting bored with our relationship so I'm pleased he was listening.' Sarah's speech speeded up in excitement. 'I looked it up online,' she said and continued without taking a breath, 'and you can have six courses. I don't think you get large portions but you get speciality cooking with great flavours. You are looked after from the moment you enter the restaurant. I'm so excited!'

'I can tell,' Dolly replied. 'Do you think after that you'll be able to lower your standards to visit here again? My cakes will look very plain.'

'Of course, you represent normality Dolly,' Sarah replied with a smile, 'and I'm guessing he will be very poor for a while. Also Le Petale de Lys doesn't have a resident Agony Aunt like here.'

'That's true. I do my best,' Dolly laughed.

It was almost 5 o'clock and time for Brenda to drive Gary to his social evening at the Bowling Club. As long as the road is clear it only takes around five minutes to drive there, fifteen minutes to walk. Gary would need a lift home as he planned to enjoy a drink or two which would leave him unable to drive, or walk in a straight line. As Brenda drove, a cyclist cut out in front of her car and she braked hard to avoid him. Gary immediately leant forward to press the horn on the steering wheel but Brenda pushed him away.

'No Gary,' she shouted, 'what do you think you are doing?'

'But he cut in front of you, the idiot!' Gary replied, still angry.

'Yes he did and yes he is but,' she started, 'I'm the one who's driving, not you. So don't honk my horn! You can only honk the horn when you are driving.'

'You didn't say that last night,' Gary joked. Brenda smiled.

'Stupid!' she said.

'I hope you don't let anyone else honk your horn,' Gary said, trying not to laugh.

'Of course not,' she replied, 'I may allow people to twiddle with my indicators but never let them go as far as honking my horn.' Gary and Brenda were both laughing as the car pulled into the Bowling Club car park. Gary leant over and gave Brenda a kiss leaning on her breast accidentally as he did.

'Have I told you lately you have a lovely pair of headlamps?' he said. Brenda laughed as he got out.

'You are stupid but I love you. Bye!' she giggled. 'Give me a call when you need picking up.'

'I will, bye love,' he said.

Gary walked into the Clubhouse. Anthony, Brian, Cyril, Paddy, Phil and Tim were already sitting at a table. Gary joined them making sure he picked up a pint of beer from the bar first.

'It's nice to have a social evening and open up our bar,' Cyril said, 'and it's good most of us could be here.'

'Having the bar open might have encouraged a few of us,' Anthony said.

'Yes, cheap booze does it for me,' Tim agreed.

'Surely it is the thought of talking tactics for our next game and not the alcohol that encouraged you here?' joked Gary.

'Emm let me think,' said Brian, 'no, it's the drink for me too.' The others smiled.

'It's nice to meet up socially,' said Phil, 'although I can't have much to drink as I'm at work tomorrow.'

'That's brave Phil,' Gary remarked.

'I made sure I will be a working from home,' Phil said. 'I'm not that stupid.'

'Do you have to stipulate which room you are working from?' Brian enquired.

'No, why?' replied Phil.

'So you could be working from bed then?' Brian said, with a cheeky smile. 'Working on how to sleep off a hangover.'

'I wouldn't risk it,' Phil admitted. 'They can tell everything now. When you are on your laptop, how long you've been off the laptop, so they can probably tell which room you are in.'

'Are you okay, Paddy?' Gary asked. 'You're quiet as a mouse this evening.' Gary smiled at the others knowing that Paddy would react.

'Mice aren't that quiet so that's another stupid simile,' Paddy moaned. 'They made a lot of noise when the buggers were in my loft.'

'What's one of those when it's at home?' Phil said.

'It's a small furry creature, likes cheese and gets the better of Tom the cat,' Gary explained.

'I know what a mouse is,' said Tim, 'but what's the simile thing?'

'And it's not at home!' said an irritated Paddy.

'Calm down Paddy,' Cyril pleaded. 'You're off on one early this evening. Gary stop winding him up by mentioning quiet mice. And Tim, a simile is a figure of speech, it's a comparison using like or as, for example, as cool as a cucumber, as cunning as a fox.'

'As irritating as a Paddy!' Phil said, interrupting Cyril.

'Very funny,' Paddy moaned while the others laughed.

'Haven't you been away on holiday, Gary?' Cyril asked changing the subject.

'Yep, only came back late yesterday,' Gary confirmed, 'we went to Paris.'

'Was it good?' Phil asked.

'Very good, thank you,' Gary replied.

'Paris?' Paddy said, 'full of foreigners I expect.'

'Yes, that's true Paddy,' Gary said. 'It's a lot like Oxford in the summer. All those foreigners looking for Inspector Morse.'

'They bring money into Oxford though, so we should be glad they are here,' Cyril said, spoken as you'd expect by a retired bank manager.

'And fellas, I've got some news. That wedding I was telling you about, you know the wedding of my great niece later this year? The one I was worried about?' Gary asked, 'It's off. Seems the bridegroom turned out to be a bicycle who's in a relationship with another bicycle.'

'Oh no!' Anthony said. 'Still at least you can cancel the new suit. Every cloud, silver linings and all that.'

'That's true,' Gary agreed. 'Right then, Cyril do you want to discuss tactics for our next match?'

'Good idea,' Cyril responded. 'So as I see it what we need to do is win. That's it really. And after that hard training programme I suggest we get another drink.'

'Well, you can't argue with the Captain, can you?' said Phil.

'No,' agreed Anthony, 'great idea, Captain.'

Brenda was enjoying the peace of having the house to herself. She had been busy all afternoon with household chores and washing the holiday clothes so, by 9 o'clock, she was quite tired. She hadn't found anything she wanted to watch on the popular television channels, so searched through the others. She found an episode of Vera on ITV3. Brenda loved this programme so settled down to watch it. She didn't mind that it was a repeat because even though she'd seen all episodes, she could never remember who committed the murder until ten minutes before the end of the story. This particular episode was a little scary with scenes of creepy woods lit by the full moon with some areas covered in mist. What made it more terrifying was the very clever accompanying music so Brenda muted the sound. That was much better, after all you don't need spooky music to watch someone get bashed across the back of the head, do you? When the story had moved on and it was now a daylight scene with DCI Stanhope standing over the body, Brenda felt brave enough to unmute the sound. She picked up the remote control but before she had a chance to take any action there was a tremendous crashing noise coming from her back garden. She froze with fear. It was by now quite dark outside as the August evenings had started to close in earlier. Thoughts started racing through her mind. Had she locked the back door? At which point should she dial 999? Then there were further noises of people running around the side of her house and shouting. She was still too afraid to move when the doorbell rang. Wow, she thought, the police got here really quickly. Then she remembered she hadn't called the police. Should she answer the door? Would people push their way inside the house if she did? Why did Gary have to go out tonight? Oh no! Suddenly there was a knock on the kitchen window and she heard Kristian shouting,

'Brenda? Gary? Are you in there?' The sense of relief felt at hearing a voice she recognised was only matched by the strength of stupidity she felt for over reacting to the situation. She walked to the back door and opened it. Apparently First Class had been sitting on the fence which divides Gary and Brenda's home from Kristian and Joshua's. Satan, the big burly German Shepherd dog, had spotted this and decided to chase him, jumping the fence and running up Brenda's garden. First Class jumped into his own garden at the top and, thankfully Satan decided to stop his pursuit at that point. Kristian and Joshua had been in hot pursuit of their dog but didn't fancy jumping the fence themselves so ran around the side of the house.

'Brenda, I'm so sorry about this,' Kristian said, standing at the backdoor holding one guilty looking Satan by his collar. 'I can't see properly as it's dark, but I think he may have trampled some of your lovely begonias.' Brenda was so relieved she wasn't under attack that the loss of a few plants seemed trivial.

'I'll take a look in the morning,' she said, 'but don't worry about it.' She looked at Satan. 'Is he friendly? Can I stroke him?'

'He's very friendly, although that poor cat might not agree,' Kristian replied. 'Yes, he loves being made a fuss of.' Brenda stroked Satan's fluffy head and it was love at first touch.

'Oh, he's gorgeous,' she said, 'and he's so soft!' The love appeared to be mutual as Satan lapped up the attention and wagged his tail furiously. Kristian took Satan home and Brenda walked back inside. She turned the television off blaming the creepy scenes she'd watched for her gross over reaction to the noise outside. She sat back on her sofa and fell to sleep only awoken at 10:30 by Gary ringing to say he was ready to be picked up. Well he actually said he was 'picked up for ready' which allowed Brenda to assume he was very drunk.

The car journey to the Bowling Club was peaceful with very light traffic at that time of night. The only other thing Brenda saw was a hedgehog crossing the road. The journey back was less peaceful as Gary talked incessant nonsense in his drunken state. When they got home Brenda entered the lounge and threw the car keys into a bowl on the side. About five seconds later Gary staggered in behind her.

'Well, do you think you can make it to the sofa, Gary?' she said teasingly.

'Sure er honey suck, honeysuckle, um sucklehoney er, love,' Gary replied unconvincingly.

'How much have you had to drink?' she asked.

'Not too, err, what did you say? What sweetie?' Brenda couldn't be angry with him being drunk, after all it hadn't come as a surprise. He was so vulnerable when in that helpless mess.

'I think it's time you got to bed,' she said. 'You never call me sweetie.'

'Bombon then?' he replied, as an alternative.

'I thought you were going to be talking tactics for winning your next game?' she said. Gary laughed and he tried to explain,

'We did, we did er, did discuss ticky tackytics. The main ticky tac was how to get three pints from the bar bit to our table without a tray!'

'C'mon Mr Tickytacky, let me help you upstairs to bed,' Brenda said, as she didn't think she'd get any sense out of him. Then she realised she could use this to her own advantage. She could get his agreement to almost anything now and he wouldn't remember a thing in the morning. It would be her word against his that he'd agreed.

'Gary,' she started, 'I want a dog.'

'A what?' he replied, 'Did you say a doggy-woof woof thingy?'

'Yes!' she said. 'A dog I can take for walks and that will protect me when I'm here on my own, like this evening.'

'Well,' he said, trying to remember what they were talking about, 'well I suppose that's a change from wanting a baby called

Natalie.' That remark cut into Brenda's heart. They had planned to call their daughter Natalie but lost her at twelve weeks of the pregnancy. She knew this was the drink talking though, so pulled the knife his words had placed in her heart straight out, with no ill effects.

'We could train it to bring you beer from the fridge,' she continued knowing that would appeal to Gary at that moment.

'Oh yes!' he squealed. 'What a bwill, bwilliant, em great idea! Yes let's get a woofy!' Gary then got up from the sofa and staggered into the hall and opened the cupboard door.

'Where are you going?' Brenda asked.

'For a wee,' Gary replied.

'No, that's the cupboard!' Brenda shouted. 'The toilet used to be there in our old house but it's not now.'

'That's cunning, that is,' Gary remarked, 'moving it, moving it, moving it when I'm not looking!'

'What moving it three times!' Brenda laughed. 'I'll take you upstairs and you can use the bathroom.'

'Okay sexy lady,' he said. 'Did you have a, er, thingy good evening sweetie poops?'

'Yes, thank you,' Brenda replied, 'apart from hooligans trampling the garden and scaring me by shouting and bashing on the door.'

'Ah, very good,' Gary replied. He started to sing as he staggered to the top of the stairs, 'You are my sunshine, my only sunshine... I can't remember the words.... you are.'

It took a little while to help Gary to the bathroom and then on to bed but once in bed he appeared to fall to sleep easily or that's what Brenda thought. However, after just a couple of minutes of lying in the darkness in silence, Gary started to giggle.

'Brenda? Brenda?' he giggled, 'Brenda?'

'What?' she asked.

'Brenda,' he continued, still giggling.

‘Gary you are drunk, go to sleep!’ she replied, but he didn’t. Instead he continued,

‘Brenda, Brenda, listen! About your sexxxxxy headlamps. Why are they no longer on full beam but always dipped?’

‘What?’ Brenda said, rather shocked even after allowing for his drunken state.

‘That’s okay though my honey sucklething . . . it just means they are no longer as dazzling as they used to be.’ Oh that poor pillow suffered again as Brenda hit him hard with it.

‘Ouch, what’s that for sweetie?’ Gary moaned.

‘Shut up Gary or you may end up sleeping in the shed playing with your rod!’ she shouted.

‘Ohh! Did I say something not quite righty!’ Gary replied innocently, as he fell asleep.

Chapter Nine

September
Oh, bowls to prompting!

September found Gary and Brenda still dogless. Although Brenda had got a drunken approval from Gary to get a dog, she never pursued it. She had been looking out of an upstairs window the morning after that drunken evening and noticed Kristian walking around his garden picking up dog poo. That vision of dog ownership put her off the idea! Luckily, Satan was happy to allow her access to his head, should she feel the need for contact with a canine. So far he had not jumped the fence again but First Class was keeping a respectful distance.

There was massive excitement on 3rd September when Izzy gave birth to a baby girl. Camille was born three weeks early but weighing a healthy 6lb 2oz. Mother and baby were fine although Camille had to remain in hospital for a couple of extra days as she was jaundiced, that was the only hiccup with the premature birth. Brenda was so excited and spent a lot of time with Izzy and Camille, which was a blessing for Izzy as she was struggling to adapt to the demands of motherhood. By the middle of September all was calm. It was early evening when Gary returned home after an afternoon of bowling.

'Brenda love,' he started to say, 'the greatest bowling club in the south needs your assistance.'

'What?' Brenda replied, 'The South Marston Team needs my help?'

'No, us!' Gary protested, 'I'm insulted you didn't immediately think I was referring to the team I play for.' Brenda smiled as she enjoyed winding him up.

'Well you did say greatest team in the south and you are always running your team's efforts down so why would I assume that?' she replied. Gary thought for a second and then felt she had a point. 'So how can I help?' she continued. 'Before you ask I'm not making sandwiches for the matches. I had enough of that last time when my cheese and pickle sandwiches got slated by the opposition. Those idiots called them bogies with diarrhoea sandwiches.'

'We were winning at the time so they had to pick on someone, sadly it was you,' Gary said sympathetically.

'They called me Bogie Brenda! I laughed it off, ha, ha, what a joke but, to add insult to injury, you let them win!'

'What I'm going to ask has nothing to do with sandwiches,' Gary reassured her. 'It's to do with boosting the number of female members of the team. We have never had more than five female members since 2016 and now they've all left.' Brenda looked horrified.

'Oh no, Gary,' she insisted, 'I'm not being recruited to a bowling team, well not the same one as you anyway. I think it's healthy for our marriage if we have different hobbies. That way I get some peace in the house.'

'That's charming, thanks a lot!' Gary moaned. 'I'm not looking to recruit you. Me and the boys . . .' He started but before he could go any further Brenda laughed.

'Boys?' she said. 'You may have a mental age of boys but I don't think . . .' And this time Gary interrupted her.

'Okay, if you are going to be picky,' he continued, 'the old blokes and I were wondering if we could attract any of your WI lot to join us.'

'What, you aren't serious, are you?' replied a stunned Brenda.

'Why not?' Gary asked. 'We've got our club's open evening tomorrow and you've got a meeting tomorrow so you could persuade them to come along afterwards. You said your meeting starts at 6 o'clock and will probably be over in an hour so why couldn't they come along to us afterwards?'

'We are popular all of a sudden,' Brenda said. 'You know that Aggie is coming along tomorrow to talk to the members about Amateur Dramatics, don't you?'

'Poor members, how frightening for them,' Gary replied. 'So they could come along to us afterwards, at least we are friendly. What do you think?'

'Oh Gary, I'd love to help but,' she replied, 'it's very short notice. Still I suppose it is possible as after Aggie's talk we were going to have a meeting on updating procedures and I know that has been postponed. So I'm expecting to be finished by 7.'

'That sounds promising,' Gary said.

'I can ask everyone for you and it's up to them what they want to do. Your bowls lot do surprise me though as I'd have thought you would like a men only club,' Brenda said.

'Yes we do like it but it looks bad if we haven't got anyone to make sandwiches and wipe the bar down.' Gary joked. Brenda looked concerned but before she could say anything Gary continued, 'It's a joke! After forty years of marriage you are still so easy to wind up. So you'll invite them all?'

'I will,' Brenda replied. 'Aren't there any others going?'

'I doubt there will be many so you will try to make it sound exciting, won't you? You know, really sell it to them?' Gary said, almost pleading. Brenda smiled.

'Bowls exciting?' she said.

'I don't see why that's amusing. It's no less exciting than WI after all you know what they say a WI woman is, don't you?' Gary replied, but he immediately knew he'd made a mistake.

'No Gary, I don't know, what is a WI woman?' Brenda asked calmly.

'Nothing, it's just a silly man thing, just a silly man joke,' Gary replied, trying to take her away from the subject, but Brenda was intrigued and wouldn't let this go.

'Pretend you are on Mastermind and you've started so you'll finish! What does WI stand for?' she insisted.

'Woefully irritating,' Gary replied, cringing as he said it. He was expecting some fallout.

'Very funny,' Brenda replied. 'So why do you want woefully irritating women in your bowls team?'

'Beggars can't be choosers!' was the reply. 'No seriously I'm joking. Your ladies will have a lovely evening and if they decide it's not for them then nothing has been lost. There's a free drink in it for them.'

'That'll do it!' Brenda conceded, 'especially with the younger, skint members!'

'Thanks love,' Gary said. He was now smiling and announced,

'You know I think my WI woman is wickedly intelligent. Wicked as in 'wicked', down with the kids speak.' Brenda smiled sympathetically, he was trying hard.

'Gary,' she started, 'don't start that again as you definitely aren't down with the kids except in mental age of course.' At this point the doorbell rang and the wicked one called Brenda sent Gary to answer it. He returned with Aggie. In her usual forthright manner she didn't allow Brenda time to say hello before speaking.

'Sorry it's a little late, Brenda,' she started. 'I hope you weren't getting ready for bed.'

'Hello Aggie. It's only 8 o'clock so a bit early for bed time. Is everything okay?' Brenda asked.

'Oh yes, fine thank you. I just wanted to pick your brain,' Aggie announced. Gary smiled and felt obliged to make a joke.

'Won't take long then!' he said. Brenda said nothing but stared disapprovingly at Gary who decided retreating from the room would be the best strategy. 'I'll leave you ladies to it as I've got things to do,' he said.

'Like what?' Brenda asked deliberately to make him squirm but he was already leaving the room.

'Err, I've err, I've got to check the bath for spiders!' he shouted as he climbed the stairs.

'Oh dear, I really frighten him, don't I?' Aggie remarked, 'I'm not looking to recruit you two, I know that bird has flown. I scared you both off when you got attacked by flying teeth. Unless you've changed your mind?'

'No Aggie, thank you but no!' Brenda replied, forcefully. 'Now what do you need my opinion on?'

'It's about my talk to the WI tomorrow,' Aggie went on, 'I'm going to tell a few stories relating to my experiences with AmDram.'

'Not the one about flying teeth ending up in my cleavage, I hope?' Brenda asked.

'Well no, as that would be insensitive to you,' Aggie replied. 'Do you think a few stories will be enough?'

'Absolutely Aggie,' Brenda said, 'short but interesting is what's needed. WI hasn't attracted so much attention for years. Wantage Lawn Bowling Club is also looking for new members.'

'I hope I get some interest,' Aggie continued. 'Thank you Brenda, I'll see myself out. See you tomorrow.' With that the hurricane that is Aggie left the lounge. As she passed the stairs she shouted,

'You are safe now Gary, you can come down, spiders permitting!' Brenda was still smiling to herself when Gary reappeared.

'She didn't get you then?' he said, as he walked back into the lounge.

'No she didn't,' replied Brenda, 'but that's no thanks to you, running off like that!'

'Sorry,' Gary replied, looking guilty. 'By the way there is a spider in the shower, a great big black hairy one. Can you get it out, please?' Brenda stared at Gary open-mouthed as he continued, 'You know I hate the things and I can't shower until you've got rid of it.' Brenda stopped concentrating on spiders and the like as she was distracted by the clock. She looked at it noting the time.

'What are you worrying about the time for?' Gary asked.

'Well I have to keep checking as I can't believe how quickly time goes when I'm with you,' she joked and Gary fell for it.

'Really?' he said.

'No of course not,' Brenda replied. 'I keep wondering how Sarah and Steve are enjoying Le Petale de Lys.'

'I forgot about that,' Gary said, 'well let's hope his visa card isn't being rejected right now.'

'It's a lovely gesture though, isn't it?' Brenda remarked.

'What, running out of money?' Gary asked. 'The cost of living can easily arrange for us to run out of money!' Brenda didn't find that amusing.

'You know what I mean. The meal in a posh place is romantic. Why aren't you still romantic like that? You used to be. You've given up trying!' she moaned.

'I am still romantic!' Gary insisted. 'And when I am you ignore it.'

'What do you mean by that?' Brenda asked.

'Who do you think sent you that Valentine's card?' he said in a slightly aggrieved tone. Brenda was shocked, it was from him!

'What the one with . . .' she started but the sentence was finished by Gary,

'the funny pig who wanted his oink squeezed? Yes, that was from me,' Gary confirmed. Brenda smiled.

'Shame!' she said, 'I thought that was from Harrison Ford.'

'You didn't even mention it, did you?' said a hurt Gary.

'I didn't know it was from you and I didn't want you thinking I had a secret admirer in case you got upset,' Brenda tried to explain. 'We've been married so long what were you doing sending an anonymous Valentine's card?'

'Just trying to keep romance alive to mark the first Valentine's Day in our new home,' Gary insisted. 'Totally ignored!'

'Well you should have put your name in it,' Brenda said.

'But they are supposed to be a mystery,' Gary replied.

'Thank you love,' she started, 'to tell you the truth I'm relieved it was you as I was afraid it was from one of your creepy bowls mates. Okay Mr Piggy Valentine,' she continued, 'where's this huge spider then and, more to the point, where's your oink?'

The next morning at almost 11 o'clock Sarah walked into DDs. There were a few customers drinking and eating at tables while Dolly was tidying behind the counter.

'Hello Sarah, no work today?' Dolly asked.

'No Dolly, I booked today off as I thought I might like to lie-in after my evening out,' she replied. 'Trude is meeting me here at 11.'

'Ah yes, the big evening out. How did it go?'

'It's a wonderful place. The food is so different, full of lovely flavours. It was great,' Sarah said but despite her positive words, Dolly could sense she was a little subdued.

'So why can I sense that you are a little down today?' Dolly asked. 'Is it just the anti-climax?' Sarah looked confused by the question.

'No, it was nothing to do with the sex,' she replied. Dolly was surprised by that snippet of information which took her off guard, leaving her rather embarrassed.

'I was referring to the occasion actually and the grand venue,' Dolly explained.

'Oh sorry, of course you were,' Sarah replied. Both women smiled awkwardly. Trudie walked through the door just in time to break the tension.

'Morning ladies!' she said. 'Well Sarah, I want all the details! How did it go?' Dolly winked at Trudie and announced,

'The sex was good apparently, but she hasn't said much about the meal.'

'Were you talking about starters?' Trudie asked.

'No, more like afters!' Dolly laughed.

'Stop it you two!' Sarah pleaded. It took a lot to embarrass Sarah but this had done it.

'I'm only pulling your leg, lass,' Dolly explained, 'go and sit down and I'll bring your coffees over.' They walked over to a table near the window and sat down.

'So what's wrong then?' Trudie asked.

'Nothing really,' Sarah said. 'The place was lovely. Even the toilet or powder room thingy was out of this world with different soaps, moisturisers and everything. It was so posh. The food was so tasty, little portions of full flavour. We chose our wine after a wine tasting too.'

'Why are you a little down then?' Trudie asked. 'Everything sounds perfect from what you've said.'

'It was a lovely restaurant,' Sarah said, 'it wasn't the place I had the problem with, it was Steve. He meant well but he did some embarrassing things.'

'Like what?' Trudie enquired.

'He didn't understand the wine tasting and just gulped it down. He picked up some food with his fingers instead of using the cutlery and kept addressing staff as 'love' and 'mate'. And the number of times he said, right you are, began to really irritate me!' Sarah blurted this out so fast she was left out of breath. Dolly carried the coffees over and Trudie pulled a face at her and mouthed 'thanks'. She put the cups down and retreated to the counter.

'Oh dear,' Trudie said to Sarah, 'but he won't have meant anything by it. That's just TAS being TAS, I mean Steve being Steve. It isn't very often any of us get to go to a place like that, is it?' Sarah thought quietly for a few seconds and then smiled at Trudie.

'You are right, Trude,' she said. 'I should be more grateful, shouldn't I? He looked smart in a suit and everything. It cost him a lot of money too. I'm just worried that we don't have a lot in common for us to work.'

'Oh dear,' Trudie said and with a smile she winked at Sarah before saying, 'Right you are!'

'Stop it!' Sarah said, laughing at the joke. Then her expression returned to deadly serious.

'I'll tell you something though, I swear that two of the waiters fancied me,' she announced.

'Oh, here we go!' Trudie moaned but before she could say anymore Brenda walked in.

'Hello ladies,' she shouted across the café. 'Did you have a good time yesterday, Sarah?' Sarah was now in a more positive frame of mind and replied accordingly,

'Yes, thank you. It was lovely.' Brenda was happy for her and continued to the counter.

'Hello Dolly,' she started, 'please can I have a coffee to go? I feel like something to drink on my walk home. I've just been to the jeweller to collect a present for Camille.' Brenda pulled a child's gold bracelet out of a box.

'That's cute, isn't it? So dainty,' Dolly said.

'Thank you Dolly, I like it,' Brenda said. 'I have had her name engraved on it.' She pointed to the neat engraving. 'It's on the band, see, Camille. Of course, she won't be able to wear it straight away but her mum can keep it for her until she's about four or five and not putting everything in her mouth.'

'Well that's a little way off,' Dolly remarked, 'but time goes so quickly it'll be here in a flash.'

'Yes, I know but I wanted to get her something special now to mark her birth. She's got a lot of teddy bears already. She'll be able to keep this forever.'

'It's lovely. I'm sure mum and baby will appreciate it,' Dolly said, handing Brenda her take-out cup of coffee. 'I'll see you later at WI.'

'Yes, see you later,' Brenda said and she shouted across to Sarah, 'see you at WI this evening Sarah!' Sarah was still in deep conversation with Trudie but waved her hand to acknowledge Brenda's words.

Brenda had a nice relaxing walk towards home via Izzy's house. She knocked on the door and Izzy answered looking tired and a little bedraggled. She welcomed Brenda inside.

'I hope I haven't called at a bad time, Izzy,' Brenda said.

'No, you're fine, Glenda,' she said. 'Camille is sleeping now but she has been crying a lot. I won't bring her down, if you don't mind, as I don't want to wake her.'

'That sounds very sensible to me,' Brenda said. 'Well I won't take up a lot of your valuable time. I know you don't get many breaks so you need to take advantage of when Camille is asleep.' She handed Izzy the box containing the bracelet. 'It's a little present for Camille,' Brenda started to explain. 'You'll need to keep it for her for when she's older but I wanted her to have something special.' Izzy opened the box.

'It's beautiful, Glenda,' said an excited Izzy. 'Thank you so much. I'll keep it safe for her. It's got her name on it, how nice. If I get our phone number put on the back, it could be an identity bracelet for if she gets lost.' Brenda was a little puzzled by that remark. Izzy doesn't *do* jokes but surely she was joking, right?

'Perhaps you could get her microchipped at the vets,' Brenda joked.

'Will they do that?' Izzy asked. Brenda smiled and felt that it was perhaps time to go. She was pleased that Izzy liked the present. She started to walk towards the door when the loud shrill of a baby crying rang through the house. Camille had woken up. Izzy's face told a story, she looked exhausted and ready to scream when Camille started to cry.

'Oh, Glenda,' she said, 'she doesn't stop. She's not due a feed but she cries so much and I'm exhausted.' Izzy looked as if she was about to cry.

'Let me take her for a couple of hours,' Brenda offered. 'You go to bed and get some sleep.' Izzy's face lit up as much as an exhausted face could light up.

'Ah, would you?' Izzy sighed. 'Two hours of sleep would be so good.'

When Brenda got home, she arrived with a baby much to Gary's horror. Just as Izzy didn't *do* jokes Gary didn't *do* babies! As he put it, he can't tell one end from the other until they are walking! Brenda however was in her element, cooing over and kissing the little bundle of joy. Gary disappeared into his shed for a couple of hours but had to return to the house when he found it too cold to sit in his picnic chair any longer. It was a cold September day, the temperature was below average for the time of year. Izzy turned the two hours into three and appeared at Brenda's front door at almost 3 o'clock to reclaim her daughter. Gary was more than happy to hear the ring of the doorbell and let her in. They walked into the lounge where Brenda was holding Camille.

'Hello!' said Izzy, 'I hope you've been a good girl.'

'You'll be lucky,' Gary replied with a smile, 'my wife is always a little devil.' The extra sleep must have recharged something inside Izzy because she appeared to understand the joke.

'Are you a devil, Glenda?' she laughed. 'Thank you for looking after her, you are very kind.'

'That's okay,' Gary joked, 'after all she is my wife!' Izzy just looked blank for that one. Perhaps she needed five hours of sleep to be able to understand two jokes in a row!

The women of the Wancott WI gathered for their meeting in the village hall at 6 o'clock. Present were Susan, Vera, Violet, Sarah, Marianne, Amy, Mandy, Lucy, Dolly and Brenda. There were a couple of others no one recognised, but they were welcome to sit in if they wanted to. They were older and probably just wanted the company of others and the warmth of the hall.

Aggie gave a thirty minute talk on her AmDram experiences and about the theatre group she had set up, the Wancott Theatre Players. It had been presented well with a lot of comedy included and the women had found the topic entertaining. She ended by thanking everyone for listening and the chairperson for inviting her.

'I'm happy to answer any questions you may have,' Aggie told her audience. 'I'm particularly keen to encourage you to join us.' Nobody said a word. 'Isn't anybody interested at all?' Vera looked up.

'Do you have to act to be part of your group?' she asked. 'Could I take part in a non-acting capacity?' Mandy decided to add her opinion on this.

'It's an acting group, Vera,' she said.

'It's a theatre company,' Aggie boomed, 'but that is a good question. There are other roles, for example we need people to help with scenery and costumes. We tend to see to our own makeup individually. Of course, we always need people to act as prompters.'

'Well Vera would be good at prodding people!' Marianne remarked.

'She said prompter, not prodder,' Vera said, finding it hard to keep a straight face. 'I think I would enjoy that, if I can keep up. I'm willing to give it a prod, I mean, a go.'

'Splendid! Are you free tomorrow evening? There is going to be a rehearsal and you could have a go then,' Aggie said.

'Okay, let's do it!' said Vera. There were no other questions for Aggie so Susan, in her capacity as chairperson, decided to round off the meeting.

'Well if there aren't any other questions for Aggie we'll let her go. Thank you for coming to talk to us, Aggie.' Aggie marched out of the hall as only Aggie can march. Susan then addressed the others. 'I think Brenda has already told you that the procedures meeting has been postponed and that in its place we've been invited to the Bowling Club's open evening.'

'I hope you can all make it,' Brenda said. Most were silent although there were some non-committal noises from others. 'Everyone will get a free drink,' Brenda added. There was a complete change in atmosphere and grunts of approval filled the room.

It was only a five minute walk from the hall to the Wancott Bowling club. The promise of a free drink had persuaded all the women to attend the open evening. The Bowling Club members present to welcome them were Cyril, Anthony, Paddy, Tim, Brian, Phil and Gary. Cyril looked delighted by the number of the WI members who had arrived; most of whom went to the bar first to collect their free drink, naturally.

'Welcome everyone,' he said, 'I'm Cyril, the Club Team Captain. Thank you ladies for joining us. I hope you've all got a drink.'

'Hello,' Susan replied, 'I'm the Chairperson of the WI and on behalf of those here, I would like to say thank you for inviting us.'

'My pleasure,' Cyril replied, before starting his official pitch. 'Bowling is a gentle and enjoyable sport. We find it's a great way to meet up with friends while getting involved in some competitive action.' Before he could go on, Amy couldn't hold her tongue.

'I'm not meaning to be rude,' she started, 'but is this club only for old people?' Brenda tried to hide her smile and stop herself from laughing but it was proving hard especially as Amy hadn't finished talking. 'I'm surprised any of you can lift the bowling ball let alone roll it, it's heavy you know?'

'How old are you, young lady?' asked Cyril, smiling cheerfully.

'I'm 19,' Amy replied.

'I appreciate that when you're 19 everyone over 40 is old,' Cyril continued, 'but we oldens are stronger than you think!' Marianne then decided to get involved with the questioning.

'Do you have to work out to develop your arm and chest muscles?' she enquired. On hearing this Brenda had to turn her back on Gary as any eye contact would have made her laugh uncontrollably. The most exercise Gary ever did was climb the stairs to bed at night.

'No, you just need a normal level of fitness,' Cyril replied, politely.

'That's me out then,' Vera piped up, 'I was out of breath walking to the bar for my drink. Perhaps I'm more suited to sitting at the side of the stage reminding people of their lines.'

'You don't have to be super fit to play bowls,' Phil said, 'it's a game of skill rather than fitness, although of course we are all as fit as a butcher's dog.' That did it for Brenda who roared with laughter but luckily the other women found it funny too. Gary gave Brenda a hard stare which told her it was time to stop laughing.

'Why is a butcher's dog any fitter than a fishmonger's dog?' asked Paddy who had had his cage rattled by another simile. There was a stunned silence in the room. What on earth was he talking about? Phil looked embarrassed on everyone's behalf and explained that Paddy challenges all sayings. Violet had been thinking about Paddy's question though.

'Perhaps a pescatarian diet doesn't suit dogs?' she said. Everyone was stunned into silence again. They looked confused but were willing to let it go, except for Vera that is.

'What's a pescaterything?' she asked.

'A veggie who eats fish,' Violet replied.

'I love a good piece of cod,' Vera continued. 'If you steam it and make a lovely sauce to go with it, lovely!' That made everyone feel hungry.

'Okay ladies,' Susan said. 'Sorry Cyril, let's stick to bowling.'

'Are the bowls sticky then?' Vera joked. There were some sniggers of appreciation.

'Thanks Susan, that's no problem,' Cyril continued. 'I'm pleased everyone is relaxed.'

'I think that's probably the drink talking,' Mandy said.

'I'll let you finish your drinks and then we'll go outside and have a go,' Cyril said, enthusiastically. The silence was broken by the general murmur of everyone talking.

'I'm not sure any of these will be joining us,' Gary said to Anthony.

'Maybe not but that one's cute,' Anthony replied, looking across at Mandy.

'I don't know,' Gary said disapprovingly, 'what did poor Tess ever do to deserve being stuck with you?'

'Keep your hair on, I'm only window shopping. There's nothing wrong with appreciating the view,' Anthony replied. Mandy had noticed Anthony staring at her and was feeling uncomfortable.

'I don't like the way that one over there keeps looking at me,' she said, 'he's creepy.' Brenda looked across and saw it was Anthony.

'He is creepy!' she said. 'I'd be happier if he didn't meet up so much with my Gary as he's got some odd ideas.'

'Really?' Mandy remarked. 'Well if he comes over here I'll make sure he gets the right idea, okay!' Brenda smiled, it sounded like Anthony had met his match there.

Just across the room Amy was talking to Marianne.

'They're all ancient,' she said. 'I still can't believe they can lift and roll that heavy ball.'

'I wonder what star signs they are?' Marianne said. 'I don't think this is going to be for me though. My horoscope for today said that a challenge will come my way and I should take the bull by the horns and I will succeed. I can't see anyone here I'd describe as a bull, can you? More like old donkeys.'

'No, the evening is bull-ocks though,' Amy declared, which resulted in both women smiling.

Some of the other WI members were standing together. Dolly turned to Brenda.

'Who supplies the food for matches and socials?' she asked. 'You know tea and scones or whatever? It always hurts me to mention scones in Gary's presence after his efforts.'

'I can understand that,' Brenda sympathised. 'Oh he did his best but his cooking skills are non-existent. He's too old to learn things now, well broken records don't play new tunes!'

'But he's good at big bangs!' Dolly replied. 'I could provide a takeout basket of goodies for matches, if needed,' Dolly said, returning to her original question.

'I think they rely on freebies from wives and so on,' Brenda explained. 'I've told Gary I'm not doing that anymore.'

Susan, Jane and Lucy were standing by the bar.

'Well ladies,' Susan said, 'do you think you'll be playing bowls in future?'

'I don't think so,' said Lucy, 'but I'm always interested to learn about new things.'

'You know I think I might enjoy bowling so I haven't made my mind up yet,' Jane commented, 'it could be quite relaxing.'

'I'm pleased you don't think coming here is a waste of time. I think it is important to experience new things,' Susan said.

'I agree,' replied Jane, 'so what's next? Sky diving perhaps?'

'No, definitely not,' said a frightened Susan. 'I'll try anything that doesn't result in me wetting myself.' The women smiled at that thought but not for too long as Cyril tapped his glass to get everybody's attention.

'Right then ladies, shall we go outside and try bowling?' he asked enthusiastically. He led them outside and on to the edge of the green. Amy was already confused.

'Where's the bowling alley then?' she queried. 'Where are the pins we've got to knock down?'

'Oh no Amy,' said Brenda, 'it's not that type of bowling.'

'Because these oldies can't lift the bowling ball? I thought so!' Amy replied.

'No, young lady,' said Cyril, 'you have to bowl as close as you can to the jack.'

'Jack who?' asked a puzzled Amy. Cyril smiled and held up the white ball known as the jack.

'This white ball is the jack.'

'It's an oversized ping-pong ball!' Amy said. Cyril turned to the rest of his audience.

'I'm not going to bore you with all the rules at this stage,' he started. 'We'll roll this down to the bottom half of the green and both teams will aim to get as many of their bowls, also known as woods, as close to the jack as possible.' Cyril released the jack which stopped about two thirds of the way down the green. He then handed one of the bowls to Jane. 'Now have a go at bowling that down the green to get it as close to the jack as possible,' Cyril told her. She bowled and her effort stopped two feet from the jack.

'There you go!' said Anthony. 'That's very good for a first attempt.'

'Said the creepy man!' Mandy whispered to Brenda, who smiled. Cyril then passed a bowl to Lucy.

'Your go!' he announced. 'Look at where you want it to go and try to judge the power you'll need to use against the weight.' She released her effort which ran on beyond the jack by about a foot.

'That's pretty good too,' Cyril said, trying to offer encouragement. After this each woman had a go, the last one being Amy. She released her attempt and excitedly ran along the green behind it; her stiletto heels were sinking into the green. The men started to panic and shouted at her to stop.

'Stop, young lady!' Cyril shouted. 'Get off the green. Your shoes are ruining the green!' Cyril then collapsed in shock. Gary and Phil rushed over and helped him to a bench. Amy didn't stop as she was oblivious to the panic she was causing.

'Have I won?' she shouted. 'Have I won?' Her excitement faded quickly when she looked down at her feet. 'Oh no!' she screamed. 'Look at my shoes, they are filthy. I hope they aren't ruined.' Then, looking over at Cyril on the bench she asked, 'Is he alright? I told you he is a bit old for this game.' Gary looked at Anthony and sighed as he spoke,

'Oh dear, this hasn't worked out as well as we'd hoped.'

'It's certainly memorable,' Anthony replied. Everyone was ushered out of the club and there ended their experience of bowling.

The following morning Dolly was back in DDs serving her appreciative customers. Those customers happened to be the Roadeteers who had decided to take a morning break after road repairs hadn't gone as expected. They were sat at a table feeling sorry for themselves.

'I'm getting worried,' Steve announced, 'Sarah isn't picking up my calls.'

'Well when did you last speak to her?' asked Doug.

'Yesterday morning,' Steve replied, 'she was coming here to meet Trudie. I tried to phone her last night but it went to voicemail.'

'Perhaps she is charging?' Frank said, which Doug found amusing.

'Is she electric then?' he started. 'That could be very useful if she is. When she becomes annoying just take her battery out.'

'Perhaps electric Sarah is about to give TAS a shock!' Frank said. Steve didn't get the joke.

'A shock, how?' he said. 'Do you think she's about to dump me?'

'Bleedin' hell, mate,' said Doug, 'she's not answered her phone for twelve hours and you are in a panic. Play it cool, she might be put off by clingy men.'

'Let's face it, she's had a posh evening out so perhaps you've been used,' Frank suggested. 'She's had her wicked way with your wallet and now it's all over.' Steve's face dropped.

'Frank, shut up or we won't get any work out of him today,' Doug said.

'Same as normal you mean?' Frank said.

'I'm not taking any notice of you idiots,' Steve said.

'Oooow!' said Doug. Steve ignored him and shouted across the café to Dolly.

'Dolly, did you see Sarah in here yesterday?' he asked.

'Yes, she was with Trudie,' she replied. 'They were in deep conversation for about an hour.' Steve's eyes lit up at the thought of getting some information from Dolly.

'What were they saying?' he asked.

'I've no idea and if I did I wouldn't tell you,' Dolly replied. 'What's said in here stays in here.' Steve looked blank and turned to Frank.

'What does that mean, like?'

'Mind your own business!' said Frank. Steve turned to Doug.

'If he's being like that I'll ask you?' he said.

'No TAS,' said Doug, 'that's what it means, mind your own business. Women stick together you know.'

'Right you are,' Steve said, as the meaning clicked.

Back in Gary and Brenda's home the couple were drinking coffee when the doorbell rang. Brenda was surprised to find Kai and Izzy standing there with Camille. They looked serious.

'Have you got a couple of minutes for a quick chat?' Kai asked so Brenda showed them in. She was intrigued, what could this be about? She wondered if she'd done something wrong when she looked after Camille yesterday.

'Thanks for this, Glenda Brenda,' Kai said, as they walked into the lounge and sat down. Izzy looked puzzled.

'Is your middle name Brenda, Glenda?' she asked.

'No Izzy,' Brenda replied, 'it's my first name.' Izzy looked blank and then continued to say,

'Oh it's your first name but you don't use it, I see. Anyway, we want to ask you something. We've given it a lot of thought and wondered if you'd be Camille's godmother. You can think about it.' Brenda looked shocked but excited at the same time. Gary, who was standing in the corner of the room trying to blend in with the display cabinet, almost fell over.

'I rarely go to church, does that matter?' Brenda blurted out excitedly. 'And don't you think I'm too old? I'm 72 next birthday.'

'That's not old these days and you don't look 72,' Kai said. Izzy looked at him as if he'd said something really stupid.

'Well she's not 72 yet!' she pointed out. Brenda wondered if this meant Izzy thought she'd automatically age years on her birthday next June!

'You get on with Camille so well,' Izzy continued, 'I know she loved being with you yesterday afternoon, I could tell. With your old age comes experience and wisdom and you are so loving with her. Being really old isn't a problem.' Brenda enjoyed all of that until the very last sentence. Gary was grinning as he hid in the corner.

'Right, thank you . . . I think,' Brenda replied.

'So will you say, yes,' Izzy asked, 'or do you want to think about it?'

'I'd love to do it, so I'm saying yes, please,' Brenda said glowing with happiness. Izzy turned to talk to Gary whose camouflage, using the display cabinet, obviously hadn't worked.

'I'm sorry Gary but we've got a godfather already in Kai's friend Andrew,' she said, 'I hope you aren't upset.'

'Not at all,' he said. Secretly inside he was jumping with joy that he wasn't going to be a godfather.

After the three visitors had left, Gary and Brenda talked about it for a while. Brenda's joy at being a godmother was matched equally by Gary's joy at not being a godfather. What a funny pair! As they finally started to calm down Brenda's thoughts went back to the previous evening and the bowling club.

'Did you manage to speak to Cyril this morning?' she asked Gary.

'Yes, I phoned him earlier, when you were in the bath,' Gary replied.

'What did he say?' she asked.

'I didn't tell him you were in the bath, should I have?'

'Not about my bath Gary, oh sometimes!' she said. 'How was he?'

'He's fine,' Gary replied, 'I think it all got a bit much for him last night. He's over 80 years old now so he should look after himself a bit better.'

'He should,' she agreed. 'At the WI we encourage youngsters to join as it is important to have a young person's perspective on things. However, Amy, well Amy is full on and a little insensitive at times.'

'You can say that again,' Gary replied. 'Isn't she the one who told you we weren't suited as you are Gemini and I'm Pisces? She got you all worried.' Brenda was embarrassed by that memory so decided to deny it.

'I think that was Marianne but I wasn't worried,' she said.

'Really?' he said, 'I must have remembered it incorrectly then.' He decided to change the subject. 'There's one good thing from yesterday, Jane has told Cyril she is seriously thinking of joining us. So we may have one new recruit!'

'Well that's good,' Brenda began, 'but is she aware she will be the only female in the team?'

'I expect so, that's probably what attracted her; the thought of all those men around,' Gary said.

'You are funny,' Brenda laughed, 'all those old hunks, eh? Just don't expect her to do all the chores, especially making sandwiches.'

'As if!' he protested. 'Is she any good at making bogie and diarrhoea sandwiches?'

'I'll ignore that!' she said sharply. 'So last night resulted in a one all draw then?' Gary looked puzzled by this, was that a football score or something? Brenda continued, 'One new member for bowls and one for AmDram. Vera is going to Aggie's tonight to try out her skills at prompting.'

'What does that mean? What does she need to do?' Gary asked.

'I assume she will sit out of view on the night and if someone dries up, you know forgets their lines, she can let them know what's next,' Brenda replied.

'Do you think she'll be okay?' Gary asked.

'Not really,' Brenda admitted.

'That's not one all then, as Aggie may have scored an own goal,' Gary pointed out.

Later that evening, Aggie's Theatre Players were getting ready to rehearse the new play. The cast members present were Michelle, Neil and six others. Vera had arrived to test out her abilities as a prompter. They were waiting in the lounge while Aggie was taking a phone call in her kitchen. Vera was already feeling a little bored and was staring out of the window. The lounge was quiet as everyone waited patiently. Vera watched a man and woman walk by. They were talking and could be overheard.

'It'll be hard but you'll enjoy it,' the man outside said. Vera being Vera jumped straight in with,

'As the bishop said to the actress.' As soon as she said it she regretted it, she remembered she was in a room full of budding actors and actresses. 'Or he said it to the waitress,' she announced, in a desperate attempt to recover.

'Well saved,' said Michelle with a smile, 'but a lot of actresses take work as waitresses between jobs, you know?'

'Right,' replied Vera, in deep thought, 'how about bishop said to the prostitute then? If any of you identify with that please leave now.' At this point Aggie entered the room.

'Right let's get started,' she said. 'This is our first full rehearsal and I've given Vera a copy of the script but I want the rest of us to have a go at going through the play without the script. This is the play Day and Night by Aggie Parker.'

'Who's that?' asked Vera.

'Me!' said Aggie, forcefully.

'So it's the play 'what' you wrote,' Vera laughed, 'that's very clever.' They started to go through the play. All was going well until Michelle forgot her next line.

'Well it wasn't me who promised you the world was it? So you can't hold me responsible for that!' said Neil, who was word perfect.

'I know but, I can't, I can't . . .' Michelle was struggling to remember what came next and looked at Vera, 'where are we Vera?' she asked.

'In Aggie's house,' Vera replied, which brought a giggle from the others who didn't take things quite as seriously as Aggie.

'No, what's my line?' asked Michelle.

'Not sure,' admitted Vera, 'you were going too fast.' At this point Aggie jumped in,

'Vera,' she said calmly, 'we must be at the bottom of this particular page by now. What does it say?'

'Page 21,' Vera replied laughing. The others laughed too.

'Oh, for goodness sake!' boomed a very annoyed Aggie. Vera got up and handed Aggie the script.

'Here you go,' Vera said.

'What are you doing?' asked Aggie.

'If you are going to be rude and use that tone of voice with me, I don't think this is for me,' Vera started. 'Good luck, break an arm and all that, but I'd rather be a waitress or a prostitute. Did anyone see what way the bishop went?' The others couldn't stop laughing as Vera left the house. They liked Vera. In that short time they had learnt she didn't take herself too seriously. Aggie meanwhile looked completely confused as she had not been there to hear the earlier conversation. And there ended Vera's career as a prompter! She was much better suited to the role of WI comedienne, anyway.

That night as Gary and Brenda lay in bed in the darkness, Gary started thinking about Vera and the role of the prompter. This prompted him to say something.

'I reckon I could cope with being a prompter for Aggie's Theatre Group,' he said. 'Don't you think you could be one too?'

'I don't want to be one, thank you. Go to sleep Gary,' Brenda replied.

'Go on,' he persisted, 'have a go. Here is your audition.'

'What?' replied a tired Brenda.

'My line is, *you are beautiful love and I'm feeling very romantic*. What am I going to say next? Prompt me please!' Gary demanded.

'How about, *but sadly, as normal, I'm probably not up to the job*!' Brenda replied, cruelly.

'Oh, that's a harsh script!' he complained, with hurt pride. 'Can I rehearse the technique then?'

'Go to sleep! *The end*.' Brenda demanded.

'Oh right,' Gary said, 'of course I have got to wait for the winter solstice, sorry I forgot.'

Okay, I'm sure you can guess what happened next? Right, you've got it, Gary got pillowed!

Chapter Ten

October
The newbies, the brazils and nearly a Dutch artist

The daylight hours were much shorter now and the temperature outside was beginning to drop noticeably. The beautiful trees in Wancott Park started to prepare for the sheading of their leaves, many of which were beginning to turn the most beautiful shades of red, orange and yellow. Spring, Summer, Autumn, Winter; this sequence of seasons had happened every year forever and yet every Autumn Brenda was even more amazed by the beauty of nature. The only downside was that it was followed by Winter which would bring rainy, windy days and boggy grass into which her boots would sink when she was on her daily walks.

Brenda was busy, busy, busy. She was helping Izzy organise Camille's christening which was due to take place on Sunday 20th October. Dolly had kindly agreed to reopen DDs from 4:15 for the private christening party. It would close to the public, as normal, at 4 o'clock. It was now Friday 18th October. Gary had walked into town to the local newsagents to pick up a copy of his fishing magazine and he had just arrived home.

'It's nice out there, milder than I expected,' he commented as he walked into the house. 'I see the people opposite, in number 18, have moved out.'

'Yes, they moved out last week. Trudie said they've moved up north,' Brenda said.

'Ah, hardy folk!' Gary jested. 'Did anyone tell them it's colder up north!'

'They aren't going to the Outer Hebrides, Gary,' Brenda said, 'just Birmingham I think.'

'Birmingham?' Gary queried. 'That's worse!'

'We never really met them, did we?' Brenda said.

'Just as well if they are the sort of people that would go to live in Birmingham,' Gary replied.

'What's wrong with Birmingham?' she asked, preparing herself for one of Gary's special replies.

'Spaghetti Junction, Aston Villa, Crossroads,' Gary joked, 'need I say more?'

'I liked Crossroads!' she said firmly. Gary smiled as he'd forgotten that. 'It's funny isn't it, how we assume things?' she continued.

'You assumed Birmingham was nice because of the Crossroads Motel?' Gary asked.

'No, I assumed the people in number 18 were the house owners. I didn't realise it was rented until the To Let sign went up,' Brenda said.

'It's actually said Let on the board for about a month now,' Gary remarked. 'It doesn't take long to get new tenants now with the property shortage.'

'That house isn't short, it's quite tall!' Brenda joked.

'Hey, you are finally thinking like me,' Gary said, smiling.

'Heaven forbid!' Brenda said, in a pretend alarmed state. 'Still if you can't beat them join them, hey? It will be nice to see new people settle in. We won't be the newest in the Rise anymore.'

'Yes, we'll no longer be the Rise's virgins,' Gary chirped cheerily. Brenda smiled.

'That's a funny way to describe us,' she said.

'You know what I mean, they'll be the newbies now,' Gary said.

'It's good that we settled in well,' Brenda remarked.

'I told you we would,' Gary said, looking proud of himself, 'didn't I?'

'Yes, you did,' Brenda had to admit, 'sometimes I should listen to you.'

'Of course, the newbies are going to be closer to Aggie than us,' Gary observed, 'What a shock that will be for them. That's enough to drive anyone to Birmingham!'

'She's not all bad,' Brenda replied. 'She bought us flowers on our first day in the Rise.'

'But she was just checking us out for her AmDram group,' Gary said. Brenda wasn't sure that was entirely fair. She knew Aggie had a passion for, if not an addiction to, amateur dramatics but underneath all that her heart was in the right place. She'd obviously had an excellent career in teaching and had been married once. Brenda hadn't managed to ascertain whether the husband died or was divorced although Gary was convinced his murdered body probably lay beneath a stage somewhere. He had told Brenda to listen out for the howls of a ghost coming from under the stage of the Oxford Playhouse when she went earlier in the year. They had learnt that she had two sons who now lived in Scotland. The eldest had studied at Edinburgh University and the other at Aberdeen University and both had good careers. It was an eight hour drive from Oxford to south Scotland so Aggie's sons were literally at the other end of the country.

Brenda's thoughts suddenly turned to other things.

'You haven't forgotten about picking up your suit this afternoon, have you?' she asked.

'How could I forget?' Gary replied. 'You've mentioned it every hour on the hour since 6 o'clock. 'I'll see the boys . . .' He was interrupted by Brenda.

'Boys?' she queried. 'Old blokes more like!'

'. . for some bowling at 2,' Gary continued, as if Brenda hadn't interrupted him. 'Then I'll walk into town and pick up my suit from the cleaners.'

'Sometimes you need reminding,' Brenda said. 'Don't forget it as the christening is on Sunday and you'll need it.' Gary's mood changed at the mention of the christening.

'I'm still not sure why I've got to come to the christening,' he said, 'I'm not a godparent and I'm not religious.' Brenda's mood had also changed into determined wife mode!

'Well, thank you for turning up at the church for our wedding then, you atheist!' she declared.

'That was different. That was the happiest day of my life and I wasn't dreading that,' Gary replied. That knocked Brenda for six emotionally, she wasn't expecting such a romantic sentence to come out of Gary's mouth. She'd gone from determined wife mode to choked up softie.

'Oh Gary sometimes you surprise me,' she said tearfully, 'at the most unexpected time you say the most beautiful things. Thank you, I love you too.' Gary was trying hard to work out why his sentence had proved so powerful and thought he could use her change of mood to his advantage.

'Does that mean I can give the christening a miss then?' he asked hopefully.

'No, because you will be there to support me, the love of your life,' Brenda replied. 'What will people think if the godmother's other half isn't there?'

'Probably, what a sensible bloke,' he said.

'More like uncaring pig!' she said, now back in determined wife mode. Gary thought of that valentine's card, so she didn't want to squeeze his oink today then?

'Remember this is for Izzy and Kai too,' Brenda continued.

'I wonder what Izzy's parents are going to be like?' he remarked. 'Do you think her mother's strange too?'

'Izzy isn't strange, she's unique!' Brenda exclaimed.

'Unique? What, like Jack the Ripper?' Gary replied.

'Gary!' Brenda shouted in disapproval. Yep, even Gary thought he'd gone a little over the top with that one.

'Can I come straight home after the service?' he asked, almost begging.

'No!' she replied. 'There you go again! You know that there will be a little get together in DDs. Dolly's going to a lot of trouble. After she closes at 4 she'll start getting everything prepared for reopening just for the party. I need you to be there.'

'Great,' Gary moaned. 'We'll be standing around eating cucumber sandwiches, drinking tea and trying to make conversation with Izzy's dotty family and then, oh great joy, here's the vicar. Praise the Lord!'

'Sometimes you are so rude!' Brenda said.

'I agree, so best I stay away then?' Gary pleaded again.

'No, but good try!' Brenda replied. She was beginning to admire his efforts even if they weren't going to get him anywhere. There was a pause which signalled Gary had run out of strength and had admitted defeat. Oh dear, he would have to go.

'I wonder if I've got time to get another outfit in the city this afternoon?' Brenda said, thinking out loud. Gary started to look worried as that would involve money leaving their bank account.

'You've got the hat and stuff from the wedding that never was!' he declared. 'You said you were going to wear that.'

'Do you think it looks suitable for a christening?' she asked. 'It was chosen as a wedding outfit.'

'It hasn't got a veil, has it?' Gary asked. 'It's not pure white?'

'You know it's not!' Brenda replied. 'It's not a bridal dress.'

'Well then it's fine, love,' he declared, 'in fact the hat is pink if I remember correctly, a perfect colour for a baby girl's christening.'

'Oh yes, I hadn't thought of that,' she admitted, 'well done Gary.'

'It'll be perfect,' Gary confirmed.

'Perfect to look at or perfect for our bank balance?' she replied.

'Both love,' he admitted. 'You'll look lovely and I won't look pale on receipt of our bank statement.'

'Idiot!' Brenda replied, with a smile. 'Oh sometimes, Gary!'

It was now 12:30 and in DDs Dolly was talking to Trudie and Sarah.

'I wish I hadn't taken on this christening party now,' Dolly said. 'It's quite a responsibility really.'

'You'll do them proud, Dolly,' Trudie said, 'you know you will. What's worrying you?'

'I don't really know Kai and Izzy that well so don't know what their preferences are,' she replied.

'Preferences?' Trudie queried.

'You know, do they like cups and saucers or mugs?' Dolly said. 'Do they like crusts left on their sandwiches or cut off?'

'Ah, I see what you mean,' Trudie said, as the penny dropped. 'Perhaps you should ask them.'

'I tried yesterday when Kai brought my post in,' Dolly said, 'I asked him and he stood there looking confused. You'd have thought he was on a major quiz show or something.'

'Perhaps you'd be better talking to the brains of the family, Izzy,' Trudie said.

'Trouble is,' Dolly admitted,' I don't know Izzy at all, I've only met her once when Brenda brought her in here last week. I couldn't make her out. I'll see if I can ask Brenda to find out.' As Dolly was finishing the sentence Brenda walked through the door.

'Hello ladies. Ask Brenda to find out what?' she asked.

'Ah, Brenda lass, what cup do you favour?' Dolly asked. Brenda looked puzzled by the question.

'That's a bit personal Dolly but as you've asked, I'm a D cup,' she replied. The other women started to laugh.

'No, I meant cups and saucers or mugs,' Dolly explained.

'Oh my,' Sarah said as she laughed. 'Dolly are you going to serve the hot drinks in bras!' Brenda joined in with the laughing but felt rather embarrassed.

'Sorry,' she said, 'I don't know why I thought you meant that. Still if you did serve the food in bras it might encourage Gary to come to the buffet reception, he's always on about my headlamps.' Sarah burst out laughing again.

'No, no, stop it Brenda!' Sarah said desperately. 'Oh ladies I've got to pop to the loo, but I'll be back soon. Oh Brenda you've made my day!'

'Don't fall down the hole in the middle while you are laughing so hard,' Trudie said. Sarah left the others and walked off to the far end of the café to the toilets.

'Right then Brenda, back to the important question, do you prefer cups or mugs?' Dolly asked.

'My preference changes all the time,' Brenda admitted. 'It depends on the occasion. If my parents were visiting it was always cups and saucers, otherwise I would have got grief from my mother, but if it were Gary's parents it was mugs. Gary's Dad said you got your money's worth out of a mug.' She looked sad as she continued, 'they are all dead now so it doesn't matter about cups and mugs.'

'Ahh that's sad, sorry,' Trudie said.

'Yes it is,' said Brenda, 'but Gary's father's desire to get his money's worth out of everything lives on in Gary . . unfortunately!' They smiled.

'I wasn't sure which were best for Camille's christening party, cups or mugs?' Dolly asked.

'Oh definitely cups and saucers, Dolly!' Brenda replied. 'It's a special occasion. Mind you, you could serve Gary's in a mug as he spills so much when he tries balancing a cup on a saucer, I don't know what's wrong with him.'

'It's his Dad's spirit saying, why aren't you getting your money's worth, son?' Dolly joked.

'You are probably right!' Brenda admitted.

'Perhaps the clue is in the name?' Dolly said. 'A mug for a mug!' Brenda saw an opportunity to pull Dolly's leg and turned from jovial to deadly serious immediately.

'Oh no, my Gary's not a mug!' she announced. Dolly fell for it and was worried she had caused offence.

'Sorry Brenda, lass, I didn't mean . . .' she started but got interrupted by Brenda.

'Yes he is! Who am I kidding?' she said and laughed.

'Oh you!' said a relieved Dolly. 'You got me proper there!'

'My David prefers mugs too,' Trudie said, 'he's never mentioned headlamps though!' she laughed. 'Well ladies I must leave you as I'm on the afternoon shift. Say bye to Sarah for me when she gets back. I think she might have fallen down the hole in the middle, you know!' The ladies exchanged goodbyes and Trudie left. Dolly turned to Brenda.

'Seriously though,' she started, 'could you have a word with Izzy for me to find out her preferences? I've got a list here. You know what Izzy's like, she never got whether I was joking or not when you brought her in last week.' At this point Sarah returned from her expedition to the toilet.

'Leave it with me, I'll see what I can find out,' Brenda promised Dolly.

'Thanks,' Dolly said, 'oh, but I don't need her bra size.' Sarah started to giggle again.

'I'm never going to live that down, am I?' Brenda replied. As she finished her sentence Doug and Frank walked into DDs and headed for the counter.

'The Three Roadeteers are down to two,' Dolly started, 'you've lost one! Where's TAS?'

'We've messed up and left him guarding our mistake,' Frank explained. 'Could we have two coffees and a tea to take out please?' Brenda was interested by this.

'How have you messed up?' she asked.

'That's a good question, that,' Frank said.

'Yep, a very good question, that,' Doug repeated.

'And what's the very good answer to my very good question?' asked an impatient Brenda.

'Well it's like this,' Frank started, 'we were supposed to dig this hole for a pipe repair in Horse Chestnut Street but we misread the instructions and the hole is currently in Horse Chesham Street.'

'Being guarded by TAS,' Doug confirmed. 'We've had a shite day so far.'

'It sounds like it,' Dolly agreed, 'I can't imagine it's much fun if you live in Horse Chesham Street either.' Frank then turned to look at Sarah directly and asked,

'What's going on between you and TAS then?'

'That's our business,' Sarah replied, sharply.

'It's ours as well when he starts sulking and walking around in a trance,' Frank commented. 'We've got to work with him. Have you dumped him?'

'We're on a break,' Sarah said. Doug smiled at Frank and winked.

'What like an away day to Blackpool?' he joked. Dolly and Brenda found that amusing and smiled at each other.

'No, not like an away day to Blackpool!' Sarah snarled back at Doug.

'Right you are!' Doug and Frank said in unison and with that picked up their hot drinks and left. Dolly couldn't leave the subject of Sarah's love life alone.

'A break Sarah!' she joked, 'you've only been together five minutes!'

'I'm trying to let Steve down gently,' Sarah replied. 'He doesn't know that the small break is already an irreparable fracture! As far as I'm concerned we are finished.'

'Oh dear,' Dolly said.

He's not the one,' Sarah continued, 'and Brenda will have to do better when she picks my men in future.'

'What?' said a shocked Brenda. 'Now don't blame me. He was your choice, I was only driving past him remember? I hope you haven't been hurt by this.'

'No, don't worry Brenda,' she replied, 'it's all okay. There's this bloke at work, Simon, who's cute and I can tell he fancies me.'

'Here we go!' said Dolly.

'Well it's good to see you aren't heartbroken!' Brenda said.

At 1 o'clock in Seymour Rise new tenants for number 18 had arrived. Archie and Lily Clarke, both aged 42 years, were standing beside a van which was parked outside their home to be. A few boxes had already been unloaded and had been placed by the front door. Aggie came out of her house and marched along to meet them.

'Hello, I'm Aggie,' she boomed in her normal fashion. 'I live next door and just wanted to welcome you to Seymour Rise.'

'Thank you, I'm Lily,' replied Lily.

'I'm Archie, that's an Arch with an eeee,' replied Archie. That confused Aggie who spelt out his name.

'Oh, so A-r-c-h-e?' she said.

'No,' he corrected her, 'Arch with the letters making the 'ee' sound.'

'A-r-c-h-y?' she said. Lily was tired of this.

'Oh Archie,' she complained, 'why do you do this every time?'

'What's that, princess?' he asked, innocently.

'Confuse everyone,' Lily said. 'He is Archie with an i and e on the end.'

'That's what I said,' Archie insisted. Aggie looked bewildered by this first impression she was getting of her new neighbours.

'Right, well it's nice to meet you both,' Aggie said. 'You'll be busy moving in so I won't get in your way.'

'We can't get in yet,' Lily explained. 'The agent has sent our keys over to their Faringdon office in error.'

'Unbelievable isn't it?' Archie joined in. 'Wrong post code apparently.'

'What, sent them to postcode Y instead of IE?' Aggie joked, with a wry smile. It took Archie a few seconds to get the joke.

'Oh yeah, I like it!' he said, when the penny dropped.

'You asked for that, Archie,' Lily was quick to point out.

'You are definitely in the correct road then?' Aggie asked.

'Oh yes, defo!' Lily replied.

'Yes, the agents are a load of brazils!' Archie moaned.

'It's a good job it's not raining,' Lily commented.

'Yes it is or your belongings would get wet,' Aggie said.

'No, we'd leave them in the van,' Lily replied, 'I just don't like the rain, it's depressing, so it's a good job it's not raining!'

'What's that princess?' asked Archie.

'Rain's depressing,' she said.

'Oh yes!' Archie agreed. 'They are a blooming load of brazils those letting agents. What a shower! Hey, just realised what I said, a shower!' Aggie had to use her best acting skills to look amused when really she couldn't care less for his joke.

'Would you like a coffee while you are waiting for the key?' she asked.

'Ah, that would be lovely, Maggie,' Lily said.

'Aggie,' Aggie said, correcting Lily.

'What's that princess?' Archie asked.

'Aggie is going to make us a coffee,' Lily replied making sure she got the name correct.

'Lovely, just the job,' Archie continued, 'milk and one sugar, ta. We'll stay out here guarding the boxes we've already got out of the van.'

'Right, I'll bring them out to you,' Aggie said and walked back into her house.

Lily and Archie sat on the front door step.

'That's nice, isn't it?' Lily said.

'What's that, princess?' Archie asked.

'Our neighbour coming to greet us and make us a coffee,' Lily replied.

'Oh yes,' Archie acknowledged, 'but she probably wants something, mind. You don't get nothing for anything these days.' Lily listened and looked amused.

'Anything for nothing you mean,' she said, correcting him.

'That's what I said,' Archie insisted. 'She'll be wanting to borrow something once we've moved in.' Lily looked confused. What did they have that Aggie could possibly want?

'Like what?' she asked, 'we haven't got anything.'

'What's that, princess?' he asked.

'Oh forget it,' Lily replied.

'Where are these agents?' Archie moaned, 'Probably in Swindon by now, load of brazils!'

At 3 o'clock Gary was enjoying a social gathering at Wancott Bowling Club. This informal meeting included the club's newest recruit, Jane. She was sitting around the table with Phil, Cyril, Anthony, Gary, Paddy and Tim.

'We try hard enough but I don't think we're getting any better at this bowling lark,' Phil said, sounding a little discouraged.

'We're as good as we are. A captain can only ask his team to do their best,' Cyril replied. Anthony smiled and added,

'Oh dear, as bad as that then!'

'C'mon fellas, you need to be more positive,' Jane said. 'I didn't think I was joining such a negative team.'

'I'd be positive with you, my dear,' Anthony said, creeping up to Jane.

'How's Tess doing these days?' asked an irritated Gary.

'Okay Gary, keep your knickers from twisting!' Anthony fired back.

'It's don't get your knickers in a twist, mate!' Gary said, his blood pressure rising by the second. Things didn't improve when Paddy asked,

'Do you wear knickers then, Gary?' The others laughed.

'Yes, I expect he wears Brenda's underwear,' Anthony said. Jane had heard enough.

'Please! You lot are worse than children,' she shouted. 'I didn't take this afternoon off work for this nonsense. Don't worry Gary, Tess has nothing to fear I can assure you.' Jane smiled at Gary as she appreciated his good intentions and Gary smiled back.

'Oh yes, all friendly, cosy you two. How's Brenda, mate?' Anthony jested.

'Looking for her knickers,' Paddy said, making everybody, including Gary, laugh.

'I'm not sure it was right to encourage women into this club after all now,' Cyril sighed.

'Not just one anyway, not when Anthony's around,' Phil agreed.

'Don't worry,' Jane replied, 'I can look after myself!'

'Well Jane,' Cyril continued, 'you are most welcome.'

'Especially as you are a better player than most of us,' Tim said, 'I hope you'll stay.'

'I'm really enjoying it, thank you,' Jane said.

'The bowls or putting Anthony in his place?' Brian joked. At this point Tim looked at his watch and rose from his chair quickly.

'I'm sorry guys, and girl,' he said, 'but I've got to go. I'm taking Belle to the hairdressers for 3:30 and there will be hell to pay if I'm late.'

'Hell to pay?' said Paddy, 'who collects that then, Satan?' Gary smirked as he thought of the dog next door.

'What, you don't mean the dog next door to me?' he asked Paddy, who looked more puzzled than ever.

'What?' Paddy asked.

'That's got you Paddy, hasn't it?' Gary said, feeling pleased with himself. 'Anyway I've got to leave you now too. I've got a christening to go to on Sunday and my suit is at the cleaners. I'm dreading it as I don't like these church things.'

'Can't you get out of it?' asked Tim.

'I've tried, believe me I've tried hard,' Gary replied.

'Are you a godparent?' asked Tim.

'No, thank God!' Gary began, 'Trouble is I'm the husband of the godmother.'

'Brenda's godmother?' asked a shocked Anthony. 'Shouldn't that be god-grandmother? She's a bit old to be a godmother, isn't she?'

'Would you like to discuss that with Brenda?' Gary asked. 'But I warn you, if you do you could end up discussing it directly with God after she's killed you.'

'God bless you, my son!' Anthony replied. Gary smiled as he left the room with Tim.

Gary walked to Wancott Dry Cleaning Services and picked up his suit before making his way home. He entered the house carrying it in a sealed gold bag with hanger, all supplied by the dry cleaners.

'Is that you, Gary?' Brenda called from the bedroom.

'If it isn't I want to know who he is!' Gary shouted back.

'I thought it might be Anthony,' Brenda said jokingly. 'He often pops round when you're out.'

'Very funny,' Gary replied. 'I've got my suit.'

'Good,' she said, as she came down the stairs, 'hopefully we're ready for the big day now. Hey, I noticed that the new people have moved in over the road.'

'Have they?' Gary asked. 'Have you spoken to them?'

'No,' she replied, 'but I saw Aggie take them coffee. They stood on the pavement for a couple of hours.'

'What for?' asked a bemused Gary.

'Admiring our house I expect,' Brenda said, with a straight face.

'Really?' Gary asked.

'No, Gary! It looked like they couldn't get in.'

'Well I'm sure we'll meet them in time,' Gary continued, 'and we'll look normal compared with Aggie.'

'Poor Aggie! She gets a hard time but she's got a lovely heart,' Brenda said. 'She welcomes everyone new to the Rise.'

'Yes, because she's looking for new blood for her AmDram group!' Gary insisted.

'Do you think I ought to go over and introduce myself to them?' Brenda asked.

'Oh yes,' Gary replied, 'and be a good neighbour by warning them about Aggie's AmDram!'

'No,' she started, 'I'm not stirring up trouble! I'd just see if they needed anything or perhaps . . .' Before she could say anymore the doorbell rang.

'You're closest, you answer it,' Gary said.

'Yes Sir!' Brenda replied and walked to the door. On opening it she found a woman in her early forties staring back at her. It was Lily but Brenda didn't know that yet.

'Hi, I'm sorry to trouble you,' she started, 'but I've just moved in over the road. I've tried Aggie's door and the other side but they are out. I noticed your dad walk in five minutes ago so I knew someone was in here.' Brenda smiled the broadest of smiles. Oh my goodness, her new neighbour thought Gary was her dad!

'It's no bother,' replied Brenda, still smiling. 'I'm Brenda by the way. How can I help you?'

'Oh, thank you. I'm Lily. Would you have some sugar I could have please? I've unpacked most of our things and I can't find the sugar. I only need a little.'

'Of course, that's no bother. Come in, Lily!' Brenda opened the door up wide to allow Lily to walk through to the lounge. Gary was sitting on the sofa holding his dry cleaning in its gold bag. He was waiting for the coast to clear so he could take it upstairs.

'Gary, this is Lily from over the road,' she announced, 'Lily this is Gary, my dad.' Brenda managed to keep a serious facial expression although she was giggling inside.

'I'm what?' a puzzled Gary asked.

'I'm sorry,' said Lily, who had realised her mistake, 'I only saw you from the back err, Gary.'

'Gary's my husband, of course he is much older than me,' Brenda laughed as she walked into the kitchen.

'Sorry!' Lily said to Gary, again.

'Don't worry, no harm done,' Gary replied. 'Have you moved in on your own?'

'No, I'm with my hubby, Archie,' Lily replied. Brenda then reappeared with a cup full of sugar as the doorbell rang again.

'Excuse me, I'll just get that,' Brenda said as she left to answer the door again. This time she found Archie standing there.

'Sorry love, but you haven't got my wife in there, have you?' he asked.

'Are you Lily's husband?' Brenda asked.

'You what love?' Archie replied. 'Sorry, I'm a bit deaf.'

'Have you moved in over the road?' Brenda asked, speaking a little louder.

'That's right. I'm Archie, that's Arch with an eeee,' he replied. At this point Lily shouted from the lounge,

'Don't start that Archie! Sorry, he always does this when he meets new people!' Archie followed Brenda into the lounge.

'Yes sorry,' Archie began, 'I think it's partly nerves plus the fact that we've had an awful day. We were shut out for two hours because the agents lost the keys. They are a useless lot, a load of brazils!'

'Sounds bad,' Gary said.

'Let's go Archie,' Lily said abruptly, fearing that they were boring their neighbours. 'Thank you Brenda, I'll drop your cup back tomorrow.'

'Why didn't you bring one of our cups?' Archie asked.

'I forgot,' she replied.

'You're a brazil then!' he said.

'It's no trouble, honestly,' Brenda said and Gary called after them,

'Well it's nice to meet you.'

'Thank you, and likewise,' Lily added and Archie chipped in with, 'Yeah, ta.'

Brenda walked them to the front door and watched them cross the road towards their house.

'Nice people,' Lily said.

'Yeah,' said Archie, 'but why was he sat on the sofa cuddling a dry cleaning bag?'

'Where did you want him to sit, on the floor?' she replied.

By 2 o'clock on the Sunday afternoon of the christening, Brenda had already got changed into her outfit. She came downstairs talking on her phone, while Gary was sitting on the sofa reading the Sunday paper.

'I'm sure it will be fine, Dolly. I saw the cake yesterday and I think it's fantastic and Izzy does too,' she said. 'What? . . . the sandwiches? No don't worry I'll pop in and give you a hand before the service. Yes . . . . no . . . yes, I'll see you soon.' The call ended.

'Trouble at mill, or should I say DDs?' Gary asked.

'No, it's just Dolly making sure everything is okay. She wants everything to be perfect,' Brenda replied.

'I could make her some of my scones if you like,' he joked. 'They will go down with a bang!'

'That wasn't funny,' Brenda said. 'That evening still haunts me!'

'No, sorry,' Gary said, realising he'd hit a raw nerve. Luckily for him Brenda changed the subject.

'I'm going to go to the church via DDs so I can give Dolly some support. I'll see you at the church at 3:30, okay?'

'If you insist,' he replied. 'How will I find you?'

'I'll carry a copy of the Radio Times and whistle *she'll be coming round the mountain when she comes*,' she said sarcastically. 'It's a church Gary, not a football stadium! I'll be somewhere near the font as it's a christening! Oh Gary, sometimes!'

'Right, okay love,' he replied. 'By the way, you look lovely.' Brenda's tone changed immediately on receiving that compliment.

'Ah, thank you, love,' she said. 'You'd better get ready now. Don't leave it to the last minute.'

'I've got plenty of time,' he replied. 'Best not get the suit on too early as I'll probably spill something down it.'

'True, but don't leave it too late,' she repeated. Brenda gave Gary a kiss, picked up her handbag and headed out of the door. 'See you later,' she called as the front door closed. Gary continued to read the paper muttering to himself,

'How much? These footballers are so overpaid. He earns what?'

Brenda had arrived at DDs within ten minutes of leaving home. There were a few people at the tables. Dolly was in the back and Brenda walked through.

'Are you okay, Dolly?' Brenda asked.

'Oh Brenda, I hope so, I think so,' she replied. 'I've got everything spread out back here so I can just walk it through once I close at 4. It'll all be out there by 4:15.'

'It all looks great,' Brenda observed, trying to offer encouragement. 'Gary offered to come and make some of his special hot cross scones,' she continued, trying to lighten the mood.

'Oh my goodness, no!' Dolly said. 'That's all I need, exploding microwaves!' Both women laughed. 'Thanks for popping in, Brenda. You've made me laugh already, that eases the pressure.'

'You only need encouragement,' Brenda said. 'Everything will be great.'

'I hope the service goes well,' Dolly said.

'Yes,' Brenda said, 'it's a shame you're tied up here.'

'That suits me fine,' Dolly replied. 'I'm not religious and I get the urge to laugh when the vicar talks about turning away from sin.'

'Oh yes, I forgot that bit,' Brenda said with a smile.

'You'll have a sinless life from now on,' Dolly laughed. Brenda covered the bottom half of her face with her hand.

'I always have,' she said. Dolly looked on unable to make out what Brenda was doing.

'Are you okay, lass?' she asked, 'Are you about to sneeze?'

'No, I'm just checking that my nose isn't growing like Pinocchio's did,' she replied.

'As if! There's no sin in you lass,' Dolly replied, 'have a coffee while you are here.'

'Just half a cup then please,' Brenda requested.

'Half?' said a confused Dolly.

'If I have more I'm going to need the loo right in the middle of the service, especially when the vicar starts splashing around in the font,' Brenda replied. Dolly passed over half a cup of coffee just as Brenda's phone started to ring. 'Oh, it's Gary,' she said looking at her phone, 'what's wrong now?'

'Hello, I haven't been gone long, what's up?' she said. 'Wait, I'll put you on speaker so I can drink my coffee.' She put the phone on speaker and placed it on the table.

'I can't come to the service,' Gary said.

'You are joking, aren't you?' Brenda replied.

'No, I really can't come,' he insisted, 'I've just gone to put my suit on and the dry cleaners have given me the wrong one.' Brenda saw red believing it was just another ploy to get out of going.

'Oh no you don't!' she shouted. 'You are not getting out of it now.'

'I think if you saw it you would want me out of it,' Gary replied, referring to the suit.

'Gary,' Brenda snarled, 'you will be at the service or I will leave you!'

'What?' Gary said.

'The suit you've got, is it your size?' she asked.

'I think so but . . .' Gary started to reply but was interrupted by Brenda before he could carry on.

'Then it doesn't matter that it's not yours. It's a suit so it will do!'

'But . . .' Gary pleaded.

'No buts! Be at the Church!' she demanded.

'I think you are being cruel,' Gary said, his voice quivering.

'Cruel?' she shouted back. 'You will know the true meaning of cruel if you don't show up.' Gary could take no more of this and ended the call.

'Charming,' Brenda said to Dolly, 'he's ended the call!' Dolly looked concerned.

'Poor Gary sounded distressed,' she said. 'Are you sure he's okay?'

'Dolly,' Brenda began, 'he's been trying to get out of this christening for ages. I'm not falling for it.'

'Well, he's your husband so I suppose you know what you are doing,' Dolly admitted.

At 3:30 everyone started to gather in the church for the christening. They were ready to take their seats as the vicar had arrived. Izzy and Kai and their parents were standing near the font. Izzy was holding Camille who was in a beautiful christening robe which had been passed down the generations. The godparents to be, Brenda and Andrew, were standing with the group near the font. The vicar moved closer and greeted the proud parents. Everyone sat down as he was about to start the service. Then the backdoor creaked open and out of the darkness at the back of the church Gary walked in. Everyone stared and some gasped. He was wearing a slightly too big, bright pink suit with red stripes.

'This is Gary, Mum,' Izzy explained as if Gary looked normal, 'he's Glenda's husband.' Izzy's mother stood there with her mouth open in amazement.

'Has he come as the entertainment, Izzy dear?' she asked.

'No, he's come as Gary!' Izzy said, very seriously, 'Lovely Gary!'

'Oh my God!' exclaimed Brenda, 'Oh sorry vicar for the poor choice of words,' she continued, realising the vicar was standing there. Izzy smiled at Gary.

'I love it, Gary!' she said. 'You match Glenda's hat!'

The christening went without a hitch and afterwards the guests gathered in DDs enjoying the sandwiches and tea. Gary was standing *brightly* with Brenda eating a sausage roll while spilling his tea in a saucer.

'Well, my standing here, looking like a right camp prat proves how much I love you,' he said to Brenda. 'I walked through the town centre in this suit with people laughing and pointing. I did it because I couldn't bear the thought of you leaving me.'

'Oh Gary, you know I'd never leave you, don't you?' she replied. She was feeling very guilty for forcing him into such a humiliating situation.

'I suppose there is a positive to take from this experience,' he said pondering.

'And what's that?' Brenda asked.

'That there's always someone worse off than you,' Gary explained. 'Somewhere there's a clown standing at a kid's party in a grey suit!' He laughed and pulled a funny face at Brenda.

'I hadn't thought of that,' she said. 'I'm sorry I didn't listen. I'm sorry I made you go to the service and humiliated you. Dolly thought I was being cruel, I could tell she did.'

'Don't worry, love,' said a forgiving Gary. 'It's over. Nobody's giving me a second glance now.' Brenda looked around.

'That's because they can't stand to look at you without sunglasses on,' she joked.

'All in all I don't regret going anyway,' Gary admitted.

'You don't? Really?' Brenda asked, feeling a little confused but relieved.

'I matched your hat, didn't I? Izzy liked that,' he said, which made Brenda smile.

'And despite everything I wouldn't have missed seeing everyone's reaction to that middle name. "Camille Goffette". Wow, that's gold, that!' he said.

'I know, it's a strange name isn't it?' she said.

'It certainly is, but it's nothing like the name I'm going to call those in the dry cleaners when I see them tomorrow. They are a load of idiots!' Gary exclaimed.

'A load of brazils!' Brenda laughed. 'That's the new Archie word it seems!'

It had been an exhausting day for everyone but it had gone well apart from the suit fiasco. By the time Gary and Brenda got to bed they were tired but in a good mood. The bedside lamps were switched off and they prepared to drift off into a well-earned sleep.

'You know I saw young Izzy in a new light today,' Gary whispered.

'What, the light streaming through the stained glass window, you mean?' Brenda asked.

'No silly,' he replied, 'I saw her not as a strange straight-faced young thing but as a caring no nonsense human being. She didn't flinch when I appeared in my pink and red suit. She just accepted me as I was, *no he's come as Gary*, she told her mother, *lovely Gary*. I won't mock her again.'

'Well,' said Brenda, 'she's a lovely girl. I still can't work out why she's named my goddaughter Camille Goffette though.'

'Yes, amazing isn't it?' Gary agreed. 'Do you realise how close she came to having a Dutch artist?'

'What?' asked a confused Brenda.

'Cam Goff!' explained Gary.

'Oh Gary, sometimes. . . . you idiot, my lovely idiot!' Brenda said.

'What?' said Gary, 'I'm not going to get a pillow massage of my head tonight? I must wear a pink suit more often!'

Chapter Eleven

November
The Battle of Archie, 2024

As the world moved into November, Gary and Brenda's life slowed down, although Brenda was still busy. She spent a lot of time babysitting 'Cam-Goff,' which she loved. Her bonds with both goddaughter and mum were strong. There was little gardening to do as the grass and perennials had gone to sleep for the winter, so Brenda had time to do other things. Gary spent his time finishing off the decorating; all the rooms were looking great. He enjoyed fishing in the winter so long as he wrapped up properly to stay warm. Lawn bowls had moved inside to become indoor bowling and took place in a village hall four miles down the road. It wasn't perfect but it allowed the team to train throughout the winter and, more importantly, to socialise.

This November morning Brenda walked into the lounge with her mug of coffee. It was 8:45 and Gary was sitting on the sofa eating his breakfast. I say eating, but he was actually playing with it. He had a bowel of sugar-coated puffs, known affectionately by Gary simply as 'puffs'. He was flicking the cereal into the air and trying to catch it in his mouth as gravity brought it back down again. Brenda sat next to him watching this genius at work.

'Oh nearly! I'm getting closer,' he said, having just missed catching a puff.

'When are you going to grow up?' Brenda enquired. 'You are making a mess on the carpet. It'll be sticky.'

'I'll pick it up,' Gary said, as he just missed catching another puff. 'Oh so close!'

'Why have you bought those?' Brenda asked. 'What's wrong with Corn Flakes all of a sudden? You're too old for puffs!'

'This takes me back to my childhood,' Gary confessed.

'Takes you back?' Brenda questioned. 'Did you ever leave it?'

'Me and Mary always had a puff catching competition at the weekend,' he said. 'A bit of sibling rivalry never did us any harm.' He flicked another one which rebounded off his cheek and bounced across Brenda's chest.

'That's it, stop it now,' Brenda requested, raising her voice but Gary just laughed.

'Sorry love, did I clip your headlamp?' he asked with a big smile.

'That's enough! I'm serious,' she said.

'Mary would have been proud of that one if she were here,' he commented.

'I think you will find that Mary has grown up, whereas you haven't,' Brenda said. On hearing this Gary put his right-hand thumb to his nose and wriggled his four fingers at Brenda.

'Nah, nah, nah nah nah!' he shouted.

'Gary! Are you sure it's only milk on that cereal?' she asked. Gary smiled and leant over and kissed her cheek. He had at least for now stopped flicking puffs into the air.

'Talking of Mary,' Brenda started, 'when I was speaking to her yesterday I could sense she wasn't her usual bubbly self. I think she's fed up and lonely.'

'Really?' Gary asked. 'She'd have better mental health if she was playing catch the puff.'

'I doubt that,' Brenda replied.

'I'm only joking,' Gary said. 'I hate the thought of my big sister sitting in her flat feeling lonely. Do you think we should pay her a visit?'

'I was thinking that we could invite her here to stay for a few days. She could get the train to Didcot like she used to when we were first married. She's not been to stay with us in this house.'

'Good idea,' Gary agreed. 'I'll get extra puffs in so we can have a competition.' He then noticed the stormy look on Brenda's face. 'Or perhaps not,' he added.

He stood up and immediately stood on a sticky puff.

'Gary, the carpet! Oh sometimes!' Brenda said disapprovingly.

Across the road, Archie was leaving his house to go to work. He walked out onto the pavement as Sarah was passing on her way to Trudie's house.

'Mornin' love,' he said to Sarah.

'Hi!' she replied.

'Nice day, isn't it?' he remarked as he walked on.

'Lovely!' she said and continued to Trudie's door and rang the doorbell. When Trudie opened the door Sarah rushed inside.

'Are you alright, Sarah?' Trudie asked. 'You're in a hurry.' Sarah rushed to the window that looked onto the road.

'Trude,' she said, 'who's that guy?' Trudie looked out of the window and was just in time to see the back of Archie walking into the distance.

'Oh him,' she said, 'that's the new chap in number 18. I haven't met him yet but . . .' She stopped after noticing Sarah's concerned expression and then continued, 'why, what's he done?'

'Nothing, but there's still time,' Sarah replied, her face breaking into a smile.

'You get worse with age, Sarah!' Trudie said.

'He was nice and very pleasant to me. I think he likes me,' Sarah said. Trudie started to shake her head.

'Well who doesn't?' she said.

'Don't be like that,' Sarah moaned.

'I don't want to burst your bubble but I think he's got a partner,' Trudie remarked.

'Oh really? Still it might not be a permanent thing,' said an optimistic Sarah.

'You be careful,' Trudie started, 'you shouldn't go looking for trouble.'

'I don't have to look for it,' Sarah replied with a grin, 'it manages to find me!'

'I've noticed that, remember Micky Quinn?' Trudie said, reminding her.

'That's not fair,' Sarah protested, 'I didn't know he was out on bail, did I?'

'Well that's your business,' Trudie said. 'What are you planning on doing this morning? I'm not at work until the afternoon shift. Let's walk into town and get a coffee at DDs.'

'Yep,' Sarah agreed, 'great idea and who knows I might bump into the new guy.'

'I think his name is Archie,' Trudie said.

'That's as good a name as any!' Sarah remarked.

'Well as long as he's got a deep voice and wears trousers, that's usually good enough for you,' Trudie said.

'Trude, please!' was the shocked response from Sarah.

Gary and Brenda had finished breakfast and Brenda was talking on her phone, while Gary was crawling around the floor looking for stray puffs.

'Okay then, we'll see you then Mary. Bye, safe journey,' Brenda said and Gary shouted from the floor,

'Bye Mary!'

'Well that's sorted then,' Brenda said. 'Mary will arrive at Didcot Station at 12:15 tomorrow. She's catching the 7:24 from Huddersfield.'

'That's not bad going considering she's got a couple of changes, York and London,' Gary remarked. 'It amuses me that the timetables are so precise when you know they'll be delayed, nothing runs on time.'

'She's chosen the early train so she gets here in time to do something and not waste the day,' Brenda explained. 'You'll need to get to the station on time to pick her up.'

'Yes, of course,' agreed the reigning puff catching champion. 'And by the way, it's called Didcot Parkway now; it went upmarket years ago!'

'It'll always be plain old Didcot to me,' Brenda said. 'What shall we do with Mary?'

'Stick her over in that corner as an ornament,' Gary joked. 'If anyone asks we can say it's a sculpture of the Huddersfield heroine.'

'Gary!' Brenda sighed. She knew it was a joke as Gary loved his sister and would never do anything to hurt her. 'I don't think she is visiting us to be sat in the corner all day.'

'Fair enough,' Gary replied, 'I've got plenty of puffs.' Brenda looked tense at the mention of puffs.

'I could take her into Oxford sightseeing and shopping,' Brenda announced.

'Stop!' Gary said putting his hand in the air. 'Sightseeing is fine especially the museums with free admission but shopping we can't afford.'

'I'm thinking of your sister's mental health here,' Brenda reminded Gary.

'What about my mental health?' Gary protested, as he could see heavy expenditure ahead. 'I've already developed a twitch thinking about it,' he declared.

'Don't be such a drama queen,' Brenda replied, showing no sympathy at all.

'Do you think she'd like to try fishing? I've never asked her about fishing,' Gary said hopefully. Brenda shook her head and headed for the stairs.

'Right then, I've got to tidy the spare room and make up the bed,' she said. 'A woman's work is never done!'

'More like a woman's purse is never shut!' Gary moaned.

'Has that got some hidden meaning?' Brenda shouted back from half way up the stairs.

'No!' Gary replied.

'Nothing with an Anthony meaning then?' she laughed. Gary got rather agitated by that as he thought Brenda was mentioning Anthony's name too often for his liking.

'How dare you,' he shouted, 'I'm not as crude as Anthony!'

'Okay, don't lose your marbles or should I say pound coins!' Brenda shouted from the top of the stairs.

In town Sarah and Trudie arrived at DDs and were in deep conversation as they entered.

'No, I'm just saying he's not free,' Trudie was announcing.

'How do you know?' Sarah asked. 'He might be there with his sister.'

'That would be weird,' Trudie said.

'No it wouldn't, it proves he's kind and willing to give his sister somewhere to live while she looks for her own place,' Sarah insisted.

'So why then did this sister introduce him to Brenda as her husband, Archie?'

'I didn't know that,' Sarah replied, with the disappointment showing on her face.

'What's this about, or shouldn't I ask?' Dolly enquired.

'Sarah fancies my new neighbour,' Trudie explained.

'Oh I see, and he's married?' Dolly asked. 'Well Sarah, I'd avoid that sort because if they cheat on their wife with you then they'll cheat on you with someone else later.' Trudie smiled but leapt to Archie's defence.

'Poor Archie!' she exclaimed. 'To be fair I don't think he's done anything wrong except in Sarah's imagination. He's guilty of saying *hello* that's all.'

'But it's the way he said, *morning love*, I'm not stupid,' Sarah insisted.

Dolly and Trudie looked at each other and were obviously thinking the same thing.

'Really?' they said together and then both laughed. Sarah stood there looking unhappy.

'Oh dear, well we'll have two coffees please, Dolly,' Trudie requested. 'Do you want a piece of cake, Sarah? Keep your lust fuelled with calories?'

'No thanks. I go to the gym for a reason,' Sarah said, enthusiastically. Trudie paid Dolly and they picked up their coffee and walked to a table. The café door opened and Mark walked in. Trudie and Sarah were in conversation but Sarah was looking on.

'Hello Mark,' said Dolly, 'Is it time for the windows to be cleaned already?'

'Not today Dolly, but it is a month since I cleaned them last so I'll be around on Thursday,' he replied.

'Time flies doesn't it? I can't believe it sometimes,' said Dolly.

'Too true. Could I have a takeout tea, please?' Dolly poured the tea, Mark paid, took it and headed for the door to leave. Dolly called after him.

'Bye, see you Thursday then.'

'Sure will,' he replied. Sarah watched all this.

'Does that bloke clean your windows, Trude?'

'No,' she replied, 'I clean my own but he cleans Brenda's. Yes, he is.'

'Yes, he is what?' Sarah asked.

'Yes, he is single. I'm ahead of you Sarah,' Trudie said, smiling at her boyfriend seeking friend.

'Oh really? He's good looking, isn't he?' Sarah said, enthusiastically. 'Perhaps I should pop in when he's cleaning the windows.'

'What, and offer to hold his shammy for him?' Trudie asked, jokingly.

'I don't know what you mean,' Sarah said.

'You don't know when he's going to clean the windows, do you?' Trudie asked.

'He just told Dolly it'll be Thursday,' Sarah replied.

'So while I was in conversation with you, you weren't listening to me at all?' Trudie moaned. 'You were listening in on Dolly's private conversation!'

'Private? You can't claim to have a private conversation in the middle of DDs. Get real Trude!' came the immediate reply.

'Silly me!' said Trudie. 'Well mine was private enough as nobody was listening to it.'

At 1 o'clock the next day, Brenda was rushing around the house with her duster making final preparations for Mary's visit. She wanted the place to look good as it was the first time Mary had been to their new home. She threw her duster in the cupboard when she heard the front door opening and Gary and Mary walked into the hall.

'Brenda love, we're home,' Gary shouted as they walked through to the lounge. Gary was pulling Mary's suitcase as she followed him.

'Oh Mary, it's lovely to see you,' Brenda said, walking over to embrace her. 'How was your journey?'

'Not bad, thanks,' Mary replied. 'I was telling Gary, I fell asleep for most of the stretch between Huddersfield and York.'

'Best way to tackle a rail journey,' Gary remarked. 'Dream your way through the delays!'

'Come in and sit down!' Brenda said, welcoming Mary. 'We'll get you settled in and then take your things to your room. Gary, make us a coffee! We've got a new packet of Rich Teas in the cupboard!'

'Okay love, I'm on it!' Gary replied, while walking through to the kitchen.

'How are the girls?' Brenda asked.

'They are all doing well,' Mary said, beaming with pride. 'I'm proud of them. I don't know how I managed to bring up two beautiful daughters with one having two grown up girls of her own now.'

'How is Verity?' Brenda enquired. 'Has her broken heart mended?'

'You know, I could have murdered that twit for breaking her heart like that,' Mary confessed, 'but she's fine now and going out with Pablo.' Gary was listening from the kitchen.

'Pablo? So she's over the bicycle then?' Gary shouted, above the sound of water in the kettle about to boil.

'Oh yes, well and truly,' Mary replied. Gary came back into the room carrying a packet of Rich Tea biscuits.

'Gary!' Brenda said sounding alarmed, although doing her best to hide it. 'Get them out of the packet and put them on a plate. I don't know Mary, what's he like? I wouldn't mind but what's he thinking by offering biscuits from the packet in front of mother's photo?'

'Sorry,' Gary said softly, 'but Mary's my sister not Lady Mary Muck!'

'I don't mind, Brenda,' said a smiling Mary.

'I do!' said Brenda. 'Serve them properly when we've got guests.'

'See what I've got to put up with, Sis?' Gary moaned.

'I think you've done very well for yourself so stop complaining,' Mary replied.

'I know I have, there's none better than my lovely Brenda,' he replied. That brought a smile out of Brenda and Gary retreated to the kitchen to plate the biscuits and pour the coffees.

'You must get lonely, Mary,' Brenda continued. 'Is it hard on your own in that flat?'

'Is it still hard on your own getting up to that flat?' Gary shouted, from the kitchen. 'Is the lift working alright now?' Mary started to laugh and winked at Brenda.

'You haven't got any fitter since your visit those few months ago then, little brother?' she said. 'The lift is fine, the flat is fine, I'm fine, honestly. It is lovely to have a break and visit you two though.'

'You are very welcome anytime,' Brenda said and continued, 'We thought this afternoon we'll take you into town for a little walk round and we can go into DDs for tea and cake. You remember Dolly in DDs? You've seen her every time you've visited us.'

'Oh yes, I remember Dolly. The lass from Yorkshire. She knows more about Huddersfield than me and I've lived there for forty-five years now,' Mary replied.

'And maybe tomorrow,' Brenda continued, 'we could go into Oxford and do some sightseeing.' Brenda winked at Mary and silently mouthed the words 'and shopping' so Gary couldn't hear that bit. Mary smiled as Gary walked into the room carrying the coffees.

'But not shopping,' he said, completely unaware of what had just gone on. 'Do you know how much Brenda spent on the outfit for Verity's wedding?'

'Oh dear,' Mary replied.

'Well it . . .' He was about to explain but Brenda interrupted him.

'Mary doesn't want to know about that!' she said. 'Anyway I wore the outfit to the christening so it wasn't a waste.'

'And who knows you might be able to wear it again, if Verity decides to marry Pablo,' Mary said, smiling at Brenda.

'I might need something new by then,' Brenda replied. 'Anyway at some point during your stay we will go shopping, sorry I mean sightseeing!' Both women started to laugh.

'Very good. I wonder why I haven't got a brother to back me up?' Gary moaned.

'Girl power!' Brenda said.

'Wouldn't you like to come fishing with me, Mary?' Gary asked.

'Girl power!' Mary replied.

'Oh shut up and drink your coffee!' Gary said, with a large smile on his face.

At 1:30 Seymour Rise was quiet. There wasn't a soul outside except for Sarah who was walking up and down the road very slowly. Trudie spotted her from her window and opened her door as Sarah was about to pass for the third time.

'What are you doing here today?' she asked Sarah. 'You know I've got work soon, don't you? I'm on the 2 o'clock shift.'

'Yes, no worries,' she replied. 'I'm walking up and down the road slowly, looking casual and hoping I'll see Archie. I think he might come home for lunch.'

'Don't be silly Sarah. Come in a minute,' Trudie said. 'At the moment you look like a burglar who's casing the joint! Are you 42 years old or 16 with a crush?' At that moment Archie's front door opened and he walked outside. He looked across the road at Trudie and stopped as if he couldn't quite place her and yet he was sure he knew her.

'Do I know you?' he shouted across the road.

'I'm your neighbour, although we haven't met yet,' Trudie replied, a little embarrassed at having to raise her voice. Archie still looked puzzled and walked across the road to her.

'No, that's not it,' he said. 'I know you. I'm sure I do.' Sarah was feeling a little aggrieved as she had been completely ignored.

'What about me?' she said. 'Do you know me?' Archie stared at Sarah.

'Should I?' he asked.

'No, not if you know what's good for you,' Trudie said and laughed.

'Shut up Trude!' snapped a jealous Sarah. Archie's expression suddenly changed.

'Trude? Trudie! That's it!' he exclaimed excitedly. 'You are Trudie Miller. We were at school together from infants to leaving secondary.' Now it was Trudie's turn to look puzzled.

'Miller is my maiden name,' she said, 'but I can't remember an Archie at school.' However, the penny had dropped with Sarah and she shouted,

'OMG! It's Archibald Clarke!'

'That's it, that's me, the one and only!' he said, with a broad smile. 'So what's your name, you little beauty?' Sarah was chuffed at receiving this compliment, better late than never.

'I'm Sarah Richardson.'

'Archibald Clarke!' Trudie said, 'I remember you. At infant school you ate all the crayons!'

'Only the red ones, thank you very much,' he said, with a grin.

'Well fancy you moving in here,' Trudie remarked.

'You used to fancy me at secondary school,' Sarah announced.

'Did I? I can't remember that,' Archie replied.

'Not many men she claims fancied her do remember,' Trudie said.

'Trude!' Sarah protested. 'Yes, at school you once bought me a cake from the tuck shop, it was a muffin.'

'Oh yes, was that you?' he asked. 'It's funny how things turn out isn't it? Sorry, I've got to go or I'll be late. It was nice to see you again though.' Archie walked off briskly towards the town centre.

'See you Archie, soon hopefully,' Sarah called after him.

'Sarah, he's married!' Trudie whispered as loudly as she could.

'If you say so,' she replied. 'Did you see that the spark was still there?'

'For me you mean! He didn't know who you were.' Trudie replied.

'He did. He's just playing it cool,' Sarah insisted.

'Well there's cool and there's iceberg, just saying!' Trudie replied.

It was 3 o'clock when Brenda, Gary and Mary entered DDs. Dolly was cleaning a recently vacated table and didn't hear the door or notice them come in.

'Good afternoon, Dolly,' Brenda said. 'I've brought someone to see you.' Dolly looked up and saw Gary behind Brenda.

'Oh, that's nice, hello Gary,' she said. 'Just stay well away from the microwave, there's a love.'

'Am I never going to live that down?' Gary said. Dolly looked up smiling and then noticed Mary.

'Oh, hello stranger!' she said, 'It's a couple of years since I last saw you. I'm so sorry you lost your husband.'

'Hello Dolly,' Mary replied. 'Thank you for your kind words. It's lovely to be down here again. Tell me what does my brother do with microwaves?'

'That's a long story,' said Brenda. 'I'll tell you later, Mary.'

'I'd rather you didn't, love,' Gary pleaded.

'I'm sorry Gary, it's all forgiven and forgotten now,' Dolly said. 'I'm only pulling your leg.'

'Oh please, someone tell me what happened!' Mary pleaded.

'In summary,' Brenda started, 'he took part in a cookery competition, tried to bake his scones in the microwave in which he'd left a spoon, and there was a big bang.' Mary smiled sympathetically at Gary.

'Did you win, Gary?' she asked, bursting into laughter.

'Ah shut up!' Gary replied.

'Well how are you, lass?' Dolly asked Mary.

'I'm great, thank you,' she answered, 'I'm just down for a couple of days, maybe three. It's always nice to stay with these two lovely people. And their new home is great.'

'It's lovely to have you here,' Brenda said. 'Let's have a hot drink and some lovely cake! What does everybody want? Is it tea and chocolate cake all round?'

'Sounds lovely, thanks,' Mary said. Gary nodded in approval, he hadn't spoken much since being embarrassed by the microwave story.

'Well sit down and I'll bring it over,' Dolly said. They moved to a table while Dolly went to prepare a pot of tea and cut the cake. 'So are you staying local and taking in the best Oxfordshire can offer while you are here?' she shouted across the café.

'We are probably going to do a bit of looking around Oxford and . . .' Brenda started but was interrupted by Gary,

'Spending money on shopping!'

'Oh Gary's gone pale!' Dolly joked.

'To be honest I don't mind what I do,' Mary said, 'everything is a welcome change.'

'Fishing then,' Gary said, with a smile.

'Apart from fishing,' she said instantly. 'I'm happy to come in here each day. I love watching the world go by as people come and go.'

'Oh dear, well you won't be able to visit here for two or three days as I'm having to shut,' Dolly said.

'Why is that?' Brenda asked.

'I got a call this morning from my sister in Halifax,' Dolly replied. 'She fell over her cat, landed badly and broke her leg.'

'Ouch, sounds nasty! Is she okay?' Gary enquired.

'Well, she's not out jogging, Gary!' Brenda commented, sarcastically.

'I know that, but is it a bad break?' he asked.

'From what I can gather, she had an op yesterday to insert a pin in the leg,' Dolly explained. 'They won't let her go home until she's got someone there to help her. So Ian's driving me up there tonight. I haven't had time to get cover so I'll just have to close for a couple, maybe three days.'

'Oh dear, still family comes first,' Brenda said.

'Yes,' Dolly continued, 'and my niece has got time off work next week so she will look after her mum then.'

'What about young Jodie who sometimes helps out in here?' Brenda asked. 'Couldn't she help and open up for you?'

'You mean Wat-Eva?' Dolly said. 'That's my nickname for Jodie.'

'Why do you call her that?' Mary asked.

'If you'd ever worked with her you'd know,' Dolly said and smiled. 'She's a good worker but I couldn't leave her in charge on her own.'

'Would you let me run it for you?' asked Mary.

'You?' said a confused Dolly.

'Yes, I used to run the League of Friends Café at Huddersfield General Hospital,' Mary explained. 'I did that for five years as a volunteer. I loved it as I met so many lovely people. I'm sure I could hold the fort for you here, especially if the young girl, Jodie, could lend a hand for a few hours a day.'

'I'd forgotten about you working at the hospital,' Brenda said. 'Are you sure you want to spend your time down here in DDs working?'

'I'd love it!' Mary said, excitedly. 'It'd give me a sense of purpose again and I'd meet people and your friends could let me have all the gossip on you two.'

'Well it'd save me money too; no Brenda shopping equals no money being spent,' Gary gloated. 'And there's no gossip on us!'

'Sorry Brenda,' said Mary, 'I hadn't thought of the shopping.'

'Don't worry Mary, I can spend loads on cake instead,' Brenda said, 'I'll help you in here too, if you do cover for Dolly.'

'Are you sure? That would be great,' said Dolly. 'I don't like to lose business really. It shouldn't be too busy this time of year for you.'

'That's sorted then,' said Mary. 'You just need to run through the till with me so I know how it works. Oh yes, and the security systems so I can open up and lock up.'

'That's brilliant,' Dolly said. 'Thank you. I'll give Wat-Eva a call and ask her to come in for however many hours you'd like her here. She knows the ropes. Oh, that's a weight off my mind.'

'It's a weight off my wallet too,' Gary announced rejoining the conversation.

'Shut up Gary!' said all three women in unison.

Later that evening, Archie and Lily were sitting on their sofa about to relax after a hard day at work.

'You'll never guess who I saw today?' Archie said.

'I think you're right,' Lily replied.

'What's that, princess?' Archie asked.

'I think you are right,' Lily repeated. 'I won't guess unless I'm given a clue.'

'Oh right, you brazil!' he said. 'Yes, umm, someone we were at school with.'

'Yep, think you are going to have to narrow it down a bit more than that Arch!' she said.

'A couple of girls we were at school with.'

'Why don't you just tell me?' Lily pleaded as she was tired of this guessing game.

'What's that, princess?' Archie asked.

'Just tell me who you saw, Arch!' Lily insisted as she was becoming very irritated.

'You can't guess it can you, you brazil!' he said. 'I saw Trudie Miller and Sarah Richardson.'

'Well, I've spotted Trudie through the window, she lives opposite so it's not difficult, now who's the brazil?' Lily questioned.

'Yes, but I hadn't realised she was opposite. Anyway I saw them both this afternoon outside,' Archie said.

'Trudie's okay, but stay away from that Sarah!' Lily said, bluntly.

'Why?' asked Archie.

'Because she's a man-eater,' Lily said, 'but you would be a bit tough to chew by now, I guess.'

'What's that?' Archie asked.

'She fancies herself and doesn't keep boyfriends for long,' Lily replied.

'She reckoned I fancied her at school but I can't really remember her,' he said. 'She said I bought her a muffin from the tuck shop.'

'No, you bought that for Trudie,' Lily said, remembering the event clearly. 'It was Trudie you liked.'

'Yeah, I did, that's right,' he said, 'but that was a long while ago now.'

'Sarah assumed the muffin was for her,' Lily said, 'and took it from you.'

'Is that what happened?' Archie asked. 'She's a silly brazil then, isn't she?'

'Yeah, stay away from her,' Lily warned Archie. 'I've no problem with Trudie, she's okay and has got a really lovely husband too, he's miles better than you.'

'Thanks!' Archie said. 'That's kind of you to say.'

'You know what I mean,' she replied, 'but Sarah's a funny one, so stay clear!'

'You make it sound like she goes around with a net to throw over blokes,' Archie commented.

'I wouldn't put it past her,' Lily said. 'So now we've established who you saw today, what do you fancy watching tonight?'

'What about Naked Attraction?' Archie said.

'No way!' Lily groaned, 'I don't want to see what I'm missing!'

'Thanks again!' Archie replied.

The next morning Brenda and Mary were up nice and early to ensure they were ready to open DDs on time. Although it had been Mary's idea to help out, Brenda was really quite excited by the thought of being on the other side of the counter. They opened DDs at 8 o'clock in time for those wanting an early breakfast. Everything had been running smoothly for over four hours and Jodie (Wat-Eva) had been helping out for about an hour.

'So are you happy to be running a cafe again?' Brenda asked Mary.

'Yes, it's like riding a bike, you don't forget once you've done it before,' Mary replied. 'When you've made one latte, you've made them all!'

'How have you found Jodie?' Brenda asked.

'I know she's only been here an hour but she seems fine to me,' Mary replied.

'Why do you think Dolly calls her Wat-Eva?' Brenda enquired.

'No idea,' Mary replied, 'but she's a good little worker.' At this point Mary called over to Jodie.

'When you've finished washing those tables could you refresh the cutlery in the trays please, Jodie?' she requested.

'Okay Mary, whatever,' Jodie replied.

'And the napkins, please?'

'Whatever,' Jodie said. Brenda and Mary looked at each other and smiled as the penny dropped.

'Oh that's Wat-Eva! Got it!' Brenda said. Just then the door opened and in walked Trudie and Sarah.

'Hi Brenda,' Sarah started, 'what are you doing behind the counter? Where's Dolly?'

'She's had to go away on a family emergency so Mary, Gary's sister, is looking after the place and I'm helping. Mary, this is Sarah and this is Trudie,' Brenda explained.

'I'm pleased to meet you both,' said Mary.

'Trudie lives next door to us,' Brenda said.

'I'm pleased to meet you, Mary,' Trudie said.

'Yes, I'm pleased you're keeping the cafe going,' Sarah chipped in.

'What can I get you girls?' asked Mary.

'It's a long time since I've been called a girl so thank you for that,' Trudie said.

'You are about the same age as my daughters so you're girls to me,' Mary explained.

'Well, I'll have a tall dark, rich, handsome stranger please?' Sarah joked.

'Let me think,' Mary said, 'where did Dolly say she kept those?' She looked across the café at Wat-Eva who was filling the cutlery trays and called out to her, 'Hey Jodie, do we have tall, dark, rich, handsome and, most importantly, kind men on the menu?' Jodie looked puzzled.

'What?' she asked.

'Don't worry, Jodie,' Mary continued, 'I doubt if Sarah could eat a whole one anyway.'

'Whatever!' came the reply from Jodie, which made Brenda laugh.

'Okay then,' Trudie said, 'we'll have two hot chocolates, please. We won't have cake yet as we'll save it for our second hot drink.'

'Lovely,' said Mary, 'you go and sit yourselves down and I'll bring your drinks over.' Trudie and Sarah walked to a table and sat down just as Archie walked through the door. He looked a little flustered as he was in a hurry to get back to work.

'Hello Archie,' said Brenda, 'are you settling into number 18 okay?'

'Yeah, all lovely ta, Brend!' he replied. Brenda didn't mind her name being abbreviated because Brend was at least a form of Brenda!

'Hey Archie!' said Sarah, whose day had now improved. 'Would you like to buy us a cake for old times' sake, you know like the Tuck Shop muffin?'

'You are a cheeky madam,' he replied. 'Okay ladies what cake do you want?'

'I'm fine without, thank you,' Trudie replied. She was rather embarrassed by her forthright friend but that friend hadn't finished.

'We'll both have a piece of sticky chocolate cake,' she said.

'Sarah!' Trudie exclaimed, feeling put out at having her decision to decline cake overridden so rudely.

'I'll have a tea for me to go please and two pieces of the cake they just mentioned,' Archie requested. He had only just finished registering his request when Sarah started issuing orders again.

'See if they've got any red velvet cake for you,' she joked, 'to remind you of the red crayons you used to eat.'

'Very funny,' Archie replied. Mary passed the take-out tea to Archie while Brenda handed over two plates containing the slices of cake. Archie paid and carried the cake to Sarah and Trudie's table. He put it down and was about to leave.

'Thank you, handsome,' Sarah said. 'Now sit down a minute.' Archie pulled out the chair and sat between the two ladies, looking at his watch as he did. Trudie was getting more embarrassed by Sarah's behaviour every second. Even Mary, who'd only known

Sarah for five minutes, was beginning to think that perhaps she was wrong and Sarah could manage to eat a whole man after all.

At this time Lily was walking through the town on her way to the bank in her work break. She walked past DDs and looking through the window, she noticed Archie and the women sitting at the table. She was furious. She walked inside trying to hide her anger, but she couldn't.

'Hello Lily,' Brenda said, 'how are . . .' But before Brenda could finish Lily marched straight past the counter and over to Archie.

'What do you think you are doing? After all I told you yesterday!' she screamed at Archie. The anger in her voice was so great it was amazing that smoke wasn't coming out of her ears. Archie didn't have time to reply before Sarah shouted back,

'He's having a drink with us and kindly bought us cake. Is there a problem?'

'Yes, he's my husband and I know your game Sarah Richardson,' she roared. 'You don't change, do you? He's not interested in you and never has been!' Archie was embarrassed and could feel his face turning red. Trudie just wanted the ground to open up and swallow her. Of course Sarah hadn't finished, she was ready for battle.

'Oh yes?' she cried. 'And how would you know? He bought me a cake when I was fifteen and he's bought me another piece now!'

'He didn't buy you a cake at school,' Lily replied. 'He bought it for Trudie but you ambushed him and you haven't stopped ambushing men ever since, have you!' She was happy to make that a point rather than a question. Brenda, Mary and Jodie plus the customers at the other tables looked on in astonishment. It was hard to take in what was actually occurring and Lily hadn't finished.

'Still never mind,' she said, 'have this chocolate cake now in its place.' She took the plate holding the piece of chocolate cake from in front of Sarah and rubbed it in Sarah's face. Sarah pulled her head back, her face was covered in sticky chocolate cake.

'You are a nutter!' Sarah screamed. 'Here, Trudie didn't really want hers, you have it!' She picked up Trudie's plate and pressed the chocolate cake into Lily's face.

'Ladies please!' shouted Mary, who had been entertained enough for now and was thinking of the mess this was making on the floor.

'Stop it, Sarah!' Brenda said, her voiced raised. 'What are you doing?'

'She started it,' Sarah protested. 'At least you weren't offended when you found out your Gary fancied me!' Brenda rolled her eyes in disbelief that Sarah still thought Gary had fancied her.

'You were right,' Brenda said turning to Mary, 'when you called them girls!'

'Please don't include me in this, Brenda,' Trudie begged. 'I don't want anything to do with it. My God, it's like being back at school in the playground.' Trudie picked up her handbag and left the table to stand with Brenda and Mary at the counter.

'But we aren't in a playground,' Brenda observed. 'We are inside a café. You are making an almighty mess and an even bigger show of yourselves.'

'Lily, princess, I only bought them cake,' came this little voice from Archie's mouth. He felt like he'd been through three rounds with Tyson Fury although he'd only witnessed the events.

'Why?' she asked Archie, her voiced muffled by the napkin she was using to wipe her face, 'Why? Is it someone's birthday?'

'What's that, princess?' he asked, 'I can't hear you through the cake on your face. Try to eat as much as you can as it wasn't cheap!' With that Lily saw red again.

'Don't you princess me!' she boomed. 'Get out and back to work now!' They both left with Archie addressing Brenda as he walked past the counter,

'Does this mean I'm barred?' Lily was still shouting at him as they walked in the street. The café door opened again almost immediately after they had left and in walked Mark carrying a bucket which he hoped to get filled with water.

'Hi Brenda,' he started, oblivious to what had just happened. 'I told Dolly I'd be cleaning the windows today. Could I have some ...' He stopped mid-sentence as he noticed the mess on the table and floor. Sarah was staring at him, her face still covered in chocolate cake.

'Hi Mark,' she said, as seductively as she could for someone covered in chocolate cake. Mark averted his stare immediately by looking back at Brenda, with fear in his eyes.

'Don't ask Mark, just don't ask!' Brenda pleaded. The door opened again and in walked Steve. Now Steve being Steve, (TAS remember), didn't see anything amiss.

'Hi Sarah, love,' he shouted across to the love of his life, 'enjoying some cake, are we?'

'Get out Steve and leave me alone!' Sarah replied, in a less than friendly way. Steve's expression changed from happy to upset in a split second. Everybody who witnessed this, apart from Sarah of course, couldn't help but feel sorry for him.

'Right you are,' he said quietly and quickly left followed very closely by Mark. Mark's passing words as he fled were,

'Tell Dolly I will clean the windows next week when the vampire cake-eater has gone.'

'And to think, Sarah,' Trudie remarked, 'you said you were embarrassed by Steve's behaviour at Le Petale de Lys.'

Everything finally settled down after Sarah had left in disgrace. Trudie stayed behind to help clear up the mess although Brenda and Mary didn't blame her in any way for what had happened. By closing time at 4 o'clock everyone, including Wat-Eva, was laughing about it. Mary was relieved that none of the plates had been broken.

Later that evening Brenda discovered a bunch of flowers on her front doorstep. They had been left by Sarah with an apology written in an accompanying card. As she took them in, Brenda looked to her right and saw an identical bunch on Trudie's doorstep. Not surprisingly, she couldn't see any left over the road for Lily. Considering the amount of time Sarah spent at Trudie's home it was going to be very hard for her to avoid Lily in future. Oh dear, what a mess! On a bright note the following two days in DDs went by without incident and Mary enjoyed meeting Dolly's customers. Many came in for one cup of hot drink that they made last an hour. They wanted company really and to chat to Dolly. They were pleased to see a new friendly face in Mary and share their stories. When Dolly returned she was happy as the takings had gone up. Mary joked with Brenda that they'd sold a lot of cake on the first day they were in charge. Dolly of course, didn't understand the joke at that time but soon learnt what it was about from others who had witnessed 'The Battle of Archie 2024'. Dolly did wonder if she'd ever see TAS or Mark again!

Mary's stay with her sister-in-law and little brother soon came to an end. She had stayed four nights and managed to fit in a visit to Oxford, a city full of history and beautiful architecture. This included a look around her favourite museum, the Ashmolean. That was her seventh visit to the museum in the last ten years, but Gary was really happy as admission is free. What he didn't know was both Mary and Brenda left £20 donations in the collection box upon leaving. Well, what he didn't know wouldn't hurt him! On Mary's departure day, Gary drove her to Didcot Parkway Station with Brenda also coming along for the ride and send off. Once at Didcot, Gary waited in the car as Brenda walked towards the station with Mary. Before Brenda could leave Mary turned to her.

'Oh Brenda,' she started, 'I probably shouldn't ask but now I've got you on your own I have to. It will worry me if I don't.'

'Mary, what is it?' Brenda asked. She was becoming concerned.

'What that Sarah said in the café,' Mary continued, 'about her and Gary, that wasn't true was it?' Brenda was so relieved that Mary wasn't about to announce something serious that she burst out laughing.

'Oh no, Mary,' she laughed, 'it was all in Sarah's imagination. In fact it became quite an issue for poor Gary and he dreaded going into work.'

'What a relief!' Mary said. 'If you are sure then that's good.'

'I'm one hundred percent sure,' Brenda said. 'I moan about Gary a lot, probably too much really, but he is the most faithful man around. He'd never cheat on me.' Mary smiled, hugged Brenda goodbye and carried on into the station. Brenda walked back to the car.

'What took so long?' Gary moaned. 'I've had to pay for one hour of parking!' Brenda smiled, leant over and kissed his cheek. 'What's that for?' he asked, 'And you mind my headlamps!' he continued and grinned.

'Oh Gary, you idiot,' she said smiling, 'you're my lovely idiot!'

'Thank you,' Gary replied. He wasn't sure what was happening so just lapped up the praise. The three mile drive home was fine, not a Roadeteer in sight. Back home they closed their front door behind them and headed for the sofa to relax.

'She'll ring us as soon as she's back,' Brenda said. 'It was so nice to have her here for a few days, wasn't it?'

'Yes, it was,' Gary replied. 'She's a funny one though. Who travels two hundred miles for a holiday running a café?'

'She loved it,' Brenda said, 'even the cake fighting on the first day! She felt useful with a purpose again. She adored meeting and chatting with everyone. It's a shame she didn't want to stay a couple more days. I enjoyed her company.'

'Oh, four nights is long enough for me,' Gary remarked, 'there's only so much girl power a chap can take!'

That night Gary and Brenda were lying in the darkness when Gary's voice broke the silence.

'It feels strange with the spare room being spare again,' he said.

'Yes it does, but it's called the guest room,' Brenda said, by now half asleep. 'I miss Mary already.'

'Don't worry,' Gary announced, putting the bedside lamp on. 'I brought something upstairs to help me remember her and entertain you.'

'Oh what is it now, Gary?' Brenda moaned, in a weak tired voice. Gary leant out of bed and picked up a bowl containing puffs. He sat up holding the bowl.

'Here we go,' he announced excitedly. 'I never had time to play it with Mary. Go on love, have a go!' He started throwing puffs into the air and attempting to catch them in his mouth. They were going everywhere and Brenda woke up properly with a start.

'Gary! Stop it,' she requested firmly. 'They are going under the duvet. Right that's it!'

'That's what, love?' Gary asked.

'The guest room is no longer spare!' she announced. 'You are sleeping in there tonight. Off you go!' She pushed him firmly out of bed.

'Oh puff it!' he said, 'can't you just belt me with your pillow and forget about it?'

'No, just puff off!' she shouted.

Chapter Twelve

December
Waddle I do if I lose you?

The final month of the year had arrived. It seemed like the weather came in two varieties, either wet and mild or dry and cold. Brenda preferred the latter. She loved to go for a walk early on a bright frosty morning with the hard white fields glistening in the sunlight. When she breathed her exhaled misty white breath would lead the way before her. Gary, on the other hand preferred the milder wet days, as the heating bills were lower and he had more success fishing in damp conditions.

At 8 o'clock on the evening of Tuesday 10th December, a meeting of the WI was coming to an end. The visiting speaker was about to leave and was gathering up his papers.

'Thank you Marcus, that was most interesting,' Susan said. 'I've always wondered about the workings of a nuclear power station.'

'My pleasure Susan, and ladies,' Marcus replied and left the hall. The women who had tried to listen were Vera, Violet, Jane, Dolly, Mandy, Marianne, Lucy, Sarah and Brenda. They were now looking bored and restless. Amy, also present, wasn't paying attention at all but was listening via earphones to music on her phone.

'It might have been his pleasure but it wasn't mine,' Vera said, as she watched Marcus leave. 'What were you thinking of Susan, getting a speaker to talk about a nuclear power station?'

'I'm sorry but he was all I could get,' Susan said. 'The speaker I had planned pulled out at short notice. What could I do?'

'I came today expecting a talk on how to get the most out of using seeds in bread making,' Violet moaned, 'but instead I got a talk on nuclear power.' Jane found that amusing and chuckled to herself.

'Hey Violet, from big bun to big bang!' she said.

'You can say that again,' Violet replied. 'It's all, when the wind blows stuff!'

'Well,' said Vera, 'too many seeds in your bread would give you wind.' The women smiled at this, they were grateful for some light entertainment.

'Sorry Violet,' Susan said, 'but I did send a text around explaining the change of speaker. I think it is good to get a cross section of speakers and I certainly learnt something today.'

'Yes, so did I,' Dolly sighed, 'and that is to always read your text messages before attending WI meetings!' Suddenly Amy started to sing out loud. She was still listening via her headphones and in a world of her own, totally engrossed in her music.

'Please, please, please don't prove them right,' she sang, 'and please, please, please, don't bring me to tears when . . .' Suddenly she opened her eyes and stopped singing as she remembered where she was. She pulled out her headphones. 'Oh sorry,' she said. 'I forgot I was here. Has Nuclear Man gone then?'

'Who were you listening to?' Mandy asked, 'Atomic Kitten?'

'Nice one!' Amy laughed.

'I was intrigued by the subject matter,' admitted Brenda, 'but once he started to talk it all went over my head!'

'That's a nuclear flyby!' said Vera, smiling.

'Well I'm sure you weren't the only one who got lost in the science,' said Violet, reassuringly. 'I bet none of us here could repeat anything he said.' But, of course Violet was wrong as Lucy was present.

'Heat is produced during atomic fission to boil water and produce pressurised steam,' Lucy stated confidently. 'The steam is routed through the reactor steam system to spin large turbine blades that drive magnetic generators to produce electricity. Simple really.'

'I was about to say that!' said Vera, trying hard not to laugh.

'I'm pleased you were listening, Lucy,' Susan said. 'I don't feel so bad now.'

'I enjoyed it, Susan,' Lucy continued, 'especially learning about atomic fission.'

'I've no idea if what you said made sense or not, but well done, whatever tommy vision is,' said Vera.

'No, it's atomic fission, Vera,' Lucy said, correcting Vera in her school teacher voice. Brenda thought that Lucy was probably how Aggie was twenty-five years ago. 'It's a reaction in which the nucleus of an atom splits into two or . . .' Before she could go any further Vera interrupted by singing the song Amy had been singing earlier.

'Please, please, please . . stop!' she sang. The women smiled as Lucy wasn't the most popular member of the group.

'Yes, I agree,' added Violet. 'You can keep saying it but I won't understand it.' Sarah started yawning, making no attempt to hide her boredom.

'Sorry, I'm fed up,' she admitted. 'When are we going to get a speaker on horoscopes like Amy and Marianne requested ages ago?'

'Oh yes!' said an excited Marianne. 'Someone who'd know the consequences of moons rising and so on.'

'I'm lost again, already,' admitted Vera, 'but mooning doesn't sound very polite to me.' Susan smiled as she was pleased the women were able to laugh amongst themselves about the situation. She felt less guilty. Also, Lucy had raised her spirits by demonstrating her understanding of the talk.

'It's not easy to find speakers,' Susan said. 'I could give you a talk on my experiences as a magistrate, if you are interested?'

'That could only be interesting if you give us details of who's been naughty and how you punished them,' Mandy said, 'with lots of names we can gossip about!'

'Some of that is confidential,' Susan went on, 'so I couldn't do that unless it's already in the public domain.'

'Boring!' shouted Vera. 'Do you put people in the stocks?'

'Of course we don't!' Susan replied.

'Do you whip people in public then?' Vera continued.

'No!' Susan replied, getting a little annoyed by Vera's stupid questioning.

'Some might enjoy being whipped,' Sarah observed, 'so it wouldn't be a punishment then.' Susan thought she ought to change the subject quickly as she feared where Sarah might be going with this.

'What about within our families?' Susan asked. 'Haven't we got anyone with special skills or hobbies who would like to talk to us? How about your Syd, Vera?'

'You must be joking,' Vera said, trying not to laugh. 'He'd be able to share his skills on the best position to sleep in to achieve the loudest snore. That's about it!'

'Couldn't you get Santa to pay us a visit and talk about his life in the North Pole as we are close to Christmas?' Amy asked.

'I expect she's asked him and he said we've been bad girls so he's not coming,' Sarah replied. Brenda glared at Sarah remembering the Battle of Archie 2024 in DDs; well if the cap fits and all that!

'Lucy, you and Jake both teach little ones,' Susan started, 'do you have any teaching experiences you can talk about?'

'Sorry Susan, but we are too busy to do this justice,' Lucy replied. Vera couldn't let this go as Lucy was always boasting about her job, her husband . . . atomic fission. She was just irritating.

'Too busy?' she questioned 'With all those school holidays? Whatever you say!'

'Oh, let's keep this civil, Vera,' Susan said intervening as she didn't want the start of a war in the hall, with or without nuclear weapons. 'Brenda,' she continued, 'what about Gary?'

'Yes, he's civil most of the time!' she replied, with a smile.

'But he's terrible at cooking scones!' Lucy said, demonstrating just why she was so unpopular.

'As Susan said, let's keep it civil,' Brenda replied. 'Susan, Gary's hobbies are bowling and fishing, so need I say more?'

'And we're not getting involved with bowling again after that disastrous open evening,' Amy said, pausing for a couple of seconds before adding, 'actually I think I'm barred from Wancott Bowling Club.'

'It wasn't a disastrous evening for all of us,' Jane remarked, 'as I'm now a member of the Wancott Bowling Club.'

'Good for you,' said Sarah, 'but I think I'd rather be whipped.'

'Kinky!' said Marianne.

'Let's go fishing with Gary!' Vera suddenly stated.

'Christ, you're kinky too Vera!' said Marianne. Vera winked back at her.

'Honestly, I wouldn't be able to persuade him to give a talk,' Brenda said. 'He worries too much and I'm frightened it might finish him off.'

'He doesn't have to give a talk so much as a demonstration,' Susan said, trying to reassure Brenda. 'He'd just talk to us about fishing and show us what he does.'

'Fishing though, are you serious?' Marianne asked. 'No offence to Gary but I'm not sure I'd be interested in standing on a cold riverbank watching fishing.'

'On the contrary,' Jane said. 'It would be more interesting outside by the river. We could go one Saturday afternoon at about 3:30 as it starts to get dark by then. Gary could show us what you do, casting out or whatever it is and show us his rod and tackle.' The last bit of the sentence brought a laugh from the younger members, excluding Lucy of course.

'Brenda,' Amy started to ask, 'don't you mind us looking at your hubby's rod and tackle?'

'Really, Amy?' said Brenda. In her mind she had already made allowances for her being just 19 years old so wouldn't make a big fuss.

'He's probably not got a lot of tackle,' Marianne added with a giggle. She is in her mid-20s and should have known better!

'You two!' said Brenda, with a smile. 'You'll get on well with Gary as you've got the same childish and smutty sense of humour.'

'Do you think he'd be up for it?' asked Susan. The others started laughing again. 'Up for giving a demonstration!' she continued. She was getting a little excited that she might have found someone to talk to the members.

'I'm not sure, Susan,' Brenda replied. 'He hasn't forgiven me for getting him involved in the cookery contest yet.'

'Neither have I!' said Dolly. She was, of course, joking.

'I'll go to see his demonstration, if he will Brenda,' said Mandy. 'We'll be out in the fresh air for about thirty minutes max, I reckon. Afterwards we could all go for a drink in the pub and buy Gary one for his time.' The others nodded in agreement. As the next meeting date fell on a Saturday and most weren't working, they had little excuse not to attend. Even Dolly agreed to ask Wat-Eva to cover from 3 to 4 o'clock in DDs so she could join the women. Now it all depended on Brenda persuading Gary to be free and willing on Saturday 21st December.

'Will you ask him, please Brenda?' Susan asked, almost begging.

'Tell him to get his tackle out and show the ladies how it's done,' Amy laughed.

'Oh shut up, Amy!' Brenda replied, quite abruptly.

Brenda left the hall that evening feeling anxious. She knew it would help Susan if she could persuade Gary to give this demonstration but she didn't really want to burden him again. Once inside her home she told Gary about what had been proposed.

'I don't think that's a very good idea, love,' he said.

'Why?' asked Brenda. 'It's a bit sexist if you don't think women can make good fishermen, err, fisherwomen, err, fisherpersons!' Gary smiled at Brenda's attempt to describe a woman who goes fishing.

'I don't think they wouldn't make good fisherpersons, love,' he said. 'It's just I'm not a very good speaker.'

'But you are always fishing with your mates so you must know something about it,' Brenda replied.

'Of course but I'm not a professional,' he said. 'Our fishing trips are more of a social gathering than anything.'

'You mean they are an excuse to sit around moaning about everything and then go for a drink in the pub?' Brenda said, making a point.

'You got it!' Gary replied, making no attempt to challenge what she'd said.

'Well, that's sort of what we want you to do now,' she continued. 'You can demonstrate what you have to do by the river and let them have a go with your rod.' Gary's face lit up exactly as Brenda was expecting. 'No more innuendo please!' Brenda pleaded, 'I'm sick of hearing about your rod.' Gary stopped smiling. 'And then you can answer any questions and come with us to the pub for a quick drink,' she continued.

'What questions?' Gary asked, nervously.

'When will the earth end?' Brenda joked.

'I don't know the answer to that, does anyone?' he said.

'For goodness sake Gary, it would be questions about fishing, wouldn't it?' she insisted. 'Please, pretty please, love. The WI has been let down by several speakers and we are desperate or we wouldn't ask you.'

'Charming! Anyway, I'm not sure I could cope with a load of desperate women. They might be after my body,' Gary joked.

'Not that desperate!' Brenda replied.

'Charming, again! I don't know, the things I do for you!' he said, giving in.

'So you will?' Brenda said, excitedly.

'Okay, but the demonstration isn't going to last long as there's not much to show.'

'Yes, but enough about you,' Brenda joked, 'what about the fishing?'

'Now who's being silly?' Gary asked.

'I love you,' Brenda sighed, 'I'll let Susan know.'

'Do you think she's interested in you loving me?'

The following morning Dolly was back at her post in DDs and the Roadeteers were sitting at a table drinking coffee on their morning break. They often had their breaks in DDs during the winter as the weather was too chilly for sitting in their van.

'I'm in trouble with the missus,' said Frank. 'Remind me to pick up some Maltesers or something from town before we go home. She likes them.'

'Last of the big spenders!' said Steve. 'A bag of Maltesers! I wish that'd work for me with Sarah.'

'Okay, okay, I'll look for a box,' Frank grumbled, 'there may be some in the shops now, ready for Christmas.'

'Perhaps you should limit your rows to Christmas time,' Doug suggested.

'Oh no, mate,' Frank replied, 'they seem worse at Christmas. If I can't get a box then a bag will have to do.' The men sat quietly for a couple of minutes thinking of Maltesers. Then Doug became curious.

'What have you done wrong then?' he asked.

'It was a silly mistake that a lot of men make,' Frank said, starting to explain. 'I should have been concentrating a bit harder and it would have cut out all this hassle.'

'What was that then?' asked Steve.

'We were going out for the evening,' Frank said, attempting to explain, 'and she asked me which of two dresses I thought looked best as she couldn't decide what to wear. I chose and she went proper mad.'

'Why?' said a confused Steve. 'Did she prefer the other one, like?'

'I think I was a bit quick in choosing,' Frank confessed, 'she hadn't actually changed and was still wearing her apron. It's a bloody nice apron though.'

'Oh bugger!' Doug said sympathetically 'You're proper in the shite house then!'

'Anyway, she took the apron off and threw it at me and sulked all evening,' Frank explained. 'She was still in a strop when she got home and still off with me this morning.'

'Why are women so difficult, hey?' Doug pondered. 'We never ask them an opinion on what we should wear, do we?'

'No, but they'll always give it all the same!' Frank replied.

'True, so chocolate then!' Doug said.

'Right you are!'

As the Roadeteers were pondering on how to negotiate a peace treaty with a woman, David and Joshua walked in and continued up to the empty counter waiting for Dolly to appear.

'So your degree is going well then?' David asked Joshua.

'Yes thanks,' he replied. 'The hardest part was collecting data, like the surveys. Thanks for helping me out there.'

'That was nothing,' said David. 'I only answered a couple of questions for you. Mind you your survey got Gary into a lot of hot water with Brenda.' Joshua immediately looked uneasy, it was like a flash back to that beautiful hot summer's day when it went wrong.

'Don't!' Joshua begged. 'I didn't know what to do when she started throwing tomatoes at him. So I did what most men would do and ran for it.'

'You've common sense as well as brains,' David laughed. 'A man of wisdom.'

'Well, it's gained knowledge rather than wisdom,' Joshua responded.

'What's the difference?' asked David.

'Knowledge is knowing something but wisdom is knowing what to do with it,' Joshua replied. 'For example, knowledge is knowing a pepper is a fruit but wisdom is knowing not to put it in your fruit salad.' David smiled.

'I see what you mean,' he said. 'A bit like Gary knowing a tomato is a fruit but having the wisdom to realise that if you upset Brenda it can be transformed into a weapon.' Dolly then entered the café through the kitchen.

'Sorry to keep you waiting gents, what can I get you?' she asked.

'What can I buy you as a thank you for your past help?' Joshua asked David.

'That's very kind of you,' David replied. 'I'll have a large brandy, please.'

'Nice try!' said Dolly.

'A black coffee then, please.'

'And a latte for me please,' Joshua requested. 'Can we have them to go please? I've got to meet friends soon in town.' He paused for a second looking around, 'It's nice in here isn't it?' he said, 'I don't think I've been in here before.'

'Thank you, we do our best,' Dolly said, proudly.

'Trude visits here, usually with her mate Sarah,' David said. 'They are always in here.'

'Yes, they are two of my best customers,' Dolly remarked, 'though not always without incident but, to be fair, that is due to Sarah rather than Trudie.'

'Ever thought of issuing loyalty cards?' David asked, hopefully.

'Now let me think, let me think, let me think, No!' she replied, with a smile.

'To be honest,' David continued, 'I don't think that pair increase your profits by much. They can talk for England when they get going and a coffee and cake will last a couple of hours.'

'I suppose that means..' Joshua hesitated and then continued addressing Dolly, 'sorry I don't know your name,'

'I'm Dolly,' she informed him.

'I suppose that means that you, Dolly, make them feel welcome and comfortable.'

'I've known them for a while,' Dolly replied, 'and *he-fancies-me-*Sarah is at the WI with me. So they are friends first and customers second.'

'That's nice,' David said. 'This is Joshua by the way.' Joshua cringed at this introduction and said,

'Oh, please call me Josh, only my Mum calls me Joshua.'

'Josh,' David said, deliberately emphasising the shortened name, 'lives two doors down from us in Seymour Rise, he and Kristian are next to Gary and Brenda.'

'Hopefully I'll see more of you in here then,' Dolly said.

'That would be good,' Joshua continued. 'Do you allow dogs inside?' Before Dolly could answer David butted in with,

'Well they allow Gary in!'

'You!' Dolly said, as a partial rebuke. 'Yes, well behaved ones on leads.'

'That's how Brenda brings Gary in,' remarked David, who couldn't resist another joke. There were smiles all round as Joshua paid Dolly and the two prepared to leave with their drinks.

'Nice to see you both,' said Dolly. 'I hope to see you again soon.' On the way out they met Kai at the door. He was walking in carrying a bundle of post for Dolly.

'David!' Kai said, to stop him passing, 'There's no one in at yours so I've left a parcel for you with Glenda Brenda.' David looked amused.

'Brenda?' David asked.

'Yeah sorry, Brenda,' Kai replied. 'My Izzy calls her Glenda and she won't change that now so I call her by both names to avoid confusion.' David looked confused.

'Right,' he said.

'She's our little one's god mum too!' Kai said.

'That's going to be a bit confusing for her when she starts to talk,' David said.

'Oh, Glenda Brenda's already talking,' Kai laughed, pleased with himself about his joke. He told a lot of jokes when outside his home as there was no point telling jokes to his partner.

'Good one!' David replied, making the joke so worthwhile in Kai's eyes. Kai carried on in to DDs and passed the bundle of post to Dolly.

'Thanks Kai,' she said and she started to glance through the letters.

'No problem,' Kai replied, 'Hey Dolly, that young chap with David, is that one of the guys from next door to Glenda Brenda?'

'It seems so, he's called Josh,' she replied.

'I thought I'd seen him there but wasn't sure,' Kai continued. 'They've got a huge German Shepherd dog called Satan.'

'That's an odd name, doesn't give it a warm appeal, does it?' Dolly said. 'Are you sure it's called that?'

'Oh yes,' he said, looking haunted by a memory, 'they were screaming *Satan leave him!* as it chased me from their front door. I nearly wet myself!'

'I don't like the sound of that,' Dolly said, looking worried. 'Josh asked me if we allowed dogs in here.'

'It's probably great with the normal public, just doesn't like posties!' he noted, 'Glenda Brenda dotes on it and it's great with her. If it does come in here forget fish fingers, I reckon its favourite are postie fingers!' They laughed at yet another joke from Kai.

At 1 o'clock Gary walked into his lounge where he found Brenda sitting on the sofa reading a book.

'Look who I found loitering outside!' he said. Brenda looked up to see Anthony standing next to him.

'I was visiting a friend in Turnpike Road,' Anthony started to explain, 'so thought I'd pop in and check Gary's still alright for our fishing trip next Sunday.'

'Looking forward to it,' Gary said, 'but you could have phoned and saved yourself the detour.' Anthony looked over at Brenda on the sofa and gave her a smile.

'But then,' he said, 'I wouldn't have seen your gorgeous Brenda, would I? How are you, my lovely?'

'I'm great thanks, Anthony.' Brenda replied.

'I can see that!' he said, flirting with her. Gary was already getting jealous and annoyed in equal measure.

'Hey, that's my wife,' he said. 'Cut that out!'

'Oh Gary, don't rise to it!' Brenda said. 'He stands as much chance with me as a bacon sandwich has of being eaten by a rabbi.' Anthony smiled at her again.

'I know some Jewish friends who stray occasionally and eat a bacon butty. Would you stray with me, Brenda?' he asked defiantly.

'You can stop that stupid talk!' Gary warned him. Brenda looked at Anthony and said,

'You have as much chance of success with me as you have finding a King Penguin living in our fridge. Do you want to check our fridge for any penguins?' Gary sneered at Anthony after hearing Brenda's words.

'I'm only pulling your leg!' Anthony insisted. 'You are so easy to wind up Gary! Right I'll get off but see you soon for fishing. I'll see myself out. Nice to see you, Brenda!'

'Bye,' Brenda said followed by, 'go stick your head down the loo,' once the front door had slammed.

'He's nuts!' Gary said, 'I was cleaning the car and he suddenly appeared. Anyway I'd better finish the car.' Gary left Brenda to continue reading her book.

By 2 o'clock he had almost completed washing the car, there was just a small amount of polishing to do. Aggie was walking back along the Rise towards her house.

'Hello Gary, how are you?' she asked, making Gary jump and he almost knocked over his bucket of water. 'Sorry,' she said, 'I didn't mean to make you jump!'

'Sorry Aggie,' he replied, 'I didn't see you coming.'

'Obviously not, or you would have run indoors quickly,' she said laughing. Gary felt bad hearing that. Was he really that rude, after all she was only a woman who lived over the road?

'Really, I'm sorry, am I obviously that rude towards you?' he said. 'I'm sorry Aggie.'

'Don't be silly, I understand,' she replied. 'I brought it on myself always going on about AmDram. Apart from those in the group, most people run away from me.'

'That's sad though,' he said. 'I'll be kinder in future.'

'Well there's nothing to fear now,' she continued.

'Have you given up AmDram?' Gary asked, hopefully.

'Good Heavens, no,' was the reply, 'I live for my productions! But I won't pester you anymore. You are safe as I accept acting isn't for everyone.'

'Actually you may be able to give me some tips on public speaking,' Gary said. 'Well it's not really public speaking as it's only to a handful of WI members but . . .' Before he could go on Aggie interrupted him,

'That's still public speaking, Gary,' she boomed back to normal Aggie school mistress volume. 'You are addressing members of the public and you'll look silly if you get it all wrong.' Gary started to panic. He wondered why he had allowed himself to get talked into this. 'If those words won't come out right,' she continued, 'then you'll feel stupid with everyone looking at you.' Gary began to feel sick as she continued, 'Everyone hanging on your next word which won't come out right.' All the blood was draining from Gary's face and he turned very pale. He suddenly felt an urgent need to use the toilet.

'Thanks Aggie,' he said, 'must dash, err, I left something on.' Gary ran towards his front door with Aggie calling behind him,

'Let me know if you need any advice.' Mark had just come around from the back of Gary's house to start to clean the front windows and watched Gary run by him.

'Are you okay, mate?' Mark asked.

'He's left something on,' Aggie informed him.

'What's he left on?' Mark asked. 'Is it his stomach on the deck of a ship on the high seas, perhaps?'

Brenda managed to calm Gary down by pointing out he was not going to give a talk so much as demonstrate his skills. She reminded him that he had nothing to fear from the WI members except for Amy, Sarah and Marianne and perhaps Lucy . . . perhaps she should have kept quiet as she wasn't helping really. The Saturday arrived and the day was passing by too quickly for Gary's liking; before he knew it he was standing in front of the WI members on the riverbank.

'Thank you for talking to us this evening, Gary,' Susan started. 'I understand that you are a bit nervous.'

'How can you tell?' he asked.

'Probably because you've had to go behind the bush for a pee three times already,' Amy piped up.

'Oh,' Gary replied, slightly embarrassed.

'Please don't be nervous,' said Susan, 'we'll keep this informal, it's just a chat amongst friends. Nothing to worry about.'

'Right,' Gary replied nervously, followed by a short silence when everyone stood around staring at each other.

'Okay then,' Susan said reassuringly, 'off you go.'

'Right then,' Gary started, 'hello everyone. Ermm, this is a fishing rod.' Gary held up his fishing rod, 'which has a fishing line attached to it and a reel, ermm, to release and reel in that, ermm, said line. The line has a hook attached to it.' He held up the hook. 'The hook will have bait attached to it to encourage the fish to take a bite and get hooked.'

'It looks a bit cruel to me,' Lucy suddenly declared. 'Just imagine if you were hooked up to that through your mouth. Poor fish.'

'Yes, well ermm, I don't suppose it is a lot of fun if you are a fish but . . .' he replied but Brenda interrupted him.

'Don't worry Lucy, he very rarely catches anything, well unless you count catching a cold in winter. And anything that is caught is thrown back, except the cold that is. Isn't that right, love?'

'Yes, pretty much so,' Gary said, with a smile which was met with warm smiles from his audience making him feel more at ease. Violet looked puzzled and put her hand up. Gary looked at her.

'So what's the bit a little way down from the end?' she asked.

'Ah, that's the float,' Gary replied. 'So when the line has been cast out into the water we can tell if a fish has taken the bait and got hooked as the float will move either bobbing on the top or being pulled under. You'll see it better once I cast out.'

'Okay, thank you,' said Violet, which provided Gary with a confidence boost.

'You are lucky because I'm going on a fishing trip tomorrow evening so I've got bait,' Gary said and pulled out a plastic box and opened the lid revealing the live maggots squirming around inside.

'Oh my God, that is disgusting!' said Mandy. 'What are you doing with those?'

'Well . . .' Gary started, but was interrupted by Vera.

'That's our evening snack to go with our drink at the pub,' she said, 'full of protein.' Everyone was smiling except Mandy.

'Not quite Vera,' Gary said, 'but I like your sense of humour. They are the bait. I'll attach one to the hook, like this.' Gary attached it to the hook and Mandy fainted.

'Oh heck,' said Gary, 'is she okay?' The others rushed to help her and stand her up once she came round.

'Bloomin' vegan,' exclaimed Vera, 'can't take the pace!'

'I'm sorry about that,' Mandy said. 'I'm not a vegan Vera, just don't like maggots.'

'How do you think I feel when I find them stored in the fridge?' Brenda asked which led to Mandy fainting again. 'Oh dear, sorry I mentioned it now,' Brenda said.

Violet helped Mandy to her parked car so she could sit in it and recover.

'I hope everyone's okay,' Gary said. 'Anyway, we are now ready to cast our line out, so stand back ladies.' The women moved out of the way and Gary cast out onto the water. The line had gone out about twenty feet and the float could be seen on the top of the water.

'What happens now?' asked Marianne.

'Nothing, we just wait,' Gary replied.

'How long for?' asked Amy. 'How long does it take to catch one then?'

'It depends on whether there are any there and if they are biting,' Gary replied.

'It's a bit like you picking up men in the pub, Amy!' Marianne joked.

'Ha, ha! So what do you do while you wait?' Amy asked.

'Just relax, enjoy the peace, meditate, allow your blood pressure to drop,' Gary suggested. Amy looked blank. She was 19 years old and relaxing wasn't one of her hobbies.

'Stuff that for a month of Sundays,' she said claiming one of her Gran's sayings, 'how boring is this!'

'Well it's not for everybody, is it?' Gary said, 'a bit like bowling! Would any of you ladies like to have a go? I'll reel the line back in and you can have a go if you like.'

'I'd love a go, Gary,' said an excited Vera. 'Oh, yes please.'

'That's fine, let's have a go Vera,' Gary said. He was pleased to have someone who was interested. He reeled the line back in and handed the rod to Vera who immediately flung it back and then forwards whacking Gary on the head.

'No, no, wait Vera!' he shouted. Lucy couldn't help but laugh out loud.

'Oh Vera,' she said, 'you caught a big one there! It's a Gary-Toadspikehead. That's very rare in these waters.'

'Sorry Gary,' Vera said, 'I'm too eager, aren't I?' Gary was rubbing his head.

'It's fine, Vera,' he said, 'just pull the rod back slowly, then, when we are all out of the way, exert a little more pressure and swing the rod around to cast the line out into the water.'

'Right, Okeydokey' she said, enthusiastically. 'So me lovelies, here we go.' And she pulled the rod back and threw it around with such force she did a 360 degree turn before toppling into the water while completely releasing the rod.

'Vera! Vera, are you okay?' Brenda yelled. The ladies rushed to the edge of the bank to pull Vera out of the river. Gary stared in disbelief as his rod was floating down river. The float was bobbing about frantically.

'You are supposed to use the rod to catch them, Vera,' Dolly said. 'You don't go in to pull them out yourself.' Vera was out of breath, the water was very cold and she was in shock.

'Oh my, I don't think I did that right!' she gasped.

'You don't say!' said Amy, sarcastically.

'We'll have to get you home so you can get out of those wet clothes,' Susan said to Vera. 'We don't want you getting pneumonia. Come on Vera!' Susan and Mandy led Vera to her car. Gary stood, mouth open and bemused looking out at the spot where he last saw his beloved fishing rod.

'Can you hear that noise?' a smug Lucy asked. 'Oh it's the sound of fish laughing! It's not cruel anymore.' Gary couldn't help himself as he'd grown to dislike Lucy as much as the other women in just the short time he'd been there.

'That's a very ignorant thing to say,' he said, 'especially for a school teacher. Everyone knows fish don't laugh. Check with your Jake as he's taking a cake out of the oven this evening, he'll tell you!' Brenda felt so proud of Gary. She walked up to him and put her arm around his shoulder as Lucy retreated to the car park.

'Never mind, love,' she said. 'We'll get you an even better rod to replace that one. I'm sorry, I know you loved that rod.'

'But I need it for my fishing trip with Anthony tomorrow,' he replied.

'Well you can't go fishing can you, silly,' she said, 'but don't worry you can come Christmas shopping with me tomorrow afternoon instead. I need to get a few more presents, oh yes and a new top for me.' Gary's face dropped even further.

'Oh goodie,' he said. 'What a perfect couple of days!' There was nothing else to do so Brenda and Gary headed home. Some of the younger members of the WI went to the pub as originally planned.

Later that evening Brenda and Gary were sitting on the sofa drinking a mug of hot chocolate. They were trying to make sense of their evening.

'Why do I let you get me mixed up in the WI?' he moaned. 'It's always a disaster.'

'I'm sorry, I couldn't have known Vera would do that!' she said. 'Fishing should be safe.'

'I thought Amy would be the problem, not Vera,' Gary said. 'Whatever you do please make sure Vera never gets a golf club in her hands. She could take your head off!'

'She has got a lethal swing, hasn't she?' Brenda laughed.

'It's great news that I can still go fishing tomorrow, isn't it?' Gary said, 'Good old Anthony having a spare rod. He's bringing it with him tomorrow when he picks me up.'

'Oh yes, good old Anthony!' Brenda said sarcastically. 'You're just pleased you are not going shopping with me.' Brenda's phone started to ring and she answered it.

'Hello. . . . . Oh hello Vera, are you okay? . . . . . Ah, that's good. . . . . what do you mean you smell of the sea? It was a river! You are funny . . . . Gary is fine, he's pleased you are okay . . . I'll tell him.' Brenda lowered the phone and spoke directly to Gary.

'Vera says she is very sorry about hitting your head and losing your rod. She wants to buy you a new one.' Gary's face lit up but Brenda stared at him sternly shaking her head. She put the phone back to her ear. 'Gary says, don't be silly, Vera. It was an accident and that won't be necessary . . . . yes he is sure. You get some rest and I'll see you soon. Thanks for ringing. Bye.'

'What did you say that for, you stupid . . .' Gary managed to stop his sentence before he got himself into serious trouble.

'Stupid what?' asked Brenda, looking annoyed.

'Love, stupid love,' Gary said, thinking on his feet (although he was sitting).

'You can't let her buy one,' Brenda said, 'fishing rods are expensive.'

'I know that!' Gary said. 'Well, oh stupid love, I'm going to get ready for bed. What an f-ing day!'

'Gary you know I don't like that word!' Brenda protested.

'Fishing love, I meant what a fishing day!' he replied.

Brenda slept well that night but Gary couldn't get to sleep. His head was sore and every time he closed his eyes he had flash backs of his rod being swept away downstream! It showed where his loyalties lay as he didn't once have visions of poor Vera falling into the river, but just of her releasing his rod. His eyes followed its path from then on and not Vera's dip in the river. Well, the river was shallow at that point so she was, after all, only in three feet of water so he wasn't that worried about her. The more he thought about it though, the more guilty he felt about Vera. Yes, it was shallow there so it wasn't likely she would drown, but this was December and the water was freezing cold. Vera isn't a youngster either, she is around about his age and there was probably sewage in the river. Oh no, poor Vera he suddenly thought. He would check on her in the morning to see that she had fully recovered from her ordeal and make sure she didn't feel guilty about any of it. At least he would get Brenda to check on her again. As he finally fell to sleep he swore to himself that he'd never get involved in anything to do with the WI again . . . but he'd promised himself that many times before!

At about 5 o'clock the following afternoon the doorbell rang. It was Anthony who had arrived to take Gary night time fishing. He walked in carrying a brown bag in one hand and something else under his arm. Brenda was sitting on the sofa.

'Right mate,' said Anthony, beaming from ear to ear, 'first things first, here's your rod.' He handed Gary a child's fishing net on a cane. 'You should catch a few tiddlers in that.' Brenda couldn't stop herself and laughed.

'Ha, bloody ha! I hope you've brought a proper rod,' Gary said.

'Of course I have,' Anthony continued, 'couldn't resist that though. Right are you ready? I'd take an extra jumper for under your jacket, if I were you, just in case as it's going to get very cold later.'

'Really?' Gary said. 'I'll just pop upstairs to get one then.' Gary left the room to head upstairs and Anthony walked through to the kitchen. Brenda was still sitting on the sofa and was slightly puzzled as to where Anthony thought he was going.

'Are you okay out there?' she asked, 'Did you want a drink or something?' Anthony reappeared in the lounge.

'Sorry Brenda, my lovely,' he said, 'I hope you don't mind but I thought I'd take advantage of your facilities and have a pee before we leave. Sorry, do you mind? Where's the loo?'

'Of course I don't mind but it's not in the kitchen!' she said. 'Just out there by the front door on the left. And aim properly as I washed the floor this afternoon!' Anthony just winked at her.

'Perfect shot me!' he said and walked through to the toilet. Gary reappeared in the lounge with his extra jumper in hand.

'Where's he gone?' he asked.

'He's in the toilet,' she replied. 'So are you off then? Have a good time.' Gary walked over to her and gave her a kiss just as Anthony came back in.

'Do I get a kiss too?' he asked. Brenda rolled her eyes and shook her head.

'No, it's King Penguins to you!' she joked.

'Bye love,' Gary said, 'I'll be back about midnight.' The men then left.

'What a pair!' Brenda said talking to herself as she walked into the kitchen. She fancied a milky coffee so went to the fridge to get the milk. She opened the fridge door and jumped backwards in shock as something fell out and landed at her feet. It was a 12 inch tall soft toy, a King Penguin no less! So that's what Anthony had been doing in the kitchen, it must have been in the brown bag he was carrying. So there was a King Penguin living in the fridge! It wasn't really living though, but had been beautifully made in China. Brenda took the toy into the lounge and smiled as she looked at it. If she had said she didn't enjoy the flattery then she would have been telling a lie. 'Silly sod,' she thought out loud.

Gary arrived home at 11 o'clock, he didn't make it to midnight but Brenda was waiting up for him. It had been too cold to stay out longer and he lost heart as he didn't catch any fish. Whilst he didn't get a single nibble, Anthony had caught three. Brenda told Gary about the penguin she found in the fridge hoping he wouldn't over react. Thankfully he saw the funny side of it and admired his friend's initiative and determination. He personally wouldn't have wasted money buying a soft toy which would cause laughter for thirty seconds and then be redundant, what a waste!

As they lay together in the darkness that night, Brenda cuddled up to her man.

'I'm sorry you didn't catch any fish tonight,' she said. 'It's a shame Anthony did and you didn't. What is it about that man? He attracts women and fish?'

'He's a loopy sod, isn't he?' Gary replied. 'He's trying to catch you. Fancy leaving a toy penguin in our fridge! Next time say he stands as much chance of winning your heart as I do of owning a Porsche.'

'Then he'll put a toy car on the doorstep!' she said. '*Waddle* you going to do about it if he does that?' she smiled.

'I'll get him *ice-solated*,' Gary joked, 'and send him a stern *ice-o-gram*.'

'Okay, got it!' Brenda groaned, already tired of the penguin related jokes.

'It's all a bit *fishy*!' Gary said. Brenda had no chance of stopping the king of dad jokes once he was in full swing.

'Yes, no more penguin jokes!' Brenda pleaded.